The Ordo: Rise of The Malum

L. R. Lorkin

The Ordo: Rise of The Malum

Olympia Publishers
London

www.olympiapublishers.com
OLYMPIA PAPERBACK EDITION

A CIP catalogue record for this title is
available from the British Library.

ISBN: 978-1-80074-812-5

First Published in 2023

Olympia Publishers
Tallis House
2 Tallis Street
London
EC4Y 0AB

Printed in Great Britain

Acknowledgements

Thank you to my partner, Estelle, for believing in me throughout the entirety of writing this novel.

Chapter 1

Genaya Dorsolo had only been awake in his apartment for a few minutes before something caught his eye. A small glint on a building opposite him in the distance. Genaya was preparing to commence his daily Paxian duties and was wearing his yellow Paxian suit, samurai-like in appearance and lightweight in operation. As the first light of day was seeping through his apartment window, it shone on his hazel eyes. His smooth and soft brown hair had a goldish yellow streak down the centre and was knotted in a neat bun. Genaya had a slight stubble lining and had neat arched eyebrows. He felt the warm morning sun radiate itself onto his fair skin and faint red lips.

Genaya stood unwavering, focussed on the strange glint of light in the distance. Quickly, he pieced together the cause of the glint. A figure. A small one. It was pointing something indistinguishable in his direction. Genaya ducked instantly. A bright red flash shot across from the building and pierced Genaya's apartment window, causing the glass to shatter. The bolt finished two metres from where Genaya was crouching. Genaya instantly shot up and raced towards the door of his apartment.

As Genaya reached the top of his apartment building, a suited assassin could be seen nestled on a distant building ledge. The assassin adjusted and fired his rifle again. Whoosh! This bolt narrowly brushed past Genaya's ear. Startled by this morning's unusual turn of events, Genaya used the Electromagnetic Boots on his Paxian-suit to launch himself across to a nearby building top and begin his pursuit.

Genaya once again looked towards the assassin's direction as they packed up their gear and began to flee, ensuring no trace of evidence was left behind. Genaya could see the assassin's starship in the distance, placed atop a tall glass building where the morning suns' piercing orange light reflected sharply into his eyes.

Genaya leapt across to the ledge of another nearby building, his Electromagnetic Boots propelling him through the air. The assassin was still in sight. Desperation was instilled in every step Genaya took. The lightweight suit propelled Genaya across the building tops, the city streets growing in activity below. Hovercars and people were just beginning to meander their way across the concrete jungle.

Genaya was determined to ensure this assassin would not get away from him, no matter what. He dashed around a corner, then another. The clattering of the assassin's boots on the building ledge became more profound.

"Get back here!" Genaya screamed vigorously while gasping for air. The sudden and intense pursuit so early in the day was a strain on Genaya's legs as they continued to clump across buildings. His lungs felt crisp with the cool, dry air of the morning being vacuumed through his mouth.

Genaya felt as if he were gaining on the assassin, but the assassin appeared to be hellbent on steering clear of him. Genaya felt the air brushing past his arms as the sound of city rose above him, before he witnessed the assassin reach for his utility belt. A small object was in the assassin's hands. It appeared well crafted and Genaya saw it was metallic in nature but was unsure of its purpose. The assassin threw the object in Genaya's direction.

Genaya paused, waiting to see what the curious device had in store for him. Within nanoseconds, however, Genaya felt the folly of his plan. It was a Flash Grenade.

Genaya became dazzled by the blinding light. His eyes began watering, screaming in pain and begging not to be opened. His head went into overdrive with the immense pain inflicted upon him. Determined to catch the assassin, though, Genaya rubbed his eyes, accepted the inevitable short-term suffering and went after the assassin again. But nothing changed. A thick grey colour was still visible in his eyes.

Was he blind? He asked himself.

Precariously teetering near the edge of the building now, he wobbled and mis-stepped, slipping off the ledge. As he started falling, the ledge once again became visible to Genaya, and he clutched onto it with sheer will. Much to Genaya's interest, the grey colour began to fade. Genaya felt a brief inkling to cough as a thick veil of clouds dispersed around him. A smoke grenade ailed the assassin's escape.

A sly double-move, Genaya thought to himself.

With his strength he hoisted himself up and leapt across to a large, garden-filled area on top of an adjacent building, scouting for the whereabouts of the slippery assassin. Perched high above the ground, he scoured to the south. To his detriment he saw nothing of interest. Just high-rise buildings and drone-cars crowding the skies with the morning commute. He looked to the west where Befuno's two suns had risen. More buildings, but no sign of an assassin.

Pshhhhhh! Glass from a high-rise building to the north started shimmering and clattering above him. It cascaded down like rain towards the ground below. The assassin was situated underneath the falling glass, shielding himself from the debris.

Genaya looked on as the assassin launched a grapple hook to ascend him to a higher ledge. In this brief moment, Genaya got his first look at the assailant. The assassin was a purple-skinned alien, lanky in stature. He had a red mark down the right side of his face, and he was wearing thinly suited gold-plated armour with bright red robes. Genaya watched on as the assassin shot a look in his direction, one of dissatisfaction mixed with fear, before he jolted upwards and began to rise the gently curved skyscraper to an upper ledge. Seeing the assassin's getaway plan hatched, Genaya knew he had to act fast in order to prevent an unhindered escape. He glanced around, desperate for a solution. There! A glass elevator was rising up the building. Watching the speed at which the elevator was travelling, Genaya knew he could make the jump if he timed it correctly. Genaya took a deep breath and let the adrenaline rush through his face and cause his knees to tremble. Then, he darted straight for the edge of the building. His blood was pumping in his legs and the adrenaline continued to gush through his muscles and tingle his skin.

"1, 2… Now," Genaya whispered to himself, as he soared high into the air. Genaya let the Electromagnetic Boots of his Paxian suit take hold and thrust him across the forty-metre gap. Now, the elevator was in his sight. The cityscape looked so small to him in mid-air, and his chances of overshooting the elevator became apparent. He decreased the boot's thrusters, although now missing the building altogether entered his realm of thinking.

Moving seemingly in slow motion, Genaya braced for impact. Bang! The glass wall of the elevator shattered upon impact. Genaya came flying through and thudded abruptly against the metal inner panel of the elevator wall. Only one other person was in the elevator, taken aback and thrown to the ground by Genaya's roaring entry. She lay against the far wall of the elevator, and Genaya could see the completely stunned expression on her face at what had just occurred. Genaya did feel relieved when she began to rise up. Appearing unharmed aside from a few minor scratches.

"Sorry about that, Paxian business," he said to her warmly.

Genaya felt awkward as she responded with the wryest of smiles, coated with a surplus volume of shock and disbelief at what had just occurred.

The elevator, which had now seen better days, screeched and hulled its way up the building. The cool brisk air of the city whisked its way through the large hole Genaya created, howling and rattling against the elevator. The elevator stopped at the seventy-eighth floor. Genaya could see that the lady was evidently traumatised by the brief, but sudden ordeal. Genaya couldn't help but gleam a smile, amused by her heightened fear as she ran out of the elevator without looking back.

He waited for the elevator to continue ascending. As the elevator jolted once more, glass continued to make its way out of the elevator and onto the street below as the wind tore through the remnants of Genaya's mess.

Bing! Genaya looked up at the elevator's panel to see he'd reached the top. Floor four hundred and four. Genaya pushed the panel of the elevator roof off and climbed up. He'd reached the building's roof. On the far side, was the assassin preparing to zipline across to another building, where his spaceship was waiting. Genaya began pursuit again, this time attempting to cut off the assassin. He'd been slippery thus far but was not escaping him a third time.

The assassin was about to fire the zipline across to his ship before Genaya pounced five metres in front of him: a smooth sliding entry. Genaya directed the assassin a cold, menacing look, with his hazel eyes piercing deep into the assassin's soul. Genaya's smooth and soft hair swayed in the wind like a flag. After a brief but intense pursuit, Genaya had tracked down his target. He could sense fear in the assassin, who seemed smaller than Genaya had first thought. Genaya could see that the assassin was uncertain how to approach him. He was tentative with every movement.

"Where do you think you're going so fast?" Genaya patronisingly enquired.

"Not far it seems, Paxian," replied the assassin as Genaya watched him slowly reach for his Electron Pistol.

Focussed on the assassin's sly movement, Genaya now removed the two halves of his Plasma-Blade from their holsters. The ends came closer to each other and at the click of a button, joining together magnetically. Genaya wielded the deep grey staff-like weapon readily in front of him. The ends of the Plasma-Blade had small metal fragments extrude out of both sides roughly two-fifths from the Plasma-Blade's centre. An electrical buzzing ensued at both ends, and bright yellow plasma fields came to life between the metal extrusions and arced around the ends of the Plasma-Blade. In cohesion, Genaya's samurai-like plated suit lit up across the torso, glowing in the same yellow colour of the plasma beams.

"I'd be careful about your next move, assassin. It may be your last," Genaya said firmly, staring the assassin down intently.

The assassin moved his hand away from the pistol, and slowly looked back at Genaya, raising his hands slowly.

"Okay then," he replied calmly. "Let us not be irrational." The fluid in the assassin's mouth muffled his voice slightly and gave off a slight hissing noise.

"What are you doing here and why did you attempt to kill me?" Genaya angrily demanded.

"Temper, temper. You're quite aggressive for a supposed Paxian. Although, you are about as stubborn as one," the assassin sarcastically responded.

Within an instant, Genaya wielded his Plasma-Blade and slashed it against a ventilation system beside him on the building. The plasma beams of the blade sliced and seared through the defenceless metal, leaving the remains of the ventilation panel to fall apart in cohesion. They sizzled on the ground in a molten state, forever scarred by the damage inflicted by the Plasma-Blade.

Genaya rose up intimidatingly. His stature grew with his shoulder's rolled back and his chest inflated. Genaya responded hastily, "Don't make me ask you twice!"

The assassin, intimidated by the might and power of Genaya's Plasma-Blade, shook timidly before responding. "Okay, okay, I'll tell you why I'm here. Just, don't slice me with that thing please," he pleaded timidly. "I've been sent here from the Corvaan system to eliminate Paxian, including yourself!" the assassin replied.

"Who are you?" demanded Genaya in reply.

"I am Lucifer Dunn, a mercenary. You are the third person on my list," he replied slightly wickedly.

"Why are you after me, and why am I number three on your hitlist?" Genaya asked, baffled by the new information.

"My employer is entitled to strict confidentiality, but he has a fixation with Paxian. He's from the ungoverned territory of the galaxy, outside the reaches of the Galactic Federation. He remains incognito, as his exact whereabouts are unknown," Lucifer said, with Genaya increasingly growing in shock of this unfolding accusation.

"He sent me a hologram message, asking for the deaths of four Paxian on both Befuno and Corvaan. He wasn't stingy either. He was prepared to pay a pretty price, two million Federal Units per Paxian killed," said Dunn with satisfaction.

"Why is he after Paxian?" enquired Genaya angrily.

"I'm not sure. Clearly though, he lusts for your extermination," said Lucifer, now struggling to contain his pleasure at the nervousness and disbelief erupting on Genaya's face.

"Who is this man? He's a danger to the Federation, the entire galaxy?" Genaya said before being interrupted by Lucifer.

"Look, I just work for him. He wanted four Paxian dead, that's all I know," Lucifer responded hastily.

"Wait, you said I was the third person on your list?" Genaya enquired nervously.

"Yeah, and?" responded Lucifer, unsure of Genaya's query.

"Who were the first two Paxian? This has nothing to do with the political tension between Corvaan and Dohna, does it?" Genaya asked slowly with increasing anger.

"Well, I'll leave that for you to find out, Paxian. All I'll say is that I didn't have to work hard for the two on Corvaan. Easiest four million Federal Units I've ever made," Lucifer responded, proud of his achievement and bearing a large grin.

"What did you do?" Genaya snapped.

"What I get paid to do. Kill!" Lucifer chuckled.

Genaya, now consumed with rage, paced steadfastly towards the edge of the building. He could not believe what he was hearing.

"How do I know that you are…" Genaya proceeded, before being interrupted by the swift movements of Lucifer. Lucifer had made a dash for the edge of the building, releasing his zip line in an attempt to flee the clutches of justice. Realising this cunning ploy, Genaya swiftly disengaged the Plasma-Blade's magnetic-like hold and lunged towards Lucifer. Wielding the two plasma-engaged ends of the Plasma-Blade, he lashed viciously at Lucifer. Once. Twice. The second scratched the plating on Lucifer's armour, singeing at the contact. Despite this, Lucifer managed to grab a hold of the zip line gun and lunged from the building, allowing the rope's tension and the zip line gun's mechanism to hoist him closer to his escape.

Lucifer dangled precariously over the bustling metropolis, a sense of conviction about his escape lingered in his body language. As he approached the building wall he braced for impact and thudded his feet against one of the windows, three quarters up from the building's base. Allowing the zip line to pull him upwards, he climbed quickly up the building wall and got up. Genaya looked on as Lucifer turned to face him from the building opposite. Genaya was now consumed with disbelief, anguish, and anger. Genaya turned off his Plasma-Blade and returned the ends back into their holsters glumly, almost in shame. Lucifer smiled at him and waved back at him, teasing him further, seemingly to Genaya for the sheer enjoyment.

How could I have let Lucifer slip through my fingers, Genaya thought to himself.

Genaya could not believe he'd let his emotions get the better of him once again.

"Until next time, my Paxian foe," Lucifer called out as he walked up the boarding ramp of his spaceship.

Genaya watched on as the ship's thrusters came to life, a roar of particle energy gushed from the ship and gracefully launched it into the sky. As it turned, it scattered a shockwave of noise across the Befuno capital before propelling itself faster than light speed into the atmosphere and then off into the galaxy. All that was left for Genaya was the trail of destruction he'd created in pursuing this treasonous assailant.

Chapter 2

Genaya returned home, still coming to terms with his near-death encounter. After listening to Lucifer's accusations, he realised he needed to make contact with long-time friend and neighbouring Paxian Dreyfus on Corvaan. Genaya scrambled to turn on his receiver. A hologram appeared above it, but no picture. No one in sight. He tried again. Still no response. His breathing became deeper. Any attack on Paxian was taken seriously, but assassinations on multiple Paxian were unheard of. Losing hope, he tried calling the second Paxian on Corvaan, Bido. Again, there was no response.

"Arrrgghhh, damn it!" he screamed in frustration, flinging an item off his bench in fury.

He panicked again. At least three Paxian were on the hitlist.

If Lucifer had eliminated both Paxian on Corvaan, was he being truthful about how many Paxian he was targeting, Genaya thought. *Had he not gone ahead and eliminated Befuno's other Paxian member, Ange Kah-Sa*?

Genaya's head was swarming with fears and doubts. He couldn't conceive that more than three Paxian had been killed.

But maybe they hadn't? he pondered to himself. *Maybe Lucifer was just teasing him, unsatisfied with his assassination efforts and thus resorted to taunts.*

No, Genaya thought to himself. *That's foolish thinking.*

Calming down, he attempted to contact Ange in a desperate bid for answers. His heart was thumping so hard it nearly burst through his chest. His head was light and wobbly. The anxiety of the situation was starting to get to him.

He selected Ange's contact on his Hologram Projector and waited whilst the device left a blue holographic light with an empty projection. Suddenly a face appeared. It was slim, with circles on both cheeks. It was Ange. Her eyes were deep set and prominent. A round, striped, semi-spherical head garment covered the top of her head and extended thinly downwards just behind her long oval ears.

"Hello," Ange said in soft and slightly confused tone. "Genaya is that you?"

Genaya breathed a sigh of relief, "Yes, yes, it is me. I was just checking up on you."

"Oh, why? Our weekly meeting was only three days ago," Ange questioned.

"Yes, I know," said Genaya, feeling more relaxed knowing Ange was alive. "But in the meantime, there have been serious developments. There was an assassination attempt on me by a mercenary named Lucifer Dun. He said he was working for an undisclosed figure to kill Paxian on three particular systems and he'd already targeted Corvaan. I fear that Dreyfus and Bido are dead."

"Oh really, have you contacted Dreyfus or Bido to see if they're all right?" Ange asked before been hastily interrupted.

"Yes," Genaya nervously jumped in. "That's why I called you. Lucifer suggested he has assassinated both of them. He said there were three systems and after coming for me I fear you might be a target too. I have no idea how many Paxian he has or had intended to kill, but this may be extremely serious, especially if others are involved."

"Well do you have him in custody for questioning," she

asked, much to Genaya's embarrassment.

"He… he got away from me," stuttered Genaya awkwardly.

"How?" asked Ange baffled. "You were face to face with him?"

"I know, I know," said Genaya defensively. "He distracted me, and I let my guard down. But right now, I'm very concerned about this situation. Someone is deliberately targeting Paxian in this region of the galaxy."

"Do you think it could be due to the political stoush between Corvaan and Dohna? They have been accusing each other of espionage and have escalated trade tariffs upon each other recently," Ange exclaimed.

"I'm not sure, but I suspect that's a possibility. I interrogated him about it, but he would not say."

"In any case, Genaya, I think it's paramount we contact the Ordo," she said sternly.

"No, don't bring them into it please," Genaya pleaded.

"Genaya, that's irresponsible. The Ordo are the League of Paxian. Their existence is to deal with issues like this. Just because they've turned you down as a member many times does not mean you can ignore them because you're personally aggrieved," Ange snapped, evidently frustrated with Genaya's selfishness.

"Ange please…" Genaya attempted to plead, but was interrupted by Ange hastily.

"No, Genaya, please have some maturity. Your recalcitrant view of the Ordo must be put aside, this issue has to be dealt with. I can contact Grandmaster Zeffiro for you, but you must investigate. If Bido and Dreyfus are in danger or have been killed, something sinister may be going on between Corvaan and Dohna," Ange proclaimed.

“That’s fair enough, I just don’t want to be hasty and jump for their help,” Genaya said solemnly.

“I understand that, but this is what they exist for. Matters of importance which threaten the sovereignty and peace of the Federation. More could be at stake here than just some dead Paxian. This situation seems disturbing and dangerous,” Ange replied, more serious now than ever. “I’ll keep an eye out here for my safety, but you must go now to Corvaan. We need answers, quickly,” she implored.

“Okay, I shall leave right away, I’ll let the Ordo know of my findings,” Genaya said with a hint of concern.

“Good. And be safe,” Ange pleaded, before ending the holographic transmission.

Genaya sat down after the conversation, bewildered as to what was going on around him. He knew that the security of the region and the Federation was at stake. He knew answers needed to be found. Something unusual was occurring on Corvaan.

Was Dohna behind this? Did they order a hit? he thought to himself. He couldn’t conceive the allegations he was contemplating.

Did Dohna’s Paxian know about this, he wondered.

It was too hard to tell. Genaya relied on instinct and proceeded to investigate the matter without contacting the Dohnan Paxian. He was fearful that doing so may alert the potential perpetrators behind the present state of affairs. All he knew for sure was that somewhere, someone big or small was conspiring against the Federation. The democratic peace that had held strong in the galaxy for decades was starting to cripple from within.

Chapter 3

As the day grew on, Befuno's twin stars rose higher across the sky, bearing down relentlessly on the planet's capital city of Darsala. Its wide cityscape nestled neatly on the light green plains of the planet. Befuno was a small planet situated amongst the middle rim of the galaxy. Befuno was one of many star systems located in a region known as the Trade Intermediate. The region was a gateway for goods and service exchange between the inner galaxy, including the capital Manoma, and the outer reaches, some of which were not incorporated in the Galactic Federation. Befuno served a core purpose for interplanetary and intragalactic economic stability, along with many other planets including Corvaan and Dohna. For this reason, Genaya was increasingly concerned about the movements of this mysterious mercenary named Lucifer Dunn. He couldn't figure out who his employer was or what his motives would be.

Lucifer wouldn't invest that much effort into the eradication of just a few Paxian, he couldn't, Genaya thought to himself.

Genaya knew that such a ransom for a few murders would be a huge waste of Federal Units. He felt somehow, the growing tension between Corvaan and Dohna must be behind these movements and this ploy. But yet, things still didn't all stack up, at least not yet for Genaya. He considered the possibility that Corvaan's Paxian had gone rogue. Yet, they couldn't do that. Not at least, without the Ordo finding out and getting involved. Dreyfus was a good friend of Genaya's too. Genaya was certain that Dreyfus could not be capable of committing such a treasonous act. The situation in Genaya's head grew murkier as the possible explanations for the recent events became wilder.

All the thinking Genaya was undertaking was messing with his head, and after settling down from the morning's confrontation he made his way into his Spaceship. The spaceship was silvery and near E-shaped, minus the centre bar. The ship had Pulsar Blasters on both sides and Neutron Missiles under its hull. The Spaceship, known as an SBS-fighter (Slanted Battle Space-fighter), had yellow stripes and the royal blue and kelly green coloured Federation Logo imprinted on its centre.

The Federation Logo was circular, with two white infilled ovals perpendicularly overlapping each other symmetrically. The oval lines were thick, coloured in Kelly green and extended from the oval tips to the edge of the logo circle. The centre of the logo contained the orange 'Eye of the Ordo' at its centre, with the outer four quadrants of the logo coloured a deep royal blue.

Overall, the ship was sturdy, speedy, but especially a reliable craft, worthy of a Paxian. Genaya climbed up the ship's platform and entered into its narrow cockpit, a grin gleaming from his face. One of his favourite parts of being a Paxian was piloting, exploring the galaxy. So many buttons, controls on the ship to navigate, but he simply enjoyed the basics. High speed flights, weaving through asteroid fields and the odd dogfight. Nothing could beat the smell of a fresh cockpit. It was there where Genaya truly felt at home.

Genaya climbed into the cockpit and ignited the ship's engine thrusters. A slow, beckoning hum of noise thundered from them. With their power growing and their strength just beginning to become apparent, the ship began to hover gracefully. Then the engines tilted. The air behind them gushed as the engines bolstered more power. There was a softer humming noise, as the thrusters settled in, positioned parallel with the ship. The ship swiftly began to glide through the air at racing speed. The metropolis of Darsala increasingly shrinking in a matter of moments, and the rim of Befuno's atmosphere was now all that was visible behind him. The screen of the spaceship transcended from the light blue sky to dark blue and finally black, with many systems of the galaxy twinkling away in the backdrop. As the spaceship passed beyond the atmosphere of Befuno, it glided seamlessly and elegantly across the vast void of space. Space traffic was smaller than usual. Some ships were passing through, but given the dispute between Dohna and Corvaan, less trade was occurring.

After a bit of time Genaya was finally approaching Corvaan. Now within visible distance, Genaya could see that Corvaan was a bold green planet. The thickest of clouds were only just visible. The flight path to Corvaan was a tad tricky. An asteroid field was situated both just outside and within the Corvaanian system. It had a history of creating havoc for unskilled or otherwise inattentive pilots. Many ships, mostly larger in size, had succumbed to traps in the scattering of space rocks. Their debris, along with other smaller and less hazardous rock fragments, had over time created a ring of debris around the planet. Genaya, however, navigated the field expertly. A quick weave to the left. Then right. Down through a hole. Decreasing thrusters. Shifting upwards. Increasing thrusters again while diving left. It was an intense exercise, particularly from his perspective. Yet he enjoyed the thrill of it. It kept his mind focussed.

After escaping the worst of the asteroid field, Genaya decided to decrease thrusters and engage the ship's stealth mode. As he grew closer to the planet, the atmosphere was much more visible. Small, patchy bodies of indigo-blue water littered themselves evenly across the planet, but no oceans graced the land. Large clouds were beginning to stake their dominance in Corvaan's atmosphere. They were mostly thick white in colour, however, some red clouds entangled themselves in the patterns. Genaya could never get over flying to this planet. A relatively small distance from Befuno, it had three moons, a tropical environment and its beauty rich and widespread. It was like a second home. The main settlement Nantan still appeared speckled from Genaya's distance, but the lack of space traffic coming to and from it was eerily perplexing. Genaya's heart started to pulsate faster, and his arms started to tingle. The cockpit began to feel feverishly hot from fear.

"Something is definitely not right here," Genaya muttered to himself nervously. He'd never seen the planet like this in all his travels. It was part of the Trade Intermediate, but there was no trade traffic moving through.

Surely Dohna would not be behind this, Genaya thought to himself. *What could they gain from this? They trade more than most planetary systems in the galaxy*. Genaya could tell this was certainly a fishy situation.

Suddenly the ship's system rung out. A dull beeping noise, not overly loud, was accompanied with a flashing red light which appeared on the ship's system. Genaya read the hologram projection on the dashboard, 'Fine particle filters clogged'.

"What?" Genaya remarked befuddled. "Asteroids and debris don't usually cause such fine particle infiltration." These developments were disconcerting to Genaya, even more so given the present situation. He looked at the systems' hologram again, 'Filter three clogged,' it read. All that appeared outside the ship's cabin was a standard ring of debris and some asteroids orbiting

Corvaan. But something baffling caught his eye. A glint. A silvery glint. From one of the asteroids.

"No, no way," he said in disbelief. He knew the only thing that could've caused this filter clogging was debris off a ship. But the parts he could see floating around were only used for one type of ship. "It's not possible. It can't be," Genaya said in shock and disbelief.

The remains of the ship were strewn across the asteroid and into the ring of debris shrouding Corvaan. It appeared to be a smaller ship, although given the state of the wreckage it was difficult to determine. Genaya switched a white search light on. It was thin in size and strength to ensure it didn't travel much of a distance. He then decreased the ship's thrusters further, so that he could hover around the wreckage at a close distance.

A set of spaceship engines were shattered and in separate locations on the asteroid. What appeared to be side panels of a spaceship were now shards dazzling in the searchlight of Genaya's ship. The remains were mostly charred, with some pieces still glowing hot from the carnage.

The accident was not too old. Even more unnervingly for Genaya, the ship's cabin and whatever was left of its crewmembers remained unaccounted for. Genaya brought the ship around the asteroid now, searching for a clue.

A shadow began to emerge from above his ship. The light of a nearby star diminished slowly as the shadow continued to creep over Genaya. A slow-moving object was above his ship, but the sound of screeching and creaking metal vibrated through Genaya's ears. Slowly, he looked up. The gaping hole in his mouth expanded further. The question regarding the whereabouts of the missing cabin had been answered. Lingering above him it drifted, further and further over his ship, before colliding with an asteroid. More glass and debris were flung away and towards Genaya's ship. Genaya quickly engaged the thrusters and weaved the ship hard to the left to avoid the flying shards.

One of the panels began to float in front of Genaya now, as if it were held aloft by a puppeteer on a string. It dangled and spun around teasingly, allowing Genaya to soak in more nervous tension. A jolt ran abruptly down Genaya's spine. An emblem, scratched and slightly deformed from the debris, was marked on the side panel of the ship's cabin. It was a large, round orange circle split into six evenly shaped slices. A black vertical line ran down the circle's diameter

"Eye of the Ordo," said Genaya in complete shock. The eye was the trademark symbol of the Ordo. Their Paxian Suits wore the logo as a jewel. It was the sign of order and peace in the galaxy. A sign of protection. A sign of respect.

Upon seeing the state of the ship, Genaya realised that the Ordo members' fate was no accident. Someone or something deliberately targeted that ship. Genaya wondered if Lucifer Dunn had played a part in this atrocity. No matter how much he questioned himself, he was still highly uncertain of the answer.

The mere fact that the two Paxian on Corvaan were likely dead was enough of a development to reveal unrest in the galaxy, he thought to himself. *But this?*

Genaya was paralysed, stunned with the revelations he had discovered. His face became paler, colder. His lips were crisp with fear and his eyes were sharp white, unable to quell his growing anxieties. This situation was the most dire and consequential that Genaya had ever encountered. Unfathomable it was, that an Ordo member not only was attacked so violently; but murdered ruthlessly. No way could Dohna be behind such an atrocity, such a vile act of war. As Genaya contemplated the situation, the debris continued to float around the vast space in front of him, hauntingly reminding him of the omnipresent danger that was lurking in the shadows.

His mind scrambled now, paranoid that the perpetrators of this crime were waiting to strike again. He got back in the ship's controls and flew the ship slowly away from the wreckage, parallel with the asteroid field hovering around Corvaan's outer orbit. Almost drifting through the asteroid field, he meandered his way around the obstacles whilst contemplating his next actions. He'd just begun to reach for the ship's hologram port, when a large asteroid appeared, seemingly hurtling straight for him. Genaya quickly and sharply pulled on the ship's control throttle, before lowering it again. Upon doing so, he brought his ship to a sudden and stationary holt.

Genaya remained there, staring blankly at the sight before him. His eyes, unable to widen further, gaped deeply outside the ship's window. "Oh gosh," Genaya said slowly and in complete awe. What would have been at least five, maybe ten ships, all space frigates of various shapes and structures, rested right in front of Genaya. The only distinguishable feature confirming their frigate status was the debris of goods floating around the crash sites. Their parts were scattered across the void in front of Genaya, whilst others smeared and stained themselves across the nearby rocky asteroids. One ship still had freshly glowing red embers from its demise.

These were recent trade ships, and they were destroyed; neigh, obliterated out of existence, thought Genaya.

His mind became plagued with theories.

How could such carnage have occurred? he wondered? *The ships surely had to be entering Corvaan given they were loaded with goods. However, Corvaan would have no reasoning to destroy these ships. Someone clearly did not want them around.*

The matter deeply concerned Genaya, who was now beginning to tremble in shock. He pushed firmly on the hologram port, attempting to contact Ange. The call was answered nearly immediately. Her face popped up, but the signal was weak. She flickered, and her words were scratchy and glitchy at best.

"What? Ange, can you hear me?" Genaya pleaded. But the situation did not improve.

"Ge.... yyyyy.... CHHHHH," Ange said, as the signal flickered away.

Genaya's tensions grew a step further, despite them already pushing Genaya to a near mental breaking point. The signal stopped. A brief static noise swiftly ended the call. The blue light disappeared. Genaya began to sweat. Consumed with fear, he remained unmoving. Sitting at his chair, all the while gazing traumatised at the scene in front of him. Genaya had never had the signal drop out before. Something was up. The signal from Corvaan had been cut. Sending or receiving any transmission was no longer possible.

Genaya remained hapless, helpless, and alone. He started to grow fearful, re-engaging the ship's thrusters in order to leave the warzone-like setting immediately. The information he'd uncovered, albeit unintended, had to be reported to the Ordo immediately. Unsure of when a signal would be reached, Genaya came to the realisation that he had to get back safely and in a hurry.

Nonetheless, his trepidations were confirmed, and his angst continued to fester uncontrollably. Three actively moving ships had begun flanking behind him. Genaya's SBS-fighter's alarm screeched out in panic. This time the threat was more imminent. This time more deadly. 'Missiles locked,' the message read. Genaya's fists clenched the ship's throttle firmly. His knuckles cracked from the fierce movement. He had a dogfight on his hands.

Chapter 4

The Red light continued to flash in front of Genaya's eyes. The noise from the ship's alarms were deafeningly ringing and rattling through his ears. The message still read, 'Missiles locked'. Genaya's fears now a reality, and the proposition of death hurtling through his mind, he attempted to settle. The first required action was to avoid any missile attack, although based on the inescapable reminder on his screen, his time was running out.

The three ships that were hot on his tail could not be far behind him now, Genaya thought.

Coming under fire, he navigated his ship's dash screen to get a rear view of his ship. There they were! All Cross-Fighter ships. They each had a relatively small spherical hull at their centre. Four thin, but sturdy rectangular supports extended outwards from the hull in an X-shape. At each of these ends were long, cylindrical-shaped tubes. At the rear of these tubes, was the ship's engines. The lower two to Genaya were seen tilting downwards to give the Cross-Fighters upwards thrust. On the fronts of the cylinders, were Electron Cannons, presently displaying their rapid-fire capabilities. Underneath the hull was a smaller cannon which Genaya suspected was the source of the missiles.

The other more concerning feature to Genaya was the ship's ability to rotate their thrusters. He watched as the thrusters and cannons spun around the centre of the ship's hull, rotating on what appeared to be a loose or adjustable disc mechanism.

After gaining an initial assessment, the torpedoes sprung out from behind an asteroid. Genaya watched them closely as he quickly realised, they were heat seeking and were easily avoiding even the largest obstructions in their paths. Genaya quickly swayed the ship a hard right, around the back of a large asteroid. He then decided to weave through a small gap between two other asteroids, although this gap was quickly diminishing as the asteroids were drifting into each other.

"Woooooh!" screamed Genaya, as he slipped through the tight crevasse.

Genaya looked at the ship's dash screen. His rear vision sensors showed the three torpedoes tracking a near identical path to him. However, the rear two torpedoes never made it through the asteroid gap as it became non-existent. After a split second of them disappearing from Genaya's sight, they exploded instantly upon impact with the asteroid. A large plume of fire and a bold orange-red light expanded in all directions as the fireball grew bigger. Rock debris, of various sizes began to hurtle miles through the air in all directions. The single surviving missile, however, was still hunting Genaya.

Narrowly avoiding the wave of debris careening towards him, he pulled up, turning hard to the left. The asteroid fragments persisted, now swarming around him like a tsunami. They clattered against Genaya's ship, thundering into and denting the rear hull and thrusters. Thankfully for Genaya, no substantial damage occurred. The last missile exploded behind him, the flash of light behind an asteroid confirming its fate. The system's alarm still rung out, albeit less intensely given the imminent threat of death had briefly passed. The light, now projected in a crisp and steady yellow, cautioned him that the ships shield defences were down to seventy percent. Genaya briefly acknowledged the alert but was now concerned with the disappearance of the Cross-Fighter ships.

Unsure as to their position, Genaya closely monitored the rear-view screen on his ship's dashboard. They were nowhere to be seen. Genaya kept his ship hovering amongst the asteroids, hoping they'd lost sight of him and flown away. For a few brief moments, there was stillness. Nothing but the glint of stars, the green glow of Corvaan and the now ungraceful drifting and spinning of asteroids.

"Where are you," Genaya whispered softly, a hint of angst in his words.

Suddenly, asteroids behind him began to shatter into pieces as glossy red balls of light from the Cross-Fighter's Electron Cannons began to shoot past Genaya's ship from his left. Genaya fully engaged his ship's thrusters, trying to survive a cat and mouse pursuit with the attackers. He weaved left. Then right. Up. Down. His ship then spun and twirled as he shot through a narrow gaping hole in one of the asteroids. He briefly glanced up at the asteroid's interior. Its coarse and dusty frozen surface was now clearer on close inspection.

The Cross-Fighters were flanked tightly behind him, emulating Genaya's movements in a wave-like pattern. A large ball of fire erupted from the rear of the asteroid. One of the Cross-Fighters had crashed, exploding instantly on impact. Flames spewed and further debris shot passed the remaining Cross-Fighters. They copped a substantial hit from the debris; however, it was only minor as their shield deflectors were concentrated to their rear.

Genaya was struggling to manoeuvre his way around the asteroids and the Cross-Fighter's cannon fire. His shields, also concentrated to the ship's rear, were now at thirty percent. The damage from each cannon blast was significantly deteriorating the ship's shields. Genaya turned hard again to the left into a small asteroid clearing. The two fighters followed behind him, engaging in rapid cannon fire at Genaya. He swerved, narrowly avoiding disaster and thrust the ship downwards back into the asteroid field for cover.

Genaya circled around an asteroid, the two remaining Cross-Fighters persistent in their unrelenting pursuit. Genaya gave off a slight grin.

"Perfect," he remarked coolly.

Genaya's ship ducked around another larger asteroid this time, quickly enough for the Fighters to lose sight of him. His ship came around the asteroid in a nine-shaped loop motion. Exiting the loop, Genaya flew over an asteroid and glanced up. There, in front of his eyes, were the two Cross-Fighters. The bright purple-coloured light gleamed out of both their thrusters. Genaya's grin now turned to a pleasured smile that stretched widely across his face.

"Now I've got you," he said adamantly. "Have some of this!"

Genaya fired his Pulsar Cannons with gusto, initiating their rapid-fire mechanisms. The intimidatingly bright blue balls of light from the blasters rocketed at a swift pace between the void of Genaya's ship and the Cross-Fighters. The Cross-Fighters had apparently noticed they'd been outmanoeuvred by Genaya and turned in opposite directions around an asteroid. The blasters shot off and shattered into a small nearby asteroid, breaking it into tiny fragments. Genaya, now spoilt for choice, opted to pursue the Cross-Fighter on his left. He engaged his Pulsar Cannons again, this time steadier in his aim. The Cross-Fighter's shield began withstanding the fire initially. The Cross-Fighter's thrusters began to rotate around, first about thirty degrees in an anti-clockwise motion, before swinging sixty degrees back in the clockwise direction. It repeated this tactic four times, managing to be unscathed from Genaya's attacks. Genaya then, frustrated with the Cross-Fighter pilot's stubbornness to die, opted for a more destructive approach.

Genaya slid his sweaty and fatigued hands up the dashboard towards a red button. His finger trembled as it hovered over it, almost reluctant to proceed with his fate-deciding ploy. His hand jolted and firmly, his finger pressed deeply into the button, before flicking a nearby switch and pressing a green button. The dashboard screen lit up in excitement. 'Neutron Missiles engaged,' beeped the dashboard screen. The configured image of the Cross-Fighter from the SBS-fighter's mapping system appeared on the screen now. Genaya now looked up again to see asteroids stubbornly obstructing his well-crafted plan. Genaya turned the SBS-Fighter a sharp right. Then left. Up. Then spinning his Spacecraft clockwise.

"Blast," he screamed in frustration.

The Cross-Fighter would not stay steady. Again, another sharp left, only this time the Cross-Fighter led Genaya into a clearing in the Asteroid field. The screen on the dashboard began beeping a high tone now. Genaya was beginning to lock on. Then, in a pulsating moment, the screen flickered readily, 'Locked on!' Genaya's eyes lit up, excited as they had ever been. With an emphatic expression he slammed the button on top of his steering controls with his fingers. A soft and smooth noise, as if gas where being released, began to rise and fade quickly from underneath the ship's hull.

Two small, but long objects began to shoot out from under Genaya and tracked in an upwards-right motion, moving promptly towards the Cross-Fighter with a stream of blue light trailing behind it. In one final attempt at avoiding impending doom, the Cross-Fighter began to spin in a clockwise direction, hoping that the missile might be off-put by the multiple movements.

Genaya stared intently outside his cabin window watching the neutron missile slowly but surely latch onto the Cross-Fighter. A large shockwave rung out. The Cross-Fighter blew up and shattered into pieces within a split second. The debris hurtled across the clearing and deflected off Genaya's ship, which now had its shields focussed to the front. His face of satisfaction, quickly diminished and turned to intent concentration, as the other Cross-Fighter now emerged from the asteroid field, speeding towards Genaya's position head-on. Both ships began to fire their weapons, as an array of sharp red and blue light. Both ships sustained damages to their shields, but Genaya's ship was scratched by one of the bolts near the hull, leaving a searing mark on one of the panels.

Genaya ducked down and veered into the asteroid field again.

One last ship to defeat, he thought to himself.

This one though was relentless. The pilot expertly weaved through the path led by Genaya, dodging any asteroid Genaya attempted to conceal from him. The Cross-Fighters' Electron Cannons pulsated hard this time, sending bolt after bolt at immense speed. Genaya continued to spin and weave, narrowly avoiding a near certain death. The bolts continued to smash into asteroids, while the ones that didn't narrowly shot past Genaya's ship with a short, deep buzzing sound. Genaya, although exhilarated, was determined to tactically lure the Cross-Fighter into a defenceless position, but the environment he was navigating didn't lend itself to his desires.

Genaya continued to inspect the screen to see his rear view. The Cross-Fighter was closing in fast, but still incapable of striking the fatal blow. Within an instant, its thrusters began to cycle around clockwise, building speed quickly. Its Electron Cannons engaged in rapid fire, sending a hail of bolts in Genaya's direction. Genaya spun the ship and veered sharply to the right. Then down. Up. Down again. Despite this, two bolts found their target. They shattered into Genaya's ship with near-devastating force. One struck above the left engine, causing smoke to billow out. The other left a scar on the hull. The ship rang an alert out again, flashing another red light and message on the dashboard screen.

'Engine one at fifty percent,' it read.

The Cross-Fighter's spin began to slow, and the Cannon's rapid fire ceased. Genaya grew frustrated with the lack of opportunities to strike, so decided to engage in a risky move. He flew under an asteroid and then pulled upwards hard. He was travelling vertically relative to his original direction of motion, before completely shutting down the thrusters. He waited a moment, then tilted the ship down. The Cross-Fighter, now searching for Genaya, had lost view of him and was flying unknowingly ahead of Genaya's position. Genaya thrust his ship forwards as fast as it could manage with its damage. He tracked behind the Cross Fighter, which was now attempting to weave its way out of trouble. Genaya began to fire his Pulsar Cannons again, this time with more focus and precision.

"Got you!" he yelled, as some of the bolts from the Pulsar Cannons made contact with the Cross-Fighter.

Two of the Cross-Fighter's engines, to its top-left and bottom-right, exploded off of the ship. Genaya watched as the engines burst apart and shot away across the asteroid field. The Cross-Fighter, now worse for wear and operating with two less engines weaved back, slipping through the asteroid field absconding from Genaya's sight, heading back towards Corvaan. Genaya had a brief premonition to pursue, but given his plucky survival of the dogfight, he thought better of it. Genaya continued to monitor his rear view, ensuring the Cross-Fighter did not feebly, but bravely attempt to re-engage the battle.

Once the threat of the Cross-Fighter had passed, Genaya began to travel as fast as he could towards Manoma. He once again tried to make contact with Ange. The signal this time began to strengthen as he progressed further away from Corvaan. Ange's face appeared on the hologram, displaying a large sense of relief.

"Genaya, oh thank goodness you're alive," she exhaled as her stresses relieved. "Are you all right?"

"Yes, yes, I'm fine Ange. My ship though is a tad worse for wear," Genaya exclaimed, almost proudly.

"Where are you? Are you in any danger?" Ange asked, still with a fearful tone.

"No, at least, I don't think so. I departed Corvaan's orbit a short time ago, I couldn't get signal out there," said Genaya. "That's why the last time I tried to call you the signal dropped out; it was too weak."

"Dropped out?" asked Ange bemused. "Corvaan operates the signal though?"

"Yes, I know," rushed Genaya. "Look, Ange, what's happened at Corvaan is no dispute. Something very sinister is evolving there. A weakened signal, trade ships deliberately destroyed, and... And..." Genaya couldn't articulate the last section of his sentence, still in shock of its inevitable ramifications.

"Well, what is it?" Ange asked nervously and impatiently.

"I can't say now, I can explain it all further and, in more detail, when we meet. I need you to come to Manoma, I'm heading to the Ordo, they must know of the situation. It's paramount that they launch an immediate investigation. The situation has become dire. Did you contact Grandmaster Zeffiro?" asked Genaya.

"I did, he knew partly of the situation on Corvaan and sent an Ordo member Conraya to scope out the planet. Did you see him?" Ange asked enthusiastically.

Genaya paused for a moment in angst. He knew Conraya's fate. "I'll explain at Manoma," he said. "You must go there quickly."

"Okay, Genaya. Be safe," Ange said, giving a small hopeful grin, before disappearing off the hologram.

Genaya sat in his cockpit, hunched over. Conraya, a well-respected Ordo member, dead. He continued to sit, now in horror at the identity of the Ordo member. He could not fathom how he was to explain this to Ange, let alone to the Ordo. His address to them would have wide-reaching ramifications. Furthermore, his past encounters with the Ordo left him bitter at the possibility of never being able to be accepted into the Ordo, having already failed twice. So many things raced through Genaya's head. The only thing that stuck with certainty was that the dilemma on Corvaan had just begun.

Chapter 5

Grandmaster Zeffiro sat comfortably in his Ordo committee chair. A thick, leather-like seat coloured in deep orange. It was nicely square and had an arched back, fixed in its position in the chamber. The Grandmaster's chair was one of the ultimate symbols of respect in the galaxy, especially given the Grandmaster's position was the highest a Paxian could ever attain. Such a position was an honour and a privilege to hold and required the utmost respect and responsibility. Generally, the most wise and skilful of all Paxian held the title of Grandmaster. Zeffiro was a taller male with broad shoulders and of a fit, medium build. He had a rounded head, pointy ears, a dark brown skin complexion and wide light blue eyes. His sharp chin was coated by a thick, jet-black beard. Zeffiro's most notable feature was his Paxian suit. It was Samurai-like, as were all Paxian suits, but this one was more majestically patterned and most importantly was glazed in a crisp orange colour, with small golden lines making up the patterns.

To Zeffiro's left was Vice-Master Yaneema. An older, alien creature. He was of an average height and lanky in shape. He had rippled skin on his face and overall had a sapphire blue coloured skin texture. His emerald green eyes sparkled vividly at gaze and his rounded ears poked horizontally from his bald, circular head. One of the more intriguing features of Yaneema though was his triangularly based, elongated legs. His Paxian suit was tailored to accommodate this, and shone in deep glowing orange, as did the rest of the Ordo members except for Ange who was a guest at the meeting.

Situated to Zeffiro's right was Ange, her face now evidently a thick shamrock green colour. The circular marks on her cheeks were of a clear bright red colour. Her eyes dazzled a glossy orange, and her head garment was now evidently gold and white striped. She was of a standard human height and her figure was thinly. Her Paxian suit, however, was light blue in colour. It was representative, along with red, of Paxian with powerful strength. Ange glanced left at Zeffiro, who was looking out over the Ordo Chambers with concern and intent.

The Ordo Chambers was a large open room surrounded by smooth, cool yellow coloured stone. The meeting section was on the outer side of the chamber, which had a wall with the bottom half panelled with metal, while the other half was clear transparent glass displaying the bustling city that lay beyond. The entry side was mostly stone, but had automatic metal doors and a metal panelled wall. This is where Genaya had just made his quiet and surprisingly unnoticed entry into the chamber. He lurked at the back of the Chamber nervously, quietly continuing to inspect the set-up of the meeting.

The Ordo Chambers had two guest seats to Grandmaster Zeffiro's right, while Vice-Master Yaneema sat to Zeffiro's left. There were eight other seats, gathered semi-circularly around Grandmaster Zeffiro's chair. At the centre of the seating configuration between them was a small hologram pad.

The Chamber itself was located halfway up the Federation Building; the centre of the Galactic Federation and where The House of Representatives and the Ordo were situated, given Manoma was the capital of the Federation. The building itself was of a double pyramidal shape. One large square-based pyramid on the bottom, which was cut off two-thirds up, and another pyramid lay directly on top, leaving a slight overhang over the lower pyramidal section. The upper section of the building was also cut off near the top so that the building had a sufficiently sized, flat roof space.

"Let's call this emergency meeting to order," Zeffiro said in a deep crisply voice. "The matters on Corvaan are now reaching crisis point. The House of Representatives will be meeting on this matter soon, but we must ensure that in the meantime nothing else inflames the situation. A Paxian from Befuno, Ange, has informed me of some disturbing developments in recent times and her counterpart Genaya should be here shortly on return from Corvaan."

"Grandmaster, do we know the instigators of this conflict as of yet or is it still smoke and mirrors?" enquired one of the Ordo members.

"Unfortunately, we do not as of yet Hetana-Cia, hopefully we will be briefed with further details shortly," Zeffiro said.

"Do we know of the whereabouts of Conraya? He's been gone two days now and there's still been no word back from him nor any new information about the situation on Corvaan. He's effectively missing. Do we know if he's gone anywhere else?" asked another Ordo member in a deeply concerned tone.

Genaya analysed this man. He was human and had a relatively thick, black short-boxed beard and had slightly aged, dark skin. His eyes were prominent and had a wavy blue pigment. His face was oval, and his hair was jet-black and straight, sitting neatly on his head, all the while having an athletic, trapezoidal body shape. Genaya watched the man quickly glance a look at Ange after speaking, who turned away quickly at his sight.

"No, sorry, Heysen. There is no word yet on Conraya or his

whereabouts. We have not been able to make contact since yesterday," said Vice-Master Yaneema in a higher, silvery voice. Heysen's face, now observing Conraya's vacant seat, became clouded with sadness and grief. His body language displayed great fear for Conraya's wellbeing.

"Have we made contact with the Paxian on Dohna yet?" asked another Ordo member.

"No, we have not heard from them either Kiati. Their Premier has been reluctant to inform us about them and we have not been able to make contact with them," responded Zeffiro.

There was a brief pause, until Genaya somewhat sheepishly made his presence known and made his way next to Ange.

"Ah, Genaya," said Zeffiro with more liveliness, "You're back, what have you found?"

Genaya quickly settled into his spot before answering cautiously, "Err, I have found out a lot actually Grandmaster. However, the situation is much more dire than first thought."

All the Ordo members paused briefly, stunned as if something had unexpectedly exploded.

"Well… what DID you find?" asked Vice-Master Yaneema slowly and tentatively, seemingly expecting the response to inflict a panic attack from Genaya's build-up.

As Genaya went to speak, he sub-consciously noticed all the eyes in the chamber fixating squarely on him, making him feel uneasy. He felt a great deal of pressure and fear, knowing that he was about to be the bearer of extremely distressing and grim news.

"I made it to Corvaan's asteroid field, however, I was ambushed by unknown assailants," he said sheepishly. "They flew Cross-Fighters. There were three of them, one escaped," said Genaya, fear dripping out of every word he spoke.

Genaya froze still as Zeffiro paused, taking in the startling information. "Have you any word on the whereabouts or travels of Ordo member Conraya?" asked Zeffiro calmly.

Genaya sat unwaveringly, despite fully knowing the answer to the question.

"Well, Genaya?" further enquired Yaneema, intent on finding an answer.

Genaya looked up now, his face unsettled by the interrogation on the matter. "He's dead, I'm sorry."

Everyone's heads in the room dropped in near unison, like a pin, sorrowed at the news.

"Are you sure about this Genaya? If what you're saying is true, this is extremely serious information so we cannot afford uncertainty—" said Zeffiro in disbelief before being interrupted hastily by Genaya.

"Yes, he is, I saw his ship. It was blown to smithereens. It had the Eye of the Ordo on it," said Genaya emotionally, already uneasy about revealing the news.

The members of the Ordo Chambers looked at Genaya in stunned expressions, completely blind sighted by Conraya's suspected cause of death.

"I am certain it was not a mere crash either. The debris was scattered, and his ship was drifting in fragments. Most of the hull was in such a state of carnage that any chance of survival would be non-existent and extraordinarily ambitious," Genaya said, increasing his voice and slowing his pace as he went.

Grandmaster Zeffiro and Vice-Master Yaneema exchanged deeply concerned looks with each other before Zeffiro addressed the committee again.

"This matter is now of extreme apprehension. We must inform Governor Pehran and Vice-Governor Ghoni urgently. It could undermine the underpinnings of the Galactic Federation and its civil peace and democracy," Zeffiro said adamantly and in a deeply serious tone.

"But wait, I have further news," pleaded Genaya. All members turned to Genaya, completely taken aghast by his claim.

"There is more?" enquired Zeffiro in sheer disbelief.

"Much more, Grandmaster. In addition to Conraya, there was litany of trade ships and other vessels, all completely destroyed. They all would've been attacked recently too, like Conraya's," said Genaya in a serious, but enthusiastic tone.

"How recently would you say these ships were destroyed?" enquired Yaneema with great disquiet.

"I would say within a day or two, some would have been very recently, destroyed shortly before or even at the time I had arrived," said Genaya, to the gasps of shock by those in the chamber.

"I also noticed that when I attempted to contact Ange about the information initially, there was no signal. I fear that someone has eliminated that signal to prevent word reaching us about the ongoing developments on Corvaan," said Genaya.

"Did you find Dreyfus and Bido?" enquired Yaneema.

No, I never made it to Corvaan, and I still cannot contact them. I believe that whoever is responsible for Conraya's death was behind Dreyfus and Bido's deaths too," said Genaya steadfastly.

"Also, there was that mercenary Lucifer Dunn," said Ange, conjuring the Assassin back into Genaya's memory.

"Mercenary you say?" asked Yaneema.

"He said his name was Lucifer Dunn, he was a pink skinned alien and wore red robes and gold-plated armour around the torso. He claimed to be from Corvaan and went on to suggest he was hired by an unknown man to assassinate four Paxian, all from Befuno and Corvaan," said Genaya, etching seriousness into each word.

"How do you know this?" asked Zeffiro probingly.

"I was one of the targets, so was Ange. I pursued him to find out answers, but he escaped during questioning. He implied he had already taken care of Dreyfus and Bido. He said the man who hired him would pay him two million Federal Units for each Paxian killed. Lucifer appeared to suggest that his client wanted us eradicated," said Genaya nervously.

Zeffiro looked stunned, knowing now that the situation on Corvaan was beyond crisis point. He paused for a minute, as if his face had reset, before turning back to Genaya in a confused and slightly aggrieved state.

"Escaped?" enquired Zeffiro with much disdain.

Genaya now froze, uncertain on the easiest way to respond. "Ye…Ye…. Yes, Grandmaster Zeffiro," said Genaya softly and with trepidation.

Zeffiro's face shifted further towards anger at Genaya's feeble response. "How could you let him escape Genaya, he is a threat and could hold the answers to this problem," said Zeffiro with haste and a touch of outrage.

"Well, to be honest Grandmaster, he was sly and caught me off guard after informing me why he was trying to kill us," Genaya pleaded to Zeffiro in an innocent tone.

Zeffiro huffed in disbelief at Genaya's response. "So, you're telling me you lost the one person who could reveal to us the reasons for the current crisis, because you let your emotions get in the way?" said Zeffiro aggrievedly.

Genaya turned slowly towards Zeffiro and shot a

displeasured look at him. "I didn't 'let' my emotions get in the way, I was concerned for the wellbeing and safety of my fellow Paxian, Grandmaster," protested Genaya, resolute that he had not done anything wrong.

"Genaya, you are still twenty-three and clearly highly skilled in the ways of a Paxian, but your emotions interfere with your job. Paxian are Guardians, protectors of their districts. There were always two on each planet for diversity in the regions and they're all skilled or knowledgeable, but most importantly highly trained in the Paxian ways. There are Paxian's of Power like Ange and Peacekeeping Paxian like yourself all across the Galaxy, all trained thoroughly to ensure they do their job properly," said Zeffiro irritated by Genaya's actions.

Zeffiro paused briefly, while Genaya looked down shamefully. "Your desire to be on the Ordo is constantly hindered by your emotional betrayals. For Paxian these indiscretions can be ignored if they occur infrequently. Although with you Genaya, they seem to occur too often. I understand your parents' death and your upbringing may affect you but in order to fulfil your requirements as a Paxian you must let go of your emotions and think more level-headedly," said Zeffiro in a calmer, more constructive tone.

Genaya, turned to look at Zeffiro, a frown imprinted on his face and his fear converted into disappointment and frustration. "Yes, Grandmaster, I understand," said Genaya defeatedly.

"Good, now given what information we have we must make a move and make it fast. The situation is evolving by the day, and if we do not do something shortly, we may not be able to contain it," said Zeffiro with a burst of passion.

"Investigations must be made, in order to protect the Galaxy and its freedom from tyranny," added Vice-Master Yaneema.

"What if we sent a small party to investigate Dohna and Corvaan, given that each side is accusing the other of treason and espionage?" asked one of the Ordo members.

"That is probably the approach we will have to take Xevo," said Zeffiro, evidently more upbeat that a plan was on the table.

Genaya looked up at Xevo, her smooth angelic voice luring his attention. She was also a human, with light brown hair at a medium length and half-up. Her round green eyes sparkled beautifully at Genaya. She had a slim figure and was slightly short. She had a heart shaped head, with brown soft arched eyebrows. Her ears were narrow, and she had a straight-edged nose and natural watermelon pink lips. Genaya had never felt such emotion so soon towards anyone, but this woman was incredibly attractive. She glanced at Genaya briefly, with Genaya exchanging a small, pleasant smile in return.

"We must send someone to investigate, Heysen is the most skilled of the Ordo. Are you okay going to Dohna and Corvaan?" asked Yaneema to Heysen with hope.

"Yes, Vice-Master Yaneema, I will," responded Heysen gracefully. Heysen felt determined to investigate the reasoning for Conraya's death and uncover the perpetrators so that they could be dealt with.

"You may want to take Genaya with you too," said Yaneema.

Both Zeffiro and Heysen glanced at Yaneema in shock.

Surely Yaneema did not reckon that he was fit for such a mission, wondered Genaya, *especially after Zeffiro's discerning disappointment of him*.

"Why is that?" queried Zeffiro.

"Well, Zeffiro, Genaya has uncovered a decent amount of information thus far, he could be of very strong use to Heysen," said Yaneema calmly.

Both Zeffiro and Heysen paused for a moment contemplating Yaneema's suggestion. Heysen appeared to be accepting of the suggestion, however, Zeffiro was still cautious. Genaya looked on with secretive excitement, hoping that Yaneema's words may offer Genaya a chance to prove himself and gain experience amongst the other Ordo members.

"In fairness, Grandmaster Zeffiro, Yaneema makes a highly valid and reasonable point. Genaya may learn from this as well and develop his skills further," suggested Heysen with increased enthusiasm about the idea.

Zeffiro stared at Heysen sceptically for a few moments. Genaya could see Zeffiro's face screw up slightly as he contemplated the idea of incorporating him into Ordo business.

"That request may be suitable, however, his tendency to allow his emotions to interfere with his duties may jeopardise the entire operation. He has only been a Paxian for two years," Zeffiro advised.

"That may be true Zeffiro, but he will be with Heysen the entire time. And besides, he is no older than Xevo and not much less skilful than her, even with his flaws," mentioned Yaneema.

Yaneema and Zeffiro both looked towards Heysen questionably. Genaya could tell that Heysen knew exactly their intentions.

"I can assure you, Grandmaster Zeffiro, he will not intrude, he is a Paxian after all. That title is by no means an easy feat to achieve," said Heysen pleasantly, now looking at Genaya who was developing a bold grin. Heysen responded likewise.

"Very well. You two must go to Corvaan and Dohna and investigate the cause of this, and to find Dreyfus and Bido and any other additional information. You must leave with haste, we have no time to lose," stressed Zeffiro.

"Sure thing, Grandmaster. Come Genaya, we have business to take care of," said Heysen with a more energetic tone.

"Very well then, I will keep you all posted on any new details that come to light. In the meantime, keep your eyes peeled. I fear there is more going on than the naked eye can see," cautioned Zeffiro, as the Ordo members got up and began to exit the chamber.

As Heysen made his way towards the Ordo Chamber exit, Genaya remained seated, listening into Yaneema and Zeffiro's conversation in the backdrop. Zeffiro's facial expression of worry and concern imprinted itself at the front of Genaya's mind.

"The boy will be fine, Zeffiro, I'm sure," reassured Yaneema to Zeffiro. "Whilst he may have problems with his emotions, they are but minor flaws. He is already one of the most powerful and skilful Paxian I have ever seen, especially at his age," said Yaneema.

"No, no it's not that," shrugged Zeffiro.

"You know, Zeffiro, you have been Grandmaster for twenty-two years. One cannot possibly expect to be without fault after all that time. You have done a lot for the Ordo after all," said Yaneema optimistically, hoping to quash Zeffiro's worries.

"I know, but I fear the greatest challenge may be yet to come," said Zeffiro.

"Look, I know the situation with Corvaan and Dohna seems pessimistic and daunting at best, but I feel we should not rush into things too abruptly or we may fan the flames of war when there is a chance they could be avoided. Diplomacy always comes first and that is partly our duty," said Yaneema.

"That may be true, but I cannot help but fear over what Genaya said. A mercenary named Lucifer Dun, Conraya murdered, as well as other ships. And… a patrol of Cross-

Fighters navigating Corvaan?" questioned Zeffiro tensely.

"I must agree those developments were extremely startling and are highly disconcerting," said Yaneema, "We must not be paranoid, although I have lived one-hundred and thirteen years and only seen this type of situation once before."

Genaya's eyes lit up at the information. His ears pricked higher with intrigue. He settled himself enough as to not actively reveal his presence.

"You're not suggesting, are you?" asked Zeffiro in disbelief.

"We cannot rule it out, we only thought they were gone," said Yaneema softly.

Zeffiro paused looking at Yaneema with great concern.

"Do you think they could have possibly survived?" asked Zeffiro.

"We cannot say for sure. Most of them appeared gone, but the outer reaches of the Galaxy are a realm of illusions and are not scoped by the Federation. There is every chance they festered there and are now rising back to strength," said Yaneema.

"If the Malum are involved, we would have to declare war immediately, the effects could be far reaching. The response would be miles beyond what we could even normally consider reasonable, but for them it would be justifiable. They may even be manipulating the Federation as we speak?" suggested Zeffiro with deep concern.

Genaya's eyes nearly popped out of their sockets due to the sheer excitement and intrigue of Yaneema and Zeffiro's discussion. He began to make his way silently to the Chamber's exit with the last remaining Ordo members.

"Perhaps," pondered Yaneema. "Although time will reveal the perpetrators of these crimes and any masterminds at the helm. We just need to ensure the Federation and its people are protected from what may ensue."

"I'll visit Governor Pehran and Vice-Governor Ghoni in the Governor's Office later tonight and inform them of the situation. They need to know so that they can be mindful of any unusual behaviour or activity in The House of Representatives," said Zeffiro.

"Good, good. Do not forget your rest either Zeffiro," Yaneema smirked.

"I shall not," softly laughed Zeffiro.

"Good," said Yaneema beginning to leave, before pausing and turning towards Zeffiro with concern growing from his face. "If what you suggest is true, and that The Malum did survive..." Yaneema paused, almost as if his fears had shut down his bodily functions.

"Yes, Yaneema," asked Zeffiro worriedly.

Yaneema looked up at Zeffiro with a face that had nervousness and concern trickling through it. "I fear the volume of anguish and tyranny inflicted by them is yet to begin," said Yaneema, before turning and proceeding out of the chamber. "Stay safe, Zeffiro," said Yaneema calmly as he began to exit the Chamber.

"You too my old friend," said Zeffiro, before Zeffiro turned to gaze out of the window panel at the city of Manoma.

Genaya glanced back one final time to witness Zeffiro staring intently at the capital, watching the world go by him. Genaya turned back quickly after Yaneema looked at him quizzically, before pondering with deep concern the near imminent threats the Federation faced. The only thing that eased Genaya's mind was the stern calling of Heysen, frustrated by Genaya's sluggish and distracted movements. He was going on an adventure that could change not only his fate, but that of everyone in the Federation. That excited him most of all.

Chapter 6

Genaya excitedly made his way with Heysen through the Federation Building, navigating the extensive network of corridors that filtered traffic all around the building. Their Egyptian blue coloured floors and walls were soothing and welcoming. The lights on the walls were like shells, directing light up the wall in a whitish colour.

"Have you ever embarked on anything like this before?" asked Genaya excitedly.

"No, and don't get too worked up, Genaya, we are on important business," said Heysen nonchalantly. "You're only coming because you have intel," said Heysen politely, though much to Genaya's dissatisfaction.

"Well, if you put it that way," said Genaya insisting Heysen was acting as a buzzkill. "But nonetheless I am going on an official Ordo mission for the first time," stated Genaya joyfully.

"Yes, but I assure you that Zeffiro will be analysing the mission's success deeply and with great concern. Especially now that you're involved too," said Heysen, attempting to quell Genaya's delight and remain focussed on the task at hand.

"Well, I don't anticipate disappointing him," said Genaya a little smugly.

"Where to first do you reckon?" asked Heysen, trying to cold shoulder Genaya's unnecessary arrogance.

"Ah, I think Dohna would be best. We have no information there," said Genaya, distracted by all the various rooms and offices he was passing by.

"I suppose you've never really trekked through this building much before?" laughed Heysen. "Oh, and yes that sounds like a good idea."

"No, I have. I just have never been this way before. The Public Hangar is in the other direction. Even Paxian are not allowed to use the Ordo Hangar," said Genaya in awe of his surroundings.

"Well, that is true, but you still seem so surprised and amazed by all this," said Heysen cheerfully.

"I cannot help it. The Federation Building is so much larger than I first thought," said Genaya, before looking up consolingly at Heysen. "I'm sorry about your friend, Conraya, he seemed to be a good Paxian," said Genaya remorsefully.

"He was a good friend," said Heysen sombrely, a touch of emotion in his voice. "I'm upset that he's gone, but I know he would want me to find those responsible and continue to do my job properly."

"I'm sure he would," said Genaya earnestly.

"Say, when Zeffiro was talking about your emotions, he mentioned your parents," said Heysen inquisitively, before they both stopped walking and looked at each other. Genaya turned to Heysen, unsure of how to react.

"What about them?" asked Genaya slightly defensively.

"Oh, I didn't mean to bring up a sour topic. It just seemed to me that he was giving you a bit of a hard time. I was wondering if there was anything I should know?" questioned Heysen.

Genaya paused and assessed Heysen, before turning away. They continued walking towards the hangar.

"I suppose, if we're going to be partners, I should tell you," said Genaya acceptingly. "My parents died when I was three years old."

"Oh, I'm sorry to hear that," replied Heysen heartfeltly.

"It's okay. Zeffiro at the time had only recently ascended to the role of Grandmaster. My mother was Vice-Master at the time, stepping down from the role of Grandmaster to look after me," said Genaya emotionlessly. Heysen turned in disbelief at Genaya's remarks.

"Your mother was Grandmaster Dorsolo? Delisi Dorsolo?" asked Heysen in bewilderment.

Genaya looked up at Heysen's face, which was reacting as if he'd had claimed to be one hundred feet tall.

"Yes," replied Genaya, perplexed at the reaction.

"You do know that your mother was one of the greatest Paxian to have ever graced the galaxy?" enquired Heysen.

"I am aware, but I do try not to think about it too much," replied a more hushed and dismal Genaya.

"Well, you should be very privileged to be related to such a noteworthy figure," said Heysen. "What did your father do?" asked Heysen, now engrossed in Genaya's origins.

"He was a diplomat. He worked here in this very building too," said Genaya casually. "According to Zeffiro, many were critical of their relationship. A diplomat and an Ordo member, let alone Grandmaster, together. Apparently, it was highly scrutinised, and my mother was subject to much criticism, yet still continued to be a worthy Grandmaster regardless," said Genaya.

"A fine one she was. I was only ten years old when they passed away in that hovercar accident. I always dreamed one day of being an Ordo member. She inspired me to become a Paxian, even though it's only for those naturally gifted," Heysen said with a touch of smugness. "Did you know that your suit colour is the same as your mother's?" asked Heysen.

"What?" enquired Genaya perplexedly.

"You know when you get assigned as either a Paxian of Power or Peacekeeping Paxian, that the gem in your Plasma-Blade connects with you spiritually. It chooses a colour of either red or blue for Power Paxian and yellow or green for Peacekeeping Paxian," said Heysen.

"Yeah?" further enquired Genaya, unsure of Heysen's direction of conversation.

"Well, your mother supposedly was also a Peacekeeping Paxian, like yourself. She had a yellow suit and a yellow Plasma-Blade. I just find it intriguing that you're following in her footsteps," said Heysen with admiration for Genaya.

"Oh, well that's good," said Genaya more upbeat.

"Don't take that the wrong way Genaya, you still have plenty to learn," said Heysen smirking at his younger counterpart.

"I won't," replied Genaya with a grin.

"Good, good. I'm still a tad unsure as to why Zeffiro seems to be giving you a bit of hard time?" asked Heysen with bafflement.

"Oh, I know why that is," said Genaya adamantly. "My mother was his mentor, I believe that there must have been some sort of tension there," said Genaya. "He did also help look after me, and that was before being my mentor so he must be tired of me, or just Dorsolo's in general," said Genaya a touch pessimistically.

Heysen appeared surprised. "Wow, I did not know that," he said. "So, he does know you well though," said Heysen.

"Yes, I guess he does," said Genaya. "But still, I feel he is still a bit overly harsh on me. Maybe he wants me to be like my mother, I don't know," said Genaya, feeling disappointed by

Zeffiro's treatment of him.

"Genaya. I've been on the Ordo for three years now. I know Grandmaster Zeffiro well enough. Yaneema was my mentor, and he is very good friends with Zeffiro. He would never hold a grudge. He would only do things if he believed they would help people become better," said Heysen convincingly.

"Yes, but I feel he just thinks I keep failing," said Genaya slightly aggrieved.

"Genaya, failure is merely an opportunity for us to grow, to become the best version of ourselves we can be," said Heysen with a serious tone. "Never be afraid to make mistakes, it happens to the best of us, even myself," said Heysen now encouragingly. "I'm certain Zeffiro sees great opportunity and strength in you, but your emotions interfering with your work would be seen as a weakness Zeffiro would want to remove from you," said Heysen.

"How so? Wouldn't he be letting his emotions get in the way by judging me so—" said Genaya aggravatedly before being interrupted by Heysen.

"Genaya!" said Heysen in a soft, stern voice. "I can assure you Grandmaster Zeffiro would never do that. He is highly regarded for a reason. He has been on the Ordo for twenty-five years. He is one of the most skilled Paxian there is, hence, why he is still Grandmaster," said Heysen now slightly bothered by Genaya's attitude.

"I guess so," said Genaya, now deflated.

"I know so," said Heysen now concerned. "This is exactly what he was talking about when he said you have a tendency to let emotions interfere. You must be careful, Genaya, allowing fear and hatred into you is not only against Paxian values, but it also extremely dangerous. Do not let yourself be consumed by fear, it makes us do horrible things."

"I won't, Heysen. I'm sorry, you were right. I just try really hard to succeed is all," said Genaya partly deflated.

"I can tell," said Heysen jovially, grinning at Genaya.

Genaya looked up at Heysen now grinning back, "Is it within the Paxian ways to be patronising?" said Genaya sarcastically.

"It can be," said Heysen now bearing a large smile on his face. "You have much to learn," Heysen laughed, as both he and Genaya entered an elevator.

It was of a similar colour to the halls; however, this was a brighter and whiter blue colour. The doors themselves were twin sliding doors and they were of a crimson red colour.

"It appears so, but I'm sure I will learn plenty on this mission," said Genaya with a smirk.

"Right you are," smirked back Heysen in reply. "Now, we're almost at the hangar," said Heysen with a more business-like tone.

"Oh, are we?" asked Genaya excitedly.

"The Federation Building isn't that big, Genaya," replied Heysen patronisingly.

"Fair enough," said Genaya admittedly.

"Now, if I'm correct, there should be three spaceships available to us. A V-craft, an H-craft and a D-craft," said Heysen, excited by the range of choice.

"Oh, wow! Well, I don't know which to pick," said Genaya addled by the various types of spaceships.

"Well, we're nearly off the elevator, when it stops, you'll be able to see for yourself," said Heysen reassuringly.

The elevator thumped as it reached the hangar, coming to a sudden halt. Genaya looked up as the crimson red elevator doors opened elegantly like stage-curtains, unveiling some of the most prized starships in the galaxy. The hangar contained three of each type of spacecraft, as well as two larger command ship vessels, able to hold many more troops on board. To the left was the widest platform space, for the V-craft. It was a craft in a V-shape formation with engines on both tips of the 'V', able to tilt downwards to allow the craft to hover. The Laser Cannons were on the front tips of both wings, which also accommodated guided neutron missiles. It was of a sleek silvery chrome design and highly reflective. The cockpit had room for three people and the wings were rotatable around the entire axis of the hull, similarly to the Cross-Fighter. However, from Genaya's observation it appeared the engines could not overlap each other. In addition, each wing had the Ordo logo imprinted on it.

The Ordo logo was circular in shape. It had a smooth, silver and irregularly-shaped 'X' figure. At its centre, surrounded by a metallic gold curved square, was the Eye of the Ordo; a simple orange circle divided into six even pieces, and connected by two thin vertical lines at either end. The rest of the logo was metallic gold in colour.

Directly in front of Genaya and Heysen were the H-craft. These were sleeker, simpler designs of spaceship and were of a golden colour. On the backs of the ships were two engine thrusters. The H-craft also had much tinier thrusters underneath, which propelled gas out below the spacecraft, allowing it to hover. On the front of the 'H' designed ships were Laser Cannons again, and the Ordo logo was located on the spaceship's hull. The cockpit was clearly smaller, but still allowed two people to operate the thrusters and the Laser Cannons.

The other spacecraft, the D-craft, was a different type of vessel. These ones were evidently larger, able to hold more than half a dozen people. It's D-shape allowed the ship to have its thrusters lined along its rear and gas compressors underneath the hull to allow the ship to hover. The Ordo logo was situated on top of the space craft. A cockpit was located at the centre of the 'D-curve' of the ship, with an amply sized glass shield for viewing. The ship also had two manually controllable Laser Cannons situated under the ship on either side. The D-craft also had a rectangular protruding panel centre of these Laser Cannons, where Gluon Bombs were located and able to be fired from. This ship was coloured a deep sandy orange and was bulkier than the other two ships but carried a sleeker design.

"Well, I reckon we take either a V-craft or an H-Craft, given that we're not travelling too far," said Heysen.

Genaya was still admiring the massive command ship vessels. Turrets were littered across the ships' exterior. It looked big enough to house an army, yet they still barely took up any room in the Hangar.

"Genaya!" said Heysen more loudly, smirking at Genaya's intrigue.

"Oh, yes, sorry Heysen," said Genaya, snapping back to reality.

"What ship do you reckon will be best?" asked Heysen.

"Well, I'm not entirely sure. I'm not familiar with the ships myself. However, I would say given the firepower of what I encountered, a ship with good defensive and offensive design would be ideal," Genaya said.

"Okay, so I'd say we'll need a V-craft," said Heysen confidently.

"Why is that?" asked Genaya curiously.

"Because the V-craft is more versatile than the H-craft and it has Laser Cannons and Guided Neutron Missiles," said Heysen positively. "The D-craft is probably too big for the mission, and the H-craft is too singular in shape and ability to be used."

"That's fair enough," said Genaya convinced, impressed by Heysen's thorough detailing.

Genaya and Heysen veered their direction of motion left towards the V-craft. Genaya began analysing the hangar and the massive hangar doors lining the outside of the Federation Building, right near its base. The hangar appeared as a giant open room, but different platforms were strewn across it. Some landing platforms were protruding the walls to the left and the right, allowing the temporary parking of ships. The catwalks and the platforms themselves, as well as the main one where Genaya and Heysen were on, were lit up in bright, orange-coloured lights, and the platforms themselves were in a similar blue to the Federation Building hallways, only fainter. Genaya and Heysen gathered by the side of one of the V-craft's hulls, analysing the vessel for any potential advantages or damage.

"Is it all good to go?" asked Genaya.

"It should be, I can't seem to find much wrong with it anyway," said Heysen critiquing the ship.

Heysen pulled out a shiny ring bearing the Ordo logo from the thin utility belt fastened around his orange Paxian suit. He then proceeded to hold it beside a small Ordo logo next to the V-craft's main hull door. A small beeping noise then arose from the ship, and the doors unlocked themselves, allowing Heysen to open it up and inspect the ship.

"Now, just wait outside a second, I'm making sure the ship is ready for flight," said Heysen, before climbing into the ship and wandering around the cockpit. Genaya continued to absorb the magnitude of the hangar and the array of ships parked within it.

Heysen returned quickly to the ship's doorway. "Okay, all

good, come on in," said Heysen encouragingly.

Genaya placed his left foot in first, before grabbing a hold of the doorway and thrusting himself into the cockpit. The first thing noticeable to Genaya was the hard metal flooring of the cockpit ringing against his yellow Paxian Boots. He gazed around, there were three seats; two at the front, and one guest-type seat situated a bit further behind, near the storage supply area at the back of the cockpit. The cockpit was not small, but it certainly was not roomy either. Genaya analysed the seating. Large, leathery black chairs teased their comfort with every second of his analysis. Cup-holders, a full white navigational dashboard with overhead screens, as well as two large screens on the dashboard itself. The entire ship was evidently high-tech and Genaya was beyond impressed.

Genaya rushed towards the storage space to assess it. *There was certainly a lot of it*, he thought to himself. There was also an ultra-mini kitchen on-board, so meals could be prepared and eaten. The interior had a darker vibe, and it was coloured as such in a rich shade of black. The only negators of this setting were the white dashboard and the orange-coloured lights on the ceiling.

"Wow, this is awesome," said Genaya, completing his initial inspection.

"It's pretty good, I'll admit," said Heysen in agreeance, "This ship is one of the more recent designs as well. It can jump at least twenty thousand light years in fairly quick time, a bit longer for bigger jumps," said Heysen, admittedly impressed with its figures.

"Wow, how long is the recharge time?" asked Genaya.

"It's not too bad, but I still would wait half a Manoma day before attempting it. Wouldn't want to blow the engines," said

Heysen admonishingly.

Genaya looked at Heysen in agreeance. Genaya settled into the main cockpit chair in front of the V-craft's main controls. The chair's feel was leaps above its visual aestheticism. It was such a soft, smooth and cushiony piece of furniture, clearly designed to withstand even the hardiest of traveller. Genaya closed his eyes and slumped himself in the chair, feeling the warm and cosy embrace of heaven. He was, however, rudely interrupted from the serenity quickly by a hand tapping his shoulder.

"Out!" said Heysen softly and cordially, a smile rising on his face.

Genaya rolled his eyes and shot up out of the chair with reluctance. "You know I can pilot spacecraft," said Genaya.

"I have no doubt. But this is an Ordo ship and given you certainly haven't flown a V-craft before, I'm jumping ahead and saying now is probably not the time to learn," said Heysen slightly irked by Genaya's overenthusiasm and lack of seriousness.

"I need you to man the weapons controls," Heysen followed up. "This here is the Laser Cannons while this one here launches the Neutron Missiles," said Heysen, directing Genaya to the relevant controls on the ship's dashboard.

"Okay, thanks," said Genaya appreciatively.

Heysen flicked a couple of switches and pressed a few buttons before grappling the V-craft's navigational joystick and tilting it towards himself. The ships' engine boomed to life in quick time. A blue flame-like colour began shooting out of the engines as they tilted downwards. The engines were now thrusting directly against the ground and the V-craft lifted gracefully off the hangar floor. Heysen then flicked another switch, and pressed two buttons, before gently leaning the joystick forward. The ship slowly made its way out towards the hangar entrance. Heysen now pressed the black audio control button on the dashboard.

"This is Heysen Jogja, Ordo V-craft One requesting clearance to fly," said Heysen professionally. Both he and Genaya waited a little bit, looking at each other with slight angst, before a voice came over the radio.

"Heysen of Ordo V-craft One, this is Ordo Control. Permission to fly granted," said the voice through the radio.

Heysen and Genaya then looked up as the large hangar doors opened up fairly quickly, the fading golden sunlight of Manoma flooding into the hangar. Genaya looked out and saw all the large high-rise buildings, as well as the increasing traffic weaving throughout the city's airspace. The artificial lights of the concrete jungle created their own enticing atmosphere, with advertising boards charismatically highlighting themselves amongst the elegant backdrop.

Heysen began throttling the joystick further forward and the ship boomed louder as they made a swift and quick ascent out of the hangar and above city. Genaya looked back in awe at the speed of the spacecraft, now already exiting the Manoma atmosphere with ease. He looked at Heysen, navigating the ship with vigour and control, before turning to view the galaxy. This was going to be a new kind of mission. Even though it was the most serious he'd ever embarked upon, he knew he was going to thoroughly enjoy it.

Chapter 7

The bright cantaloupe colour of Dohna beamed straight into Genaya and Heysen's eyes. The planet was spectacularly coloured, with streaky purple clouds hovering around its rich atmosphere. Unlike Corvaan, there was no asteroid field orbiting around the planet. Hence the journey was much less hazardous, at least from natural causes.

"We're coming up into the planet's jurisdiction shortly," said Heysen to Genaya.

"There's still plenty of trade ships operating and commuting through here," said Genaya in shock.

"What do you mean?" asked Heysen confused by the statement.

"When I went to Corvaan, there were no trade ships moving through at all, with the exemption of the ones blown up," said Genaya with increasing angst.

"I agree that the signs all point to Corvaan, but Zeffiro sent us here to investigate. We cannot rule out the possibility Dohna is manipulating the situation on Corvaan," said Heysen with sincerity.

"That's true, but the situation here is warmer and much less eery, or at least that's how it seems," said Genaya with conviction.

"Nonetheless, we're here, and we'll be landing in a sec, so buckle up," said Heysen.

Both Genaya and Heysen fastened their safety belts and

settled in, awaiting a near imminent landing on Dohna. "Now, when we land, I'll do the talking. We are here on strict business," said Heysen sternly.

"So, I can't say anything," asked Genaya aggrievedly.

"I didn't say that, but as I am the Ordo member here it would be appropriate for me to lead," said Heysen sincerely, despite Genaya still feeling discontent.

The Planet was now at the forefront. It uniquely had no moons, and more surprisingly no noticeable bodies of water. The view outside of the V-craft became more and more apparent as the depth of Dohna's atmosphere became sharper. Now isolated settlements were becoming more visible. The ripples of lightly coloured sand dunes became much clearer and more patterned. A larger, more permanent settlement was in one of the larger valleys in the sand. This settlement was somewhat open but had a larger dome like structure at its centre, surrounded by four candle-like towers. The structure was apparently of sandstone in a starfish orange colour. The rest of the settlement had evidently been built around this mecca of a Government Building.

A large open space, big enough for some larger spacecraft, was vacant to the left side of this building for visiting spaceships to dock whilst attending the Dohnan Government Building. The space itself was fairly desolate and sandy but was made of a very coarse sanded tarmac so that harsh winds would not jeopardise the surface's integrity.

Genaya's muscles grew impatient with excitement as Heysen pulled the ship around, selecting a position on the tarmac to land the V-craft. He began to steady the ship so that it was hovering eagerly over the selected space. Heysen then flicked a switch and began decreasing thrusters slowly, whilst tilting the engines downwards so that all motion was directed vertically.

The V-craft slowly lowered down towards the tarmac, still positioned stably over Heysen's desired landing position.

Gracefully, the ship gently and softly clunked as it contacted the tarmac, and the engine's thrusters quickly came to rest. Heysen pressed a few more buttons, allowing the cabin lights to illuminate further now that the ship's engines were no longer active. Nonetheless, natural light was still pouring in through the cabin windscreen. Heysen and Genaya undid their safety belts and got up out of their chairs. Heysen made his way towards the ship's storage, whilst Genaya stood back watching Heysen with intrigue. Heysen opened up one of the storage drawers, withdrawing two large and thick wheat-coloured cloaks.

"What are those for?" asked Genaya slightly hesitantly.

"These," said Heysen drawing out the word, "are protection."

"From?" asked Genaya, now slightly confused from Heysen's vague answer.

"The sun, and the wind, and the sand," said Heysen. "I didn't get them out because I was feeling cold," said Heysen sarcastically.

Genaya rolled his eyes at Heysen's mockery, before grabbing one off Heysen. Both Paxian slid on the cloaks, then reached for the cloak-hoods and placed them over their heads. The material was well-woven and fairly smooth across Genaya's neck.

"Now remember, stay calm and I'll do the talking," said Heysen seriously.

"Yes Heysen," said Genaya dissatisfied by Heysen's seriousness.

Heysen walked towards the V-crafts door, pressing a button adjacent to where it opened. Suddenly, the door's hatch jolted and folded downwards onto the coarse, sandy tarmac. The sediment crunched aesthetically as it was firmly crushed by the door, and the bright sunlight of Dohna raced into the V-craft cabin. Heysen, followed closely by Genaya, began pacing down the ramp of the door hatch and onto the tarmac below, letting the dry sand squish roughly against their smooth, high boots. They made their way across the tarmac, where spacecraft of various sizes and shapes were docked whilst visiting the desert planet.

As they made their way through the settlement, they passed sandstone huts and houses, used as shops as well as places of residence. Genaya noticed that some of these were underground, evidently to provide shelter against the drier, hotter season's sun. Many locals, however. were still actively operating about their economy, paying no interest in the unusual interlopers.

The Dohnans were a reptilian-like species of alien, having silky dark brown and scaly skin. They had two, sharp black eyes, but they were not big. Their tongues were long, thin and serpent-like, however, were of a deep blue colour. They didn't have any obvious ears, but clearly were still able to hear things around them. They also had two short and scaly arms. In addition, they had two legs and moved similarly, albeit less naturally, than humans did. Genaya was amazed, never having seen a species like them before and only hearing and reading of them. Whilst there was a large contingent of natives, there were still many assorted aliens and humans frolicking around the marketplaces and open areas of the city.

After a little bit of walking, Heysen and Genaya entered through the large, dome-shaped Government Building, which was being guarded by Dohnan soldiers. They briefly analysed Heysen, before allowing them to pass through. Upon entering the building, both Paxian swiftly removed their cloak-hoods off their heads and inspected the building's surroundings.

The entryway was not large, but there were two curved staircases that ascended to a level above the main floor. The ceiling was very high, given the sheer size of the building. Many offices were situated upstairs, however, the main Government Chambers were deeper into the building on the ground floor. The walls of the building had colourful, mosaic artwork patterned across them, with an emerald green floor to accommodate.

A Government Official, wearing a bright red jacket and professional jet-black pants approached Heysen and Genaya.

"Gmacha, Julis Jorna tuf goomai," said the Dohnan Official with a thick lisp and reptilian accent.

"Greetings to you, we're here from Manoma representing the Ordo," said Heysen pleasantly.

The Official stopped, looking sceptically towards Heysen and Genaya, before prompting them to wait while he discussed with other officials.

"You understand Dohnan?" asked Genaya to Heysen highly surprised.

"Yes, most Ordo have to understand a certain number of languages. This one isn't as common, but it's easier to grasp," said Heysen.

Genaya acknowledged Heysen, before proceeding to ask another question. "What's going on?"

"Not too sure. I don't know if we're going to like it either," said Heysen concerned. "They seem to think we may be some sort of threat, or rouse. Tensions must be very high," said Heysen with increasing angst.

The Official finalised discussions with his colleagues, before he approached Genaya and Heysen once more with a look of fear and anger. "Quaibacci! Quaibacci!" yelled the Official.

Genaya began to panic. Dohnan guards were emerging from the palace corners and descending slowly around Genaya and Heysen. "What's he saying?" asked Genaya anxiously.

"Get out!" said Heysen, displeased with the response of the Official.

The guards came closer. Genaya began feeling tense. They were swarming. Corralling around him and Heysen.

"Calm, Genaya," said Heysen with fear.

Genaya started hyperventilating. The guards were armed with blasters.

Were they about to be captured as bait? That would be no way to die, feared Genaya.

Genaya's instincts kicked in. He threw off his cloak and reached to his back, unsheathing his Plasma-Blade ends. Genaya quickly clicked the magnetiser bringing them together and ignited his Plasma-Blade. The beaming yellow plasma fields hovered and glowed around the ends of the weapon. The humming noise of the blades was rich and crisp, echoing throughout the domed room. Genaya's suit begun illuminating its yellow radiance as he stood in an attacking stance.

The guards reacted unfavourably to this move. They aimed their blasters in attack positions and screamed at Genaya, seemingly to put the Plasma-Blade down.

"Genaya!" Heysen yelled quietly in a highly angered tone. "Put it away, before you get us both killed!"

Genaya looked at Heysen with confused fear. "But Heysen, they'll kill us?" he pleaded.

"Just do as I say!" barked Heysen hastily.

Genaya reluctantly unignited his Plasma-Blade before demagnetising the weapon's ends and sheathing them back into their holsters. The guards, however, were still yelling at them.

"Boshna! Boshna!" said Heysen hurriedly with decreasing fear. The guards lowered their blaster aim at Heysen and Genaya, a little surprised by the foreigner's use of their language. "Huchna ki bom santrai Qi Lok," said Heysen more relaxed.

The guards turned to the Official. The guards parted themselves, creating a pathway so that the Official could once again approach Genaya and Heysen.

"What did you tell them?" asked Genaya.

"We mean no harm," said Heysen more calmly.

"Fu, nochi rye hensa," said the Official.

"He's asking us to state our business," Heysen said to Genaya.

"We are here on Ordo matters, like I said before this unnecessary stand-off," said Heysen to the Official passively, albeit professionally. "Our business is to find and solve the cause of your trade dispute and espionage allegations against Corvaan."

"Loshni, Jokku Mingga Ordo, bansala dong richta?" enquired the Official.

"Yes, we are Ordo, see," said Heysen revealing the Ordo logo on his orange samurai-like Paxian suit. "We've come to speak with Premier Sphixter."

The Official paused for a moment, contemplating Heysen's words. "Bonna," said the Official as the guards put away their weapons and stood aside. "Minsa Roi Sphixter," said the Official.

"What did he say?" asked Genaya, puzzled by the entire situation that had just unfolded.

"He's taking us to see Premier Sphixter, leader of the Dohnans," said Heysen.

The Official led Genaya and Heysen through the building and through a corridor, before turning left down another corridor and into a large vacant room. This room had a semi-circular table with five seats lined across it in a straight line, and a throne-like chair centred on the top of the curved side. The Official ushered Genaya and Heysen to sit down, before leaving them alone in the room, which was lined with velvet dark green carpet and had mosaic patterned walls.

"Don't stress, Genaya, he's fetching Sphixter for us," said Heysen, aware of Genaya's angst.

"Sorry, Heysen," said Genaya frustrated with himself.

"I see where Zeffiro was coming from. Your emotions took hold there way too much and way too easily," said Heysen disappointed by Genaya's actions.

"Heysen, they were converging on us. They could have killed us," said Genaya.

"Genaya, we're Paxian. We keep the peace; we don't disturb it. Recklessly throwing yourself into an aggressive confrontation like that only inflamed the hostility," said Heysen frustrated by Genaya's lack of understanding.

"But they could've killed us, I was only protecting us," said Genaya adamantly.

"They would not have killed us. I can assure you they are not the perpetrators we're after," said Heysen sincerely.

"What makes you so sure," asked Genaya annoyed by Heysen's confidence.

"If they were the perpetrators, we would have been long dead before entering this building," said Heysen.

Genaya stopped and realised that what Heysen was saying was correct. "I'm sorry, Heysen," said Genaya remorsefully.

"It's okay, but your actions were highly irrational and emotionally uncontrolled. They are not Paxian qualities," said Heysen worriedly. "Beware of your fears, Genaya, they are the greatest deception, the one true cause of grief and tyranny," said

Heysen cautioning Genaya.

Genaya looked remorsefully at Heysen, before the door mechanically shot up and Sphixter walked in, along with four bodyguards with red armour. As Sphixter sat down on the throne-like chair, the guards situated themselves evenly on either side of Sphixter.

Genaya looked at Sphixter. He was similar to the rest of the Dohnans, but bigger in size. His skin was also a scaly dark brown colour, but his eyes were slightly bigger.

"What can I help you with, Paxian," said Sphixter in a deep, slithery and serious tone.

"We are from the Ordo, we're here to resolve the conflict between you and Corvaan," said Heysen.

"Baaaahhhh, CORVAAN! What resolution could you possibly hope to achieve," screamed Sphixter, angered by Heysen's apparently ridiculous statement.

Heysen became a tad nervous and taken aback by Sphixter's response. Clearly there was bad blood with that topic.

"We're trying to figure out what is really going on. You claim they've shut down trade to you, and they claim likewise," said Heysen, maintaining a poised approach. "And then there's claims of espionage," said Heysen enquiringly.

"Ahhh yes, they've stopped our trade for ages," said Sphixter in frustration. "They missed several crisis meetings and after our insistence that they must join, they refused and shut off trade to us. We've been unable to get other ships through too, they've just gone missing," said Sphixter with hints of rage.

Sphixter's words struck a chord with Genaya. "What kinds of ships?" he asked insistently.

"Fairly standard trade ones, mainly carrying food supplies," said Sphixter.

Genaya paused, contemplating Sphixter's words.

"Wait, if you're Ordo, who is this young man?" enquired Sphixter concerned. "He does not wear the orange suit. He's merely a Paxian," said Sphixter.

"He has been granted permission to join me by the Ordo, based on his intelligence on this situation," said Heysen calmly.

"Heysen, those trade ships, some of them were bound for Dohna," said Genaya with a heightened sense of urgency.

"Yes?" asked Heysen, curious of Genaya's point.

"Well, how come they were blown up at Corvaan? They have nothing to do with Dohna's trade routes. Corvaan makes enough food, and they don't import any. So, what were they doing at Corvaan?" asked Genaya to Heysen, a great sense of fear and urgency lifting amongst both of them.

I'll get back to that in a second," said Heysen to Genaya, still intent on questioning Sphixter.

"Might I ask where your Paxian are? The Ordo has been unable to make contact with them," asked Heysen to Sphixter with intrigue.

"Our Paxian are safe. We have them here, but we've kept them under strict guard since they were nearly assassinated," said Sphixter in a genuinely angered tone.

"By whom?" asked Genaya. "Did this assassin happen to have purple skin and red robes with gold-plated armour?" Genaya followed up.

"Yes," replied Sphixter slowly and concerningly. "How did you know?

"He tried to kill me too. He claimed that he had already killed the Paxian on Corvaan. His name is Lucifer Dunn, he works for someone, but we cannot figure out who. We believe he is the man behind your issues," said Genaya hyped up by the unfolding situation.

"So, our espionage allegations are true," said Sphixter aggrievedly.

"Not quite, we cannot establish that yet," said Heysen warningly. "It's important you don't jump into things too hastily, Premier; this conflict may already be bigger than we think."

"Okay," said Sphixter hesitantly.

Genaya and Heysen got up out of their chairs. "Thank you for talking to us Premier Sphixter, we appreciate it. The Governor and the House of Representatives will keep you posted on any new information. Until then, stay safe and be wary," said Heysen sincerely.

Heysen and Genaya made their way out of the room, before leaving the Dohna Government Building and heading towards their ship. The sun had lowered, and the late afternoon/evening sky set in. A mix of red, orange and purple colours danced amongst the streaky clouds.

"I knew he was involved," said Genaya outraged. "Lucifer Dunn could not be trusted."

"That may be true Genaya, but we must focus on the problem at hand," said Heysen with concern. "The situation does, however, create more worry for what's going on away from Federation eyes. The problem is exponentially growing and the more we discover the worse it seems to get," said Heysen.

"And the trade ships?" asked Genaya.

"That I'm still contemplating," said Heysen, puzzled by the unfolding situation. "I'm still concerned as to why they are at Corvaan. From Sphixter's information, they did not even need to pass through there."

"Maybe Corvaan jammed their signal. Sent them on a detour." said Genaya suggestively.

"That's a possibility, but Corvaan could not possibly know which ships are heading towards Dohna, only the Federation itself or the parties involved could know what ship is carrying what and to where," stated Heysen reassuringly.

Genaya froze dead still in his tracks. Heysen's words were now resonating through his ears like a siren. A dark thought shot into his thinking. It clouded his judgement. Then, it sent his nerves into overdrive. He looked wide-eyed and paralysed towards Heysen, gravely uttering, "We need to get to Corvaan. NOW!"

Chapter 8

"How are the plans unfolding, Premier Finkel," said Vondur Sombria.

"Good, so far, we currently have control of the city, and the first wave of Battle-Bots should be arriving in a matter of days," said Premier Finkel.

"Excellent," said Sombria with vigour. "Keep an eye out, this operation cannot fail!" said Sombria bluntly.

"Yes, Vondur," said Premier Finkel, before leaving the Government chamber.

Sombria sat enthusiastically in her newly crafted throne chair, a crystallised black behemoth. It had three spikes at its top and was perfectly elevated, as if it were customised just for Sombria. Sombria was human, with long, streaming black hair. Her eyebrows were thin and hard angled complementing her diamond shaped head. Her complexion was fair, and her eyes were grey and empty. Her lips were marked in deep black, as was the circumference of her eyes. Her face was smooth and intimidatingly dark, partly reflective of her intentions. Her suit was similar to a Paxian's, albeit shrouded in a darker violet colour. Her inner robes were also tight like Paxian ones. However, they were black instead of white.

On the small table to the right of the throne was her helmet. A violet and chrome coloured item, perfectly curved in structure. It was constructed like an evenly sized bucket but curved to suit a human head. The body of the helmet was coloured in a rich chrome. The facial section of the helmet was of a deep, dark violet colour, slightly indented and of a condensed trapezoidal shape. It had a clear glass-like slit at the top to see through, split in the middle by a thin portion of the chrome helmet.

Corvaan's main Government Chamber was not overly large compared to most other Government Chambers. However, it had sufficient room to seat at least fifty people and had a glazed concrete floor. The walls were of white brick and a dark green rug bearing Corvaan's government logo lay in front of the throne chair.

A sinister smile was growing richly from Sombria's face. Thus far, her plan had gone perfectly. Soon she, alongside her army, would have control of the Corvaanian system.

"Jeppora, at last," said Sombria enthusiastically.

A tall, muscular alien-like creature walked into the Government Chamber. He had two legs, but four brawny arms. His head was bald, and his skin complexion was a mix of icy grey and dark burning red. His face was patterned, such that two long grey lines travelled from his chin, up through his eyes and over his head. They were joined at his chin by further grey-coloured skin. He had two grey streaks branching around the side of his head below his wide, slanted eyes. A single grey line between his nose and mouth conjoined the main vertical stripes of grey. In addition, Jeppora had a plus symbol in between his eyes, situated centrally above them on his forehead. It was also frosty grey in colour, but had a large, dark red infilling. Aside from his thin frosty grey lips, the remainder of Jeppora's face was filled by a raging deep red colour. His menacing yellow eyes sliced through the air with a vicious tone.

"I have arrived," said Jeppora in a hushed, gruff manner.

"Good, how are the Battle-Bots coming along?" asked

Sombria in an eager tone.

"They have departed Vormok. I personally oversaw them board the war-carriers," said Jeppora, "Over five hundred thousand so far, with a thousand artillery vehicles. They're being led by a large Cross-Fighter fleet in case of any threat."

"Excellent," said Sombria. "Inform Veneticus, everything is going to plan and as scheduled. Corvaan should be in our control within a matter of days. After which, we'll send another hundred-thousand Battle-Bots to Ferra. Soon the Trade Intermediate will be under our control," said Sombria vigorously.

"Sombria, I'm unsure if the factories will have sufficient material to produce that many units. We may have to deploy the Vormok army until—" said Jeppora hastily before being cut off swiftly by Sombria.

"No, we cannot!" barked Sombria. "A waste of such resources on the initial phase of the operation would be cataclysmic. We must preserve them!" said Sombria sternly.

"Yes, Vondur Sombria," said Jeppora distastefully.

Suddenly, a member of the Corvaanian Army came racing into the Government Chambers, abruptly ending Sombria and Jeppora's conversation as he knelt before them.

"Vondur Sombria, I have urgent news, of grave importance," said the Man.

Sombria thrust herself out of her throne, eyeing off the Man with disgust and anger. "You best hope this is important," she said wickedly.

"It is, our small Cross-Fighter fleet was scouring the system for any intruders or Trade ships," said the Man in an exhausted and frightened tone.

"And?" asked Sombria viciously.

"We encountered an Ordo ship, and we destroyed it. But

shortly afterwards we encountered another unknown ship. It appeared to be an SBS-fighter, possibly a Paxian's ship," said the Man weakly, with deep concern. His fatigue levels were impacting his ability to speak steadily.

Fear flickered through Sombria's eyes, and her face became pale with rage. The Man continued, "We attempted to ambush it, but the pilot was highly skilled and destroyed two of the three ships. I barely escaped," said the man paralysed by fear. Sombria could sense his fragility, his weakness as he cowered in fear at her anger.

"So, you let him go because your ship was damaged?" asked Sombria patronisingly with disgust.

"Yes, Sombria. I would not have been able to report back to you with such vital information. I would have died," said the Man, before clasping his throat in desperation.

Sombria stepped forward and grasped the Man's throat aggressively, holding him aloft. "YOU! You would put our entire operation in jeopardy because you 'might' have died?" said Sombria, rage soaring through her body.

"My chances of getting him were slim," said the Man suffocating. Sombria was literally strangling the words out of him.

Sombria withdrew one end of her Plasma-Blade, the dark-violet Plasma field lit up ferociously. She then thrust it deep into the Man's chest ruthlessly, before a wicked expression filled her face. "You put our entire mission in jeopardy because you're a treasonous coward afraid of death," she said sinisterly, the Man retching blood from his mouth.

"Don't worry though, I've made things right," she said passively at the Man as she watched his pale, fear-filled face sink as the life in it quickly diminished. Sombria withdrew her

Plasma-Blade from the Man and threw his lifeless corpse into the corner of the room, making a cluttering noise as it impacted the wall.

Sombria, breathing heavily now, disengaged the plasma beam on her Plasma-Blade and placed it back in its holster. Her wide, glaring eyes focussed on the corpse, before turning to an emotionless Jeppora.

"You!" she said menacingly. "Before you head back to Vormok, I need you to send some extra patrols to ensure no one arrives here and discovers what's going on. And if they do, make them wish they hadn't," said Sombria callously.

"Yes, Sombria," said Jeppora, "I'll personally oversee it."

"Good, we cannot fail. Inform Premier Finkel of these new developments, and make sure she doesn't send any space-fleets. We cannot afford to arouse any more suspicion. We must eliminate those attempting to uncover our operation," said Sombria, now stressed about the threat to her plans.

"And if you need to extract information from the townspeople, do what you must," said Sombria cold-bloodedly.

Jeppora nodded and vacated the Government Chamber. Sombria turned away, running her hands across her head. The last thing she needed was Paxian tearing apart the grand operation, right before her forces would be bolstered. Her rage cascaded throughout her arteries. They thumped vigorously with every breath she took. Her head pulsated in anger as she contemplated the situation. Her grand opportunity to rule Corvaan was in jeopardy. Whoever was sniffing around, would be dealt with swiftly and lethally.

Chapter 9

Heysen decreased the ships' engine output as the V-craft carrying him and Genaya started to approach Corvaan. The asteroid field was thinner and less concentrated from this trajectory, but Heysen still was forced to meander and swerve to avoid some larger chunks of space rock.

"Whoever is destroying those ships had intel from the Federation themselves. It couldn't just be Corvaan, even if they're involved in this conspiracy," said Genaya worriedly.

"Are you suggesting that it's an act of galactic terrorism?" enquired Heysen, perplexed by the accusation.

"Maybe, I'm unsure. This whole debacle seems highly coordinated for a terrorist operation. It almost seems as if it is some form of militant insurgence plotting against the Federation. What I am sure of though, is that they had help from someone on the inside," said Genaya gravely.

"If that's the case we must inform the Ordo immediately so they can let Governor Pehran know urgently," said Heysen insistently.

"It's too late now, Heysen, we're too close to Corvaan and our signal will be blocked," said Genaya hopelessly. "Besides, if we do try and send one, they may detect our presence here too soon and our fate might be the same as Conraya's."

Heysen paused a bit, reconciling his thoughts. "In that case, we must head to a remote section of the planet in the rainforest. There we can lie low for a little bit and sneak our way into

Nantan," he said assuredly.

"We might be watched the whole time, how are we supposed to get intel?" asked Genaya curiously.

"Good point, but I feel our only option is to be a fly on the wall. We shall watchfully and carefully creep our way around and try to uncover any information we can without being detected. That part is paramount," stressed Heysen.

"Do not worry, Heysen, I won't be reckless," said Genaya frustratingly.

"Your little episode on Dohna said otherwise, but regardless I just want to stress how important it is. Because if what you suspect is happening is indeed what is occurring, our lives are in great peril," said Heysen warningly.

"I'm aware of that," said Genaya sincerely.

"And if you do get into serious trouble, use your Electromagnetic Boots and take to the rooftops. That'll at least buy you some time to head back for the ship," said Heysen. "And don't forget to take the cloak off, you certainly won't need it here. You'll boil from the humidity," Heysen laughed.

Genaya looked down to realise he was still wearing his cloak from Dohna. He rolled his eyes at Heysen's bemusement before sliding off the cloak and placing it back in one of the ship's storage compartments. Genaya then turned to look out of the V-craft's window at the tropical planet that lay ahead. Out of the corner of his eye he noticed one of the three moons of spherical shape, nearby to his right. He looked intently at it, noticing some structures being developed on the moon itself.

"Hey, Heysen?" asked Genaya befuddled.

"Yeah?" replied Heysen.

"Has there always been structures on Corvaan's moon C-2?" asked Genaya, further perplexed by the sight.

"Wait, what?" asked Heysen, distracted from piloting by the puzzling and concerning question from Genaya.

"There seems to be some form of construction there," said Genaya. "I'll take the controls so you can have a look."

Heysen shot up from his chair unnaturally through haste. Genaya, however, was more astounded that Heysen had given no consideration to the fact that he was now piloting the V-craft. Genaya glanced in Heysen's direction to see Heysen standing there like a statue, staring blankly at the anomaly in the distance.

"There's only ever been a small outpost there," he said steadfastly. "This cannot be."

"How so?" asked Genaya.

"Hold on let me take the controls again," insisted Heysen as he ushered Genaya out of the pilot's seat and retook control. "They've never intended to develop there, so this must be recent. Given the current circumstances it could only be for a sinister reason," said Heysen.

"Maybe we'll find out more on Corvaan," said Genaya hopefully.

Despite Genaya's optimism, Heysen remained cautiously silent, slightly disturbed by the increasing developments.

"All right, we're about to enter the atmosphere so buckle up," said Heysen preparedly.

Genaya sat anticipatingly in the co-pilots seat, grasping the ship's weapons controls.

"One thing I find strange is that when I came here, I was attacked by a small Cross-Fighter brigade. So far here we haven't encountered anything," said Genaya confused.

"That may be so. However, we may not encounter any trouble in space. If what we suspect is indeed occurring, our adversaries lurk on Corvaan itself," warned Heysen. "Make sure you're ready to use that thing, if need be, though," said Heysen, directing Genaya's attention towards his Plasma-Blade.

Genaya nodded a little excitedly as they entered further into the thick atmosphere of Corvaan. The planet was much clearer now that there was no real air-traffic about Corvaan, even in the atmosphere. There was an eery stillness as they descended through thick cloud. Genaya felt that the extreme lack of activity was highly conspicuous. As the clouds faded quickly. Corvaan's capital Nantan was situated in the distance. Genaya's suspicions were heightened further as there seemed to be an array of ground activity there, despite the abnormal lack of activity in the atmosphere.

"I don't like the look of this," said Heysen highly alarmed. He hauled the ship around between two large hills and through a small, densely forested gorge, out of sight from Nantan.

"Do you reckon anyone saw us arrive?" asked Genaya worriedly.

"Hard to say but given the strange things occurring here I'd say they already know of our presence," said Heysen.

"Great," said Genaya sarcastically. "That seemed like a lot of people down there," Genaya stated nervously.

"I would bet they're not too friendly," said Heysen facetiously. "And if they are citizens I hold grave fears for them," said Heysen, now with a much graver tone.

The ship meandered around the gorge, which had brown bare-stone cliffs on either side, before rising above a large canopying tree.

"All right, Genaya, you can ease off the Cannons now, I've found a clearing for us to land," said Heysen half-jokingly.

Genaya slowly gave Heysen a look of mild disappointment, much to Heysen's amusement. "Don't worry, Genaya, you'll get your chance to use them," said Heysen now smiling.

The clearing where the Paxian landed was small and had thick, tall trees surrounding it. The clearing was mostly soft dirt with some small grassy patches. It was of an irregular shape but was still of sufficient size to accommodate the V-craft. Heysen brought the ship down slowly and steadily, navigating it around the tall obstacles. It then gently contacted the ground, and the thrusters decreased and hummed their way to a swift stillness. The V-craft's door hatch thrust open, and the light of Corvaan beamed in.

"Now, we MUST remain unseen. The mission and our lives are at stake if we cannot do that," said Heysen with the utmost sense of seriousness. "We will have to sneak around Nantan to gain information where we can. And we cannot afford to be split up either. There won't be a rescue party," warned Heysen.

Genaya nodded, recognising the seriousness and ever-present danger of what they were about to embark on.

"If we are sneaking, won't it be best to take the cloaks with us to help conceal our identities? I mean, don't you think two people walking around in Paxian suits will probably be a tad obvious?" enquired Genaya.

Genaya's query intrigued Heysen enough to draw a brief pause from Ordo level Paxian. "There is some validity to that, but we will suffer anyway. It's too humid out there, we'd just overheat. Besides, there is no harsh wind like on Dohna, so there is little benefit," said Heysen dismissively. "Now, stick behind me. We have some walking to do," said Heysen.

Genaya nodded and proceeded to follow behind Heysen. The V-craft's door closed after Heysen and Genaya disembarked, as Heysen used his ring, bearing the Ordo logo, to secure the ship. They began their expedition to Nantan, pacing through the rainforest and meandering over fallen tree logs and large rocks.

After some trekking through the rainforest, they emerged from it perched upon a tall hill. A sharp drop followed on the hill's forward-facing side. The view of Nantan was now much clearer to Genaya and the city was much more detailed than before. The outskirts were only a short distance away now and many features of Nantan were present. Suburban villages and housing were widespread. Those closer to the city centre were stacked against each other like sardines. All the city's structures were coloured differently; in brick reds, blacks, greys, light sandstone yellows, browns and some white.

The Main Government Building sat at the centre of the city, with the large open plaza in the centre surrounded by large buildings around fifty metres high. The plaza itself was rectangular in shape and nearly a kilometre long. It was paved with silver tiles and had small shrubbery and thin green trees lining its perimeter. However, what was also dauntingly evident to Genaya was the large procession of Corvaan's military. Large patrols marched throughout the plaza, with some vehicles moving around, carrying troops or used generally to bolster the firepower.

Heysen and Genaya quickly lay down amongst some longer grass and trees to remain hidden whilst assessing the situation.

"Looks like we've already discovered something pretty dire," said Genaya softly.

"Yes, well it's not the most comforting sight," said Heysen slightly sarcastically.

"What could they possibly be doing?" asked Genaya.

"It seems to me like standard patrols, but only for a militarised government," said Heysen curiously accessing the situation.

"That doesn't explain the volume of troops though," Genaya pointed out.

"True! That I don't have an answer for," said Heysen with deep intrigue. "My only guesses are that someone or something important is arriving. That, or they are soon to be mobilised into action."

"Mobilised on whom? Dohna?" said Genaya in a shocked, but hushed tone.

Heysen turned slowly and worriedly, "I don't know, but that may be the case."

"But why would they do that and deploy almost all their military on a system they claim is engaging in espionage against the Federation?" pleaded Genaya. "It doesn't make sense!"

"None of this makes sense, Genaya," said Heysen apprehensively. "This entire situation is beyond anything I have ever witnessed or experienced in my time in the Ordo. Just about in my lifetime, too."

Genaya looked at Heysen fearfully. "If that is the case, then what do we do?" he asked.

"Well, normally we'd send a hologram message. However, as you pointed out we cannot do that as they've blocked our signal," said Heysen frustratedly. "We still need to go down there and gather intel," said Heysen adamantly.

"Why though, we could be killed?" asked Genaya aghast at the suggestion.

"Well hold on, I thought you were the one who had a craving for life-threatening situations," said Heysen in a slightly snarky tone.

"Hold up, I only did something reckless once," replied Genaya.

"No, from my knowledge you let a now highly wanted

Assassin slip away due to pure emotion and then attempted to take on Dohna's High Army," said Heysen unimpressed by Genaya's denial.

Genaya paused for a moment, analysing Heysen's comments in frustration. "They were encroaching on us and were armed," pleaded Genaya.

"Diplomacy is paramount to civility and order," said Heysen wisely.

"Yes, well sometimes it's dilatory," said Genaya partly grumpy.

"And in those situations, by all means force is required. However, we are Paxian, and we are required to uphold the peace of this Federation. People look to us to act in correspondence to a situation. You must learn this, not only to be on the Ordo, but to fulfil your duties as a Paxian," said Heysen sincerely.

"Okay, I'll try, but how are we supposed to do our jobs peacefully down there," enquired Genaya.

"By being peaceful!" said Heysen with a smile. "The quieter we are, the safer we will be. If we ensure we have cover and avoid any large patrols, we can still get some information and make it back to the ship safely. And also, have your Plasma-Blade at the ready. You will almost certainly have to use it,"

"I've been waiting for you to say that" said Genaya delightedly, as both he and Heysen absconded back into the forest.

"That's not an excuse for violence," cautioned Heysen.

"You know I'm responsible," laughed Genaya.

"Sometimes. You have your moments," said Heysen as both he and Genaya exchanged grins. "Now if we follow this gully around the side of the hill, we should enter the city through the outer markets. There may be heavy patrols so as we exit the gully, stay low and keep your eyes peeled," said Heysen tactfully.

"Sounds good, if we reach the theatre district, there are some underground passages we could take to get near the plaza, but that'll be tricky," said Genaya.

"It may work, but for now we'll have to play it by ear. Let's go," said Heysen hurriedly.

Genaya and Heysen began to pace back into the rainforest and into a thin, winding gully. The rainforest here was dense, moist and filled with leafy green ferns. Larger, broadleaved trees provided shelter to the rainforest floor under their canopy. A small flowing creek ran along the centre of the gully, providing a sanctuary for flora and fauna alike. Genaya listened to its soft, satisfying trickle as it seeped through rock crevasses and over small sticks. Genaya was calmed by the peace of the rainforest and the soothing sound of flowing water.

Genaya noticed Heysen pause suddenly for a moment, before he ushered Genaya to crouch with him behind a thick tree stump.

"Be very quiet," he whispered ever so softly to Genaya. Heysen then turned around, peering out the corner of the stump.

"What is it? Hey—" said Genaya before being hushed by the firm hand signalling of Heysen.

Genaya followed Heysen's eyes and hand gestures and looked outwards from the tree stump. A faint, distant noise could be heard, but it was growing more distinguishable every second. Genaya could feel the moist, untouched ground below him begin to thud. The soft, damp soil shifted slightly as the vibrations grew larger. Trudge! Trudge! Trudge! Boots squished into the moist soil nearby. A squadron of around two dozen Corvaanian soldiers were making their way through the gully and up the creek.

The soldiers wore lightweight, robust, sliver coloured

armour covering head to toe. The logo of Corvaan was imprinted on the centre-chest region of the armour, both on the back and the front. Their helmets were cone-shaped and dark grey in colour. They had a cut-out part half-way down the faceward side, so that soldiers' faces were visible. The back of the helmet touched the shoulders, covering the neck down to the armour. Genaya noticed that they were armed with Photon-Guns.

Heysen and Genaya watched on intriguingly as the soldiers trekked through the dense rainforest.

"What do you reckon that ship was?" asked one of them.

"I don't know, but I hope there weren't too many people on that ship," said another.

The commander of the regiment, distinguishable by their unique golden helmet, began to speak over them.

"Listen! Premier Finkel gave us orders to kill anyone who leaves that ship. Do not thwart the mission with your relentless speculation. Do your job or I'll inform Finkel of your failure to comply, understood," said the Commander sternly.

"Yes sir," they replied.

The group continued to march away from Genaya and Heysen, their trudges became less audible the further away they got. Heysen looked in all directions before ushering Genaya out of the tree stump and back along the trail of the creek towards Nantan.

"We haven't got long," said Heysen in a hushed tone.

"What do you mean?" asked Genaya.

"If they find our ship, they'll destroy it and know who we are and we'll be stuck here," said Heysen becoming panicked. "We must find more information on what's going on and a fast form of transport to get back to the ship before they find it," urged Heysen.

"Well, it will take them a while," said Genaya confidently.

"That may be so Genaya, but the sheer fact that their mission is to eliminate us, not even knowing who we are, is highly concerning and we must get to the bottom of this," said Heysen.

Genaya nodded at Heysen, before turning and pointing at a clearing up ahead.

"There!" said Genaya. "We're in the outskirts of the city now," he said excitedly.

"Yes, keep an eye out for more patrols and for all that is good keep a cool head. We don't need to die too soon," said Heysen.

Genaya rolled his eyes at Heysen, as they emerged from the rainforest and began entering a residential section of Nantan.

Heysen and Genaya slunk across the street, taking cover where they could.

"The tunnel network starts around a small marketplace nearby. If we take a left up here and then a right, we'll be there," said Genaya.

They began moving forward again, veering left between two buildings down a small alley. Genaya thrust Heysen aside, pressing himself and Heysen firmly against the side of a building. There, they were fairly well hidden behind a corner in the wall. They both paused, hushed by fear.

A small brigade of soldiers, along with two mobilised vehicles hovering ominously above the ground, were patrolling the streets. Genaya and Heysen exchanged fearful looks. The brigade turned away to Genaya's left, down the opposite direction that he and Heysen intended to go. The pair waited a brief moment until they were sure the soldiers had passed, before pacing quickly down the same road, but in the opposite direction to the soldiers. They hugged the walls of the buildings on their right for cover, before reaching a small marketplace. The streets of Nantan were very much deserted of any citizens or traders, only occupied by the Corvaan militia.

"We must find out what had happened here," stressed Heysen in a hushed tone. This is deeply concerning. Their own citizens appear to be victims," he whispered gravely.

"We must get out of here first," whispered Genaya.

Genaya then pointed to a wooden hatch on the ground, not too far in the distance. Genaya did a quick glancing search for any soldiers, before hoisting open the hatch and directing Heysen into it. Heysen hurried into the opening, and Genaya followed close behind, warily ensuring the hatch shut silently and properly, to ensure it appeared untouched.

"Where to now?" asked Heysen.

"Not sure, we need to get near the plaza but that's a while from here," said Genaya puzzled. "It's hard to tell anything down here it's pitch black," he said in annoyance.

Genaya turned in surprise to the sound of an unsheathing Plasma-Blade. Suddenly a bright, orange light shot up from the ends of the Plasma-Blade, beaming and humming at Genaya. A firm 'Thunk!' followed, as the Plasma-Blade ends were magnetically joined together into one long staff-like shape. The energy fields around the ends danced away, their luminescence carried down a decent length of the passageway. Genaya turned to see Heysen adjacent to him, his Ordo suit lit up a deep, glowing orange.

"Thank you, Heysen, but next time do let me know before scaring me like that," said Genaya.

"You're the one complaining about the lack of light, I provided it," said Heysen, his illuminated face smirking at Genaya. "Now, where to?"

"Well, if we're under the marketplace, I think we'll need to head in a generally straight direction," said Genaya.

"Well, that's helpful," said Heysen sarcastically.

"That's the best information I have. Dreyfus knew these networks best," said Genaya defending his directions.

"All right, well, we'll try and get there, but for the love of goodness don't get us lost," pleaded Heysen. "And keep an eye out, I'm sure there'll be soldiers here too," cautioned Heysen.

Genaya and Heysen wandered around the tunnel network, slowly making their way to the centre of Nantan. After some time, they emerged at a T-junction. The left passage was short and hooked right in the direction Genaya and Heysen were travelling. The right passage had stairs leading up to a moderately sized silver door.

"If I'm correct, that door should lead out the side of a building and the Main Plaza should be close nearby," said Genaya. "Left will take us slightly further away than we'd want to be."

"Well, wouldn't that be ideal?" enquired Heysen baffled. "With the military presence in and around the Plaza we'd surely be seen. So going left would be safer and wiser, even though it's not as close," assessed Heysen.

"There's sufficient cover and there's less distance to travel to the right," said Genaya adamantly. "The other direction will take longer, and we don't really have a lot of time."

"Oh, all right," said Heysen as he disengaged his Plasma-Blade. The passages grew dark again and the pair were no longer comforted from the bright orange glow of Heysen's Paxian suit.

"I'd suggest you get yours out, there may be trouble on the other side," said Heysen warningly.

Genaya unsheathed the Plasma-Blade ends and then magnetised them together, but didn't engage the plasma beams to remain incognito. They then slowly crept up the stairs and stood leaning gently against the door. Genaya grew nervous, the adrenaline began to interfere with his thought processes. He attempted to calm himself.

His attention was quickly caught by Heysen, who was signalling him to slowly nudge the door open and peer through briefly. Genaya acknowledged the gesture, and gently nudged the door slightly ajar, waiting to see if there'd be any reaction to the movement.

No noise could be heard, no sense of urgency on the other side of the door. Most importantly, there was no alarm, no panic. Genaya then peered through the tiny crevasse between the door and the wall, hopeful of the situation on the other side. There, standing either side of the doorway, centimetres from the door space, were two Corvaanian Soldiers staring intently into the distance, away from Genaya and Heysen's position. Genaya was amazed they had not noticed the door nudge open.

The faint noise the door made surely would've given them away, he thought to himself.

His hopes though were dashed quickly, realising that they were distracted by the large fleet of soldiers not too far away in the large open plaza. It was clear to Genaya that the great noise they were creating was loud enough to muffle out any other minor sounds that may be present. Nonetheless, Genaya knew that he and Heysen could not go this way. Any sort of altercation would immediately alert hundreds of troops of their presence and their mission would certainly be over, along with their lives.

"Well, what do you see?" faintly whispered Heysen enthusiastically.

Genaya mimicked the words 'move over there quietly' to Heysen, gesturing with his finger. They slowly and lightly trod away from the door before Genaya responded.

"There are too many soldiers around, we'll be sitting ducks," whispered Genaya. "We'll have to try the long way."

"Are you sure that won't be riskier?" asked Heysen curiously.

"I cannot say, but it should give us a much better chance of escape," he said surely.

Genaya turned and went down the alternative passage. Heysen following close behind. The darkness of the tunnels provided little comfort, knowing they may be sprung at any moment. Right, left, right. This alternative route seemed like an aimless detour. Eventually though, they came upon a dim light at the end of the tunnel. Both Heysen and Genaya advanced slowly down the passage and ignited their Plasma-Blades, assured the glow created by them would not jeopardise their undercover operation. Heysen once again gestured Genaya to inspect the door. Genaya felt the black metal-ringed doorknob on the wooden doors. Slowly, he clasped its cold, hard surface firmly in his hands. Genaya then applied as little force as possible and gracefully and silently opened one of the doors to create a small gap.

Genaya could see that this entryway lead to the cellar of a building. Several cupboards, mostly for storage, along with other items were down here. More concerningly, it appeared to be a munitions storage space containing several Photon-Guns, Impact Grenades, Anti-Artillery Weapons and much more. Furthermore, there were two guards standing a tad in front of the doorway Genaya was peering through. They were facing away from the door, having a casual, indiscernible conversation.

Genaya signalled with his fingers to Heysen that there were two guards located in front of the door. Heysen acknowledged this with a grinning nod, whilst moving into an attacking stance. Genaya then gently and silently moved the door further ajar, now showing Heysen a clear view of the cellar. Both Heysen and Genaya demagnetised their Plasma-Blades and swiftly attacked the soldiers standing idle.

Shoom! The Plasma-Blades hummed and screeched as they pierced the Corvaanian soldiers' armour. The remnants of the armour were left scorched and scarred. The soldiers, impaled at the chest, fell forwards onto the floor lying dead and motionless, unaware of what had just occurred. After picking off one guard each, both Genaya and Heysen disengaged their Plasma-Blades and magnetised them back together as they cautiously analysed the cellar.

"What do you think?" enquired Genaya.

"Rather unnecessary for a political dispute," said Heysen. "I fear this stockpile is just one of many. However, we must remain cautious. There should be more guards around here.

"Agreed. I'll lead. You stay close behind me," said Genaya decisively.

Heysen agreed and they proceeded up the cellar stairs and made their way towards the ground floor of the building. The stairway led to an open entryway, situated just outside the building and a short distance away from the building's main entrance. The building had a veranda-like covering outside and around the front entrance to shield it from harsh weather. This covering extended to the cellar stairway.

Genaya could see at least two guards standing outside the front of the main building, with more assumedly situated within the complex itself. A pillar, wide enough to conceal at least one of them, was situated just in front of Genaya.

"I'll sneak over there for cover, you wait here until I signal you," whispered Genaya, as he and Heysen crouched on the stairway hiding from view.

"Are you sure you're not going to get us killed?" whispered Heysen sarcastically in reply.

"Just trust me. If we need to run, we run," said Genaya decisively.

Genaya turned back and peered above the stairway to ensure the guards were not watching. Confident he was in the clear, Genaya darted low towards the pillar and took refuge there. He scoured across the street now for any lingering danger. Another building, beside the one he and Heysen just emerged out of, had a doorway unguarded. The door was situated in a corner between the two buildings, with concealment from almost all directions. Genaya then peered out to see if there were any other troops.

Four there. Two there. Six there. Genaya paused in shock. Located a small distance down the street, was an entourage of nearly a hundred soldiers and three artillery vehicles making their way towards him. Genaya, hopeful that he had not been sighted, looked back to see if Heysen was still awaiting a signal.

Unsurprisingly to Genaya, Heysen was now eagerly seeking Genaya, asking for any update or sign for movement.

Genaya gestured with his left hand for Heysen to come, before he bolted from his cover and disappeared behind the wall on Heysen's left.

Genaya waited momentarily in fear of being sprung. But there was no disturbance. He then watched Heysen appear from behind the corner and take cover beside the pillar, using it to ensure he too was not being observed.

Genaya watched anticipatedly as Heysen assessed the pair's surroundings. Genaya could read his face instantly as Heysen discovered the scattered array of guards, relatively small in number, blissfully unaware of their presence. Heysen's face grew sour as he glanced in the direction of the approaching entourage of troops. Luckily, Genaya was hiding in a concealed porch, to the left of the street and ushered Heysen to move before they were caught out.

Genaya felt Heysen's hesitation and nervousness as he seemed to be stuck in two minds. He watched Heysen close his eyes in hope and gracefully make the brief dash to the porch. Both Paxian held their breath once again, but no alarm was raised. Now Heysen and Genaya were cornered under the shelter with troops approaching from the rear. They had nowhere to go. More troops were now approaching from the other direction, seemingly conducting their routine patrols.

It would only be a matter of time before they were caught, thought Genaya.

"Well, this is cheery," said Heysen sarcastically. "You don't suppose we could've waited a little bit?"

"Perhaps, but we cannot just wait there. Like you said, we have limited time," replied Genaya.

"I guess so, but nonetheless this is about to get messy," said Heysen concerningly. "Prepare your Electromagnetic Boots. You will need them to launch away from the troops."

Genaya nodded. His boots began to make a soft noise in the expectation of making a roaring movement. The two Paxian stood there, waiting for certain capture, maybe death; knowing that they would not be able to escape. They held their Plasma-Blades, engaged and at the ready. Their peril was just metres away.

Then the door behind them opened. Both Paxian turned in fear, wielding their Plasma-Blades in anticipation for conflict. A hooded figure appeared from the darkened room, looking at both

Paxian. The hooded cloak he wore was brown all over and shaded his face. Genaya and Heysen quickly disengaged their Plasma-Blades, as they did not believe this figure was a genuine threat. Nonetheless, they still held them out at the ready in case of an error in their judgement.

"Come in, if you wish to live," the figure muttered softly.

Genaya and Heysen exchanged looks of angst before reluctantly proceeding into the building.

Surely this man could not be any more dangerous than the fleet of soldiers that would purge them if they knew of their presence, thought Genaya.

As they entered the doorway, the man gently closed the door behind, peering out to make sure they were not seen. He then proceeded in the dark ahead of Genaya and Heysen, lighting a small lantern and taking it with him around what appeared to be a large table. He then flicked a switch, and the room became apparent.

Genaya noticed the large, circular orange table at the front. There was a meeting area in the back left corner and a red makeshift bed to his left. They both placed their Plasma-Blades back into their holsters. The features of the room resonated through both Heysen and Genaya as the man's identity became increasingly apparent. Both Genaya and Heysen stood there, facing the hooded figure gobsmacked. Their shock only increased when the figure removed his hood and revealed his pink Corvaanian skin. Standing with a large grin on his face and a look of sheer relief and pleasure, was Dreyfus.

Chapter 10

Neither Genaya nor Heysen could believe their eyes. Dreyfus, long assumed dead, stood before them cloaked and hidden away in what was left of the Old Paxian Headquarters in Nantan.

"Dreyfus… how?" asked Genaya in delighted shock.

"It's good to see you too old buddy," said Dreyfus as he removed his cloak.

Genaya saw Dreyfus' deep clover green Paxian armour now stretching from head to toe. His yellow eyes and round bald head were also visible. Dreyfus also had small and thin red eyebrows that were slightly crested. He appeared youthful, despite his age.

"Heysen Jogja, it's good to see you," said Dreyfus cheerfully.

"It's been a while, Dreyfus, glad to see you're well," replied Heysen.

"I cannot believe you're actually here," said Genaya with glee. "I tried calling you, but there was no response. We thought you were dead."

"Nearly!" said Dreyfus in a less joyful tone. He turned to reveal a long but thin scar, seemingly freshly engraved on the back of his neck.

"What happened?" enquired Heysen with concern.

"Assassin, by the name of Lucifer Dunn," said Dreyfus, the words penetrating uncomfortably into Genaya's ears.

"Yes, we know about him. He tried to kill me too, but how come you're alive?" asked Genaya.

"He missed me. He thought he had me while I was standing up. I felt the bolt graze my neck painfully, but I tried to play dead," said Dreyfus, much to Genaya and Heysen's intrigue. "He would've been too far away to tell the difference. I knew though I had to go into hiding."

"What about the body though? They would've come to inspect," said Genaya.

"They did. I managed to be able to use the body of a diseased villager and dress them up in my spare armour. I'm certainly not proud of it but they couldn't tell the difference," he said.

"Well, I'm glad you're alive, Dreyfus. Do you have any information on Bido?" asked Heysen curiously.

Dreyfus's face drooped into sorrow at the sound of her name. "She was killed," said Dreyfus dismally. I went to check up on her a while ago, to make sure she didn't succumb to the same fate. I couldn't find her," he said. "It was only when they strung up bodies in Nantan Plaza that I saw her chained to a pole they'd left there temporarily."

Heysen and Genaya reacted in horror to the claim by Dreyfus.

"What do you mean they put her on a temporary pole?" asked Genaya distraught.

Dreyfus looked up at Genaya with sadness, "They put in some poles for a bit of time, with bodies of people slain by the government, to warn others not to interfere or meddle."

"Meddle?" asked Heysen with deepened curiosity.

"The government under Premier Finkel has been undergoing suspicious activity for ages," said Dreyfus solemnly. "Those people were just some of the ones they'd claimed interfered. So, they killed them and strung them up. My decoy was there too. It was clear that they were instilling fear into any Corvaanians who disagreed with their will."

Genaya and Heysen paused, exchanging concerned looks.

"I'm highly curious though. You are very bold to be lurking around these streets, especially wearing Paxian Armour. What brings you here?" asked Dreyfus.

"We're on Ordo duties, Dreyfus. We are trying to uncover more about this disturbing situation," said Heysen seriously. "As I'm sure you know, there's been a political spat between Dohna and Corvaan over unknown origins. We hadn't found out any information, but we got a lead after Genaya confronted Lucifer Dunn. He escaped but informed Genaya of other targeted hits on Paxian. Genaya went to investigate when he could not make contact with you or Bido, but encountered opposition before reaching here. He also found Ordo member Conraya's ship destroyed, along with several trade ships that were headed to Dohna," said Heysen.

"This is indeed deeply concerning, what did you find at Dohna?" asked Dreyfus.

"Nothing unusual," said Heysen reassuringly. "The Dohnans were not acting suspiciously and cooperated well. The only intriguing point was that they were safeguarding their Paxian from Lucifer Dunn in an unknown location. They were not overly trusting of us, nor any other foreigner."

"That does not surprise me," said Dreyfus. "The day before I was nearly assassinated, I tried speaking to Premier Finkel in regard to the deteriorating situation. She would not talk to me, but her advisors messaged me saying they could not tell me why they were causing trouble or accusing Dohna of espionage. There was no warning, no indication. It was all out of the blue, unexpected."

"That's also why we're here, we're trying to uncover as

much information as we can about the matter from Corvaan's perspective," said Heysen, as they all sat down around the orange table to discuss the issue.

"Well, from what I have gathered there is much to say. I've heard much from the citizens in my ventures in recent times. I have also seen and witnessed plenty of highly disturbing things," said Dreyfus gravely.

Suddenly, a loud buzzing noise could be heard vibrating across the room and throughout the building, gradually increasing in intensity. Dreyfus quickly gestured to Genaya and Heysen to remain quiet and hide under a gap in the wall, hidden behind a camouflaged panel. They crawled in, as Dreyfus quickly flicked off the lights and joined them, grabbing the panel as he entered and fastened it into place.

Genaya felt partially claustrophobic in the nook behind the wall. There was little room. It was dark and very dusty, and they were packed into the small gap with little wriggle room. The sound was now resonating throughout the building.

"What is it?" whispered Genaya loudly, trying to overpower the buzzing noise.

"Vehicles. Artillery. They're moving them. There'll be thousands of soldiers outside right now," responded Dreyfus very softly. "Be quiet though, they'll come in for an inspection any moment."

They listened intently, as one after one, vehicles passed by, disturbing the peace of the city. As the gaps between vehicles passing grew larger, the increased sound of foot traffic by soldiers became prominent. The very notion that so many were out in force and mobilised sent fear trickling down Genaya's spine. He was certain Dreyfus and Heysen felt the same way, if not worse.

The door to the Old Nantan Paxian Headquarters was thrust

open by what sounded like half a dozen soldiers. They barged their way into the room and did a quick spot-search for any troublemakers or straddlers. Their anxiety set in further, as the glow of flashlights periodically beamed onto where the camouflaged panel was obscuring the gap in the wall. They tried holding in their breath, so as not to be heard.

After a debilitating and agonisingly long wait, the flashlight moved away, and the soldiers could be heard vacating the building, closing the door behind them. Dreyfus waited several moments before opting to slowly and gently remove the panel. The foot traffic outside had mostly passed now, nearing none at all. Upon exiting the gap, Dreyfus ushered both Heysen and Genaya out. He then made his way to the doorway, opening it slowly before peering out. No soldiers were around that were not present before, and there was no unusual activity. Upon having his trepidations quelled, Dreyfus closed the door and went to switch the light back on. The room instantly began to feel more comforting, providing a huge sense of relief for Genaya given his and Heysen's enduringly long time of unease.

"That has been occurring more frequently and more intensely in recent times," said Dreyfus disturbingly. "They don't appear to be slowing down any time soon."

"So, this has been a recurring event?" asked Heysen apprehensively.

"Much too recurring, Heysen," said Dreyfus grimly. Dreyfus looked warily towards the door before looking anxiously back at Genaya and Heysen, "These activities have been growing in number, in magnitude and severity."

"Yes, but do you know why," asked Heysen.

"Well not entirely. What was it you said about Genaya being attacked?" enquired Dreyfus.

"Do you mean by Lucifer Dunn?" asked Genaya.

"No, no, not that. In space. Just outside of Corvaan, where Heysen said you were attacked," said Dreyfus.

"Oh, that? I was in the asteroid field, and I was attacked by three Cross-Fighters. Is there something we should know?" asked Genaya confused by Dreyfus.

"Interesting," said Dreyfus with intrigue. "As you may or may not have suspected, Corvaan does not have any Cross-Fighters in its space fleet."

"No, I was not aware of that. What are you suggesting?" enquired Heysen.

"That the perpetrators pulling these strings of conflict go beyond the politics of Corvaan and Dohna," said Dreyfus grimly. "I fear that whether or not Premier Finkel is controlling this political stoush, someone else is controlling her. That she works for someone else," said Dreyfus.

"Who?" asked Genaya.

"There's another person involved here directly. And even she may not be the head," said Dreyfus.

Heysen looked blankly at Dreyfus in disbelief, "No, you're not suggesting that… No!" stuttered Heysen.

"I am. I know it's hard to believe, but it's true," pleaded Dreyfus.

"But they were eliminated. They are no longer a threat. They don't exist any more," petitioned Heysen.

"Oh, they do. And Genaya's account of those Cross-Fighters confirmed it," said Dreyfus. "I knew this had to be beyond local politics. It had no reason. No method. This is an extremely dangerous situation for the Federation," warned Dreyfus.

"Woah! Woah! Woah! Hold on. Who are we even on about here?" asked Genaya, lost by the inside discussion between

Heysen and Dreyfus.

"The Malum!" said Heysen grievously.

"Who?" asked Genaya completely confused.

"The Malum, the legion of Dark Paxian," said Dreyfus gravely. "They were once Paxian, just like us. They trained like us. They were skilled like us. At some point they also cared and protected others like us, because they were us."

"What happened to them?" asked Genaya.

"They were power hungry, manipulative and angry. They wanted the Federation for themselves. They believed the Federation was built upon lies and deceit, that only those privileged enough could achieve greatness. So, they sought to destroy the Federation and the Paxian order. Sadly, many former Paxian and sitting Paxian were emotionally curtailed into their views, their propaganda. No one was safe from it. Your mother fought valiantly to bring them down and disrupt their anarchist agenda. They aimed to create a Dark Federation, run by the Dark Paxian, or Malum. This wasn't intended to be the same setup as the Federation though. They would lure poorer systems, more impressionable systems into their scheme and prey on them. They would financially benefit from joining this Dark Federation. Your mother was Grandmaster at the time. She made a bold move, one unseen in Paxian history. She, with the approval of the Federation House of Representatives, declared war on the Malum and anyone siding with the Dark Federation. The war on Vormok was one of the biggest in Galactic history and the first time the Federation ventured war into a non-Federation system," said Dreyfus.

"Wow really? I've never known that's why it started. And what about the Malum?" asked Genaya.

"Well, they supposedly lost. The war on Vormok helped

liberate many systems from the Malum and increase the power and stability of the Galactic Federation. However, many believed some escaped, absconded from the battle before it was lost to preserve their ideology. Some Paxian have even gone missing for unbeknown reasons in recent times, potentially due to their resurgence. The Ordo has and always will be there to prevent these situations from occurring, but we cannot monitor everyone. The Malum stick in the dark sections of the Galaxy. Those ungoverned systems. I fear now that they may have infiltrated the Federation and are hatching a diabolical plan to rectify the past," said Dreyfus bleakly.

"This makes no sense though. We can monitor these things. The Governors and other politicians could not commit such acts without being discovered. Even fellow Paxian would find it hard to be so secretively sinister. They all adhere to a standard to fulfil their position. They would never be so corrupted," said an aggrieved Genaya.

"Don't be so naive, Genaya. Like you, some of these people are overemotionally attached to things. They get too concerned, too fearful of losing things such as power. Once this fear sets in, it does horrible things to people. It does corrupt them. They can be emotionally manipulated until one day they're doing things that they never thought they could do. Horrible, despicable things, just for their own personal gain," admonished Heysen.

Genaya paused in fear, disbelieving what he had just heard. "Are you sure? How could so many be corrupted so easily? It's unthinkable," he said in disbelief at Heysen's insinuation.

"Trust me, Genaya. If they have a common cause, such as power and control, anyone can be seduced," said Heysen surely. "That's why Grandmaster Zeffiro worries about your emotional attachments, your anger. It can control you if you do not monitor it and suppress it," counselled Heysen.

Genaya felt annoyed that Heysen would bring the matter up again but understood that Heysen was only being encouraging. "Are we even sure though that that's what's occurring here?" enquired Genaya.

"Well, I don't want to speak for Dreyfus. I'm not wholly convinced yet, but there's a high possibility that that is the case," said Heysen gloomily. "Their absence for the best part of twenty-three years would indicate that they do not exist. In fact, on that note, Grandmaster Zeffiro became Grandmaster right before the war ended, after your mother stepped down."

"And what happened to my mother, you know, before she died?" asked Genaya.

"She was Vice-Master," said Dreyfus informatively. "She assisted Zeffiro in restoring peace and democracy to the Federation. Unfortunately, as you know, she died along with your father a year later. Tragic it was," said Dreyfus miserably. "Nonetheless, I do not believe they eradicated the Malum. I'm certain they still exist and that some are here dictating Premier Finkel."

"If that is the case, Dreyfus, we must get out of here and report back to Grandmaster Zeffiro immediately. We've already encountered a small group of Corvaanian soldiers searching for our ship. They know we're here and are hoping to eradicate us before anyone else knows what's going on," said Heysen anxiously.

"I know, I fear something big is happening soon, there's a large amount of activity within the government that would suggest things are shifting for the worse," said Dreyfus grimly. "On the matter of your ship, it will take them some time to reach it if you've hidden it well within the rainforest. Eventually they will locate it, of course. Corvaan is only so big and there are more and more planetary patrols every day."

"Yes, but how will we get back there before they do," said Heysen slightly frustrated by the conundrum.

"Ah, that's where I can help you," said Dreyfus. "Nearby is a recreational hangar. It has all sorts of planetary cruisers and vehicles that will be able to take you to your ship."

"You conveniently forgot to mention the part where the planet is being patrolled and monitored by thousands of soldiers and artillery vehicles," said Genaya pessimistically.

"Yes, well that'll be a hassle. But if you fly low and take a slightly longer path, it will be harder for them to spot you," Dreyfus said adamantly. "Besides, once you reach the rainforest, the trees will provide adequate protection. Any Hover-speeders they wish to deploy will take some time to get to your position, so that's an advantage too," said Dreyfus.

"Are you not coming with us?" enquired Genaya.

"I want to, but I cannot leave my people to rot here. I am a Paxian after all," responded Dreyfus. "I will, however, help you and Heysen reach the hangar and escape. This is information that must reach Manoma," said Dreyfus defiantly.

"I agree with that sentiment, Dreyfus, but they will find you and presumably kill you for your treason," said Heysen.

"If there is a way, we can escape without you risking your life for us, then that is the course of action we should take," said Genaya.

"There is, Genaya, but it is inexplicably unlikely you will make it out alive," said Dreyfus grimly. "I must help you and ensure you escape, for the sake of peace and democracy in the galaxy."

"He's right, Genaya," said Heysen acceptingly. "He's risking his life so we can make it out. A very Paxian thing to do."

"But he shouldn't have to risk his life for us," pleaded Genaya.

"Trust me, Genaya, I'll be fine," said Dreyfus reassuringly. "Do not be fearful. Your lives are more valuable than mine. It's a necessary risk."

Genaya appeared reluctant in his acceptance of Dreyfus' pleas, but eventually came around. "Okay. But that still doesn't answer how we're going to escape. There are guards wall to wall," said Genaya cynically.

"That's true, and it'll be risky," said Dreyfus. "I don't see how you're getting out of here completely undetected."

"He's right, Genaya," said Heysen. "We'll be seen leaving at some point. It's best we be prepared to face them when they find us."

"There are some Drone-Speeders in the hangar, they should be able to get you out of here quick-smart," said Dreyfus. "There are Laser Cannons mounted on them as well. You'll be able to use them to defend yourselves.

"Well, that's settled, but how do we get from here to there?" asked Heysen.

"The sun should be starting to go down soon, but nightfall is still a while away," said Dreyfus. "There's still lots of light out but there will be plenty of shaded areas you can use for cover."

"Excellent, and how do we get there?" asked Heysen.

"I'll lead you. It's just down the street here and then you make a right turn, and it should be on your left," said Dreyfus.

"Good. Is there sufficient cover that way?" asked Heysen.

"I think so," said Dreyfus. "Have your Plasma-Blades at the ready though."

All three Paxian removed their Plasma-Blade ends from

their holsters and magnetised them together. Dreyfus moved towards the door, and they followed in step. Dreyfus suddenly paused and turned to Heysen and Genaya with a look of confusion. A noise could be heard outside the building. Footsteps. All three Paxian got into attacking stances and ignited their Plasma-Blades.

The door of the building was knocked down forcefully in a brief instant. The sound of the door thudding onto the ground shook the ground slightly. Quickly, the crisp orangey-pink glow of the early evening poured in. The smell of the humid air raced into the room. After a moment of shock, a small group of Corvaanian Soldiers burst down the door, pointing their Photon-Guns at the three Paxian. The three of them knew at this point, subtlety was no longer an option.

Chapter 11

"Hands up, or we will shoot," said one of the Soldiers sternly.

Genaya quickly realised that the sight of the three Paxian holding their ignited Plasma-Blades; beaming in green, yellow and orange, would be intimidating at the very least. The glow of their armour, highlighting their status, would be a further driver of the Soldiers' anxiety.

"Put the Plasma-Blades down now or we will shoot. You're under arrest for treason," ordered the Soldier, raising his voice sharply.

Genaya, Heysen and Dreyfus stood fearless to the threat of death. Genaya watched the Soldier's face turn from one of angst to one of anger in a matter of seconds.

With a loud piercing yell, he screamed, "FIRE!"

Red blasts of highly energised light began zipping out from the Corvaanian Soldiers' Photon-Guns. The deep 'Shump' sound they made echoed and reverberated around the room and outside of the building. The Paxian stood there, allied together. Their Plasma-Blades were moving left and right. The glow of their Plasma-Blades became blurred at times with the frenetic pace at which they were deflecting the Photon-Gun blasts.

After the initial fire, some soldiers began collapsing on the floor, suffering from a return of fire. Their Photon-Gun blasts were deflected straight back at them. As the number of soldiers suffering from their own bolts increased, the Paxian slowly began advancing forward to the doorway. The number of troops coming through the door was dropping by the second. Left and right, they succumbed to the expertise of the Paxian and their Plasma-Blades.

As the soldiers lay unmoving on the floor, the Paxian relaxed a little and began assessing their surroundings. Genaya stayed back with Heysen as Dreyfus opted to be the first to approach the doorway.

"We have incoming at twelve o'clock," Dreyfus yelled.

"Best get moving then, lead the way," urged Heysen, panting from the instantaneous adrenaline rush.

The Paxian made their way single file out the door. Scores of soldiers had heard the commotion and were coming out from all angles to disrupt the Paxian's advances. Most notably, a regiment of a hundred troops were making their way from the north of the street and were heavily armed. The Paxian made it outside, deflecting the bolts fired from the soldiers Photon-Guns as they came from many directions.

All three Paxian opted to ignite their Electromagnetic Boots and propel themselves onto a nearby rooftop, narrowly avoiding Photo-Gun fire as they did so. Upon landing safely, they started making their way down the street via the rooftops, hurdling across the tight-knit structures. Some soldiers attempted to fire at them from ground level, but Genaya knew their efforts were merely optimistic.

As the Paxian made it to the end of the block, they leapt across a large gap to the adjacent block, continuing their escape. Some soldiers were manned on the rooftops ahead of the Paxian and began firing in startled surprise. Heysen and Dreyfus swiftly wielded their Plasma-Blades in a near figure-eight motion, immediately removing the threat. Genaya followed closely behind them, deflecting the few Photon-Gun blasts that came his way.

Onwards they ran, leaping from block to block, before Dreyfus opted to turn left. Heysen and Genaya lagged in their response to this unexpected change of direction, but soon caught up.

"The hangar is over there, we just have to make a leap down onto the street now," yelled Dreyfus out of breath to Genaya and Heysen behind him.

"What about all the troops down there though?" asked Genaya baffled.

"We'll take care of them, don't you worry," puffed Heysen positively to Genaya, also running out of breath.

The trio leapt down from the rugged and uneven surfaces of the rooftops to the smoother, paved streets of Nantan. Palms lined the sides of the street, which was fairly narrow. The tiles of the street were deep grey, but contrasted the white-, black- and gold-coloured buildings around them. The tall thin streetlights stood firm and straight, as if they were eager to brighten up the city. The sunlight was now barely piercing the avenue, as it was shaded by the surrounding buildings. The sky was a golden crisp orange, with some parts of it fading towards a pinker tone. The shadows of the day now engulfed the street, and within them lay the threat of the Corvaanian Soldiers. Genaya watched them with angst. They were armed, prepared for battle and well equipped to deal with most fugitives. But Genaya knew that the soldiers had never fought a Paxian before, let alone three of them. They usually allied with them, not opposed them.

Given what Genaya could easily assume were tyrannical and oppressional orders, the soldiers aimed across at the fugitive Paxian and fired. The Photon-Gun blasts hailed towards the Paxian, who elegantly deflected the bolts with precision. Back-to-back-to-back, they created a perimeter where none of the bolts from the Photon-Guns could enter. The yellow, green and orange plasma fields at the ends of their Plasma-Blades danced around, repelling the onslaught of red bolts. One by one, soldiers started falling, succumbing to the same fates that their fellow servicemen had only minutes ago.

Despite the obviously folly attempts to shoot the Paxian to death, they continued. As such, their numbers decreased. Most of the fire was now coming from the western side of the street. The recreational hangar, a wide and relatively tall building with a rectangular shape, was well within distance and sight of the Paxian. Only around a hundred soldiers opposed them now. With Genaya covering the fairly soldier-bare eastern direction of the street, Heysen and Dreyfus advanced on the remaining soldiers. Many were fatigued from their tedious and vain attempts to at least subdue the Paxian. As such, they fell to the Plasma-Blade strikes with ease. A stream of corpses piled up on the road. They had quickly and harshly been dealt with by the might of the Paxian. With a final, powerful blow; Heysen demagnetised his Plasma-Blade into its two ends and slashed at the two remaining soldiers.

Genaya, now sensing the all-clear on his side, turned to find a mass grave of diseased soldiers lying defeated on the ground. “That was fun,” said Genaya joyously.

“It’s not over yet. Something is up,” said Dreyfus cautiously.

“What do you mean?” asked Genaya.

“We only got a few small regiments. That certainly was not their entire army by any means,” said Dreyfus with concern. “I thought they’d send more.”

“You’re right to be suspicious, Dreyfus. Keep your eyes peeled, they’re planning something,” said Heysen.

"How far to the hangar?" asked Genaya unfazed.

"It's just over there. We won't be able to open the main doors from the outside, we'll have to make our way through the back entrance to get there," said Dreyfus.

The three Paxian, now seemingly safe from attack, disengaged the Plasma fields on their Plasma-Blades and started running towards the hangar. They darted around a side alley and made their way to the rear of the complex where there was a small, motion-sensing door. As they arrived it opened for them, revealing a dark and eery environment.

There were vehicles here, as well as other aircraft and some spacecraft, but they were barely distinguishable. The resounding footsteps on the solid metal floor was the only thing mitigating the unnerving, prowling silence of the hangar.

All three Paxian entered through the doorway. The sounds they made upon entry shot to the other end of the hangar and back in no time, reflected by the solid enclosed walls. Dreyfus turned away briefly to the side panel, searching for the light switch.

Genaya slowly moved forward, before a small thud could be heard in the near distance. Footsteps now, slow and soft, making their way towards Genaya's position. Fearful of this unknown figure lurking in the dark, Genaya engaged his Plasma-Blade and the other Paxian, now paying attention to the luminous glow of Genaya's Plasma-Blade, followed suit.

The yellow glow of Genaya's Plasma-Blade provided a small beacon for Genaya, but now a sinister pair of yellow eyes were staring intently at him in the distance. Genaya paused, as did this mysterious figure.

What was he up to? Who was he? Genaya could barely think, paralysed with the fear and ambiguity of the individual and their set of evil-looking eyes.

The figure now took one step forward. All the Paxian were focussed squarely on him. The sound of a Plasma-Blade being magnetised resonated throughout the hangar. Genaya's eyes now lit up in fear. A graphite grey Plasma-Blade lit up at both ends, on either side of the daring yellow eyes. Suddenly, the sound of another Plasma-Blade being magnetised together shot into Genaya's ears. The echoes of fear reverberated through Genaya long after long after the sound had dissipated.

How can this be? Are there two of them? Genaya wondered. He could not believe it.

As the second Plasma-Blade engaged, Genaya watched the same graphite grey colour shimmer into his nervously dazzled eyes. This figure now appeared to possess two Plasma-Blades, one just above the other at around chest height. Now all that Genaya could see were the two ends of two Plasma-Blades, their darker colour complementing the evil yellowness of the individual's eyes.

The lights in the hangar came on, their rays scattering across the area, destroying the mystery and fear that had hidden within the darkness. A tall, muscular alien was standing several metres in front of Genaya. His two legs held him firmly in an attacking posture. However, it was clear now that the two Plasma-Blades were being held by his four muscular arms.

He had a bald head, and his skin was a patterned mixture of icy grey and dark burning red. His face had two long icy grey lines travelling upwards from his chin, through his eyes and over his head. They were joined at the chin by a grey coloured filling. He had two additional grey streaks branching around the side of his head below his wide, slanted eyes. A single grey line between his nose and mouth conjoined the main vertical stripes of grey. Furthermore, a grey plus symbol was located centrally between his eyes. The Samurai-like suit he was wearing was similar to a Paxian's, only it was of a slightly different style. The other notable feature was its glow, which also happened to be a dark graphite grey colour.

Vondur Jeppora slowly advanced on Genaya, striking some small supporting pillars and equipment as he approached, sending sparks ricocheting off them. Genaya stood firm against this daunting figure approaching him.

"Watch out, Genaya," yelled Heysen realising the seriousness of the situation.

Jeppora thrust his upper Plasma-Blade harshly against Genaya's, the forceful contact creating a sharp, screechy buzzing sound. Jeppora's second Plasma-Blade then swung around below this tussle of might, attempting to slice Genaya from his torso. Genaya noticed the movement quickly. He dropped the left side of his Plasma-Blade to make preventative contact with Jeppora's lower Plasma-Blade. In doing so, he tactically deflected the first one away with the other side of his Plasma-Blade.

Jeppora steadied from this and went to strike a deadly blow with his upper Plasma-Blade from above. Genaya was left unable to move and vulnerable to the strike. Jeppora suddenly ceased this motion. He moved his upper Plasma-Blade to his right to defend against Heysen. Heysen, noticing Genaya's predicament, went around a land cruiser to flank Jeppora and arrived in the nick of time to save him. Another screeching buzzing noise was made as Jeppora and Heysen clashed Plasma-Blades.

With Jeppora's attention diverted, Genaya forcefully pushed Jeppora's lower Plasma-Blade away from him with his own, using the chance to graze Jeppora's left ankle. Jeppora swung his lower Plasma-Blade wildly in frustration, narrowly missing Genaya, who had retreated to safer territory. Genaya could see that Jeppora's ankle had the faintest cut. But despite the apparent damage, Jeppora persisted, unaffected by the damage.

"Go Genaya! Get to the Drone-Speeder," yelled Heysen, still combatting Jeppora.

"But Heysen you're..." pleaded Genaya before being interrupted by Heysen.

"Just do it, Genaya, we don't have time," yelled Heysen, fending off Jeppora's relentless attacks.

Genaya grudgingly accepted Heysen's request and made a break for a white Drone-Speeder. It had a cylindrical, centrally located cockpit. Four circular turbine thrusters were located in a square shape around the cockpit. "Vmmmmm!" Dreyfus had turned one on. The turbines slowly and gradually increased in noise as they became faster.

Genaya noticed Jeppora's increased hastiness, seemingly sensing his near complete escape. One slash. Then a second. Jeppora could not gain the upper hand on Heysen. His skills were clearly advanced, even for an Ordo member.

The smell of searing metal filled the hangar. Remnants of debris that got in the way of Jeppora and Heysen were left smouldering and spread across the floor.

Jeppora kicked his Electromagnetic Boots into action. Over the top of Heysen he went, attempting a feebly ambitious slash at Heysen's head. Heysen deflected it easily. Jeppora then deflected an attack from Heysen as he landed. Then with his upper Plasma-Blade, Jeppora swung at Heysen. Gshhhhh! The sound of the Plasma-Blade clashes became louder with every intense attack.

Genaya could tell that Jeppora was determined to stop him from escaping. Jeppora pushed aggressively towards Heysen. He then swiped his lower Plasma-Blade at Heysen, knocking him off balance, before kicking him away with brute strength.

Genaya, just entering the cockpit of the Drone-Speeder, witnessed this in horror. Jeppora had now turned to Genaya and was running intently towards him, Plasma-Blades at the ready. The humming of another Drone-Speeder came to life. Genaya 's attention though, was solely focussed on the perseverant Jeppora. Out of the corner of his eye, Genaya could see Dreyfus moving. Genaya grew startled as Dreyfus used his Electromagnetic Boots to launch towards Jeppora and block his path to Genaya. The two began to duel, as Heysen rebounded off the ground and ran for the second Drone-Speeder.

"Heysen, we have to help him," pleaded Genaya.

"We cannot, we must leave now, or we'll never make it," urged Heysen as he scrambled into his Drone-Speeder cockpit.

"He's our friend we cannot leave him," Genaya begged.

"Genaya! No! We must leave now. That's the mission. Do not let your emotions interfere," said Heysen commandingly.

Genaya looked angrily towards Heysen, before turning and closing the cockpit canopy as the Drone-Speeder began to hover. Genaya was discomforted as Heysen returned him a serious look, one that faded into concern. Heysen's canopy lowered, and the ships began to slowly move upwards.

Genaya looked over towards Dreyfus and Jeppora. Dreyfus had led Jeppora away from the Paxian to aid their escape, their Plasma-Blades locked in a tight dual. Dreyfus pushed hard against both of Jeppora's Plasma-Blades. Jeppora released his upper Plasma-Blade, before using his lower Plasma-Blade to withstand Dreyfus's push. Dreyfus now stumbled forward, horribly off-balance. Jeppora struck, delving his upper Plasma-Blade squarely in Dreyfus' back. Genaya could barely watch on as Jeppora allowed the dead body of Dreyfus collapse on the floor, the eyes of the fallen Paxian opened wide in shock.

Genaya screamed out in mental anguish at the sight. So badly did he want to avenge his fallen friend. Genaya turned to see the hangar doors opening now. Waves of soldiers stood armed and ready to fire outside its entrance. Genaya, grief stricken, wanted so badly to make Jeppora suffer, but the threat of the soldiers convinced him internally to not pursue that path. Out of the corner of his eye, he noticed Jeppora advancing towards him.

"Go, Genaya! We need to go now," said Heysen over the inter-speeder communications.

With a firm grip on the Laser Cannon controls, Genaya wreaked hell onto the soldiers. Many shot up in the air due to the ferocity of the weapon as it released green coloured laser beams. Heysen too, started raining down a barrage of firepower. The soldiers were cleared away very quickly and very easily. Many more though, awaited the Paxian's departure.

Genaya glanced one last time, a tear in his eye, at his fallen friend as he lay bloodied on the hangar floor. Dreyfus had paid the ultimate price for their survival. Genaya was not going to let him down.

Chapter 12

Heysen and Genaya emerged from the hangar, faced with a new challenge of escaping Corvaan alive. Corvaanian Soldiers lined building tops, armed with an assortment of weaponry. Rapid-Fire Laser Cannons, Photon-Guns, even Dark Matter Torpedoes. Genaya's heart rate was pulsating as fast as it could. Death seemed like a formality at this stage.

"Genaya, engage your shields. Quickly!" barked Heysen with urgency.

Genaya directed his eyes at a blue button to the left of his dashboard and proceeded to press it. His screen came up with the message, 'Shields engaged'. All of a sudden, the Photon-Guns were being stopped right in front of the Drone-Speeder, rather than scratching its bodywork.

After Genaya and Heysen waited for the Laser Cannons to cool, they refired and proceeded to wipe out the soldiers. The blasts went everywhere. Building facades fell downwards, structurally impaired after the intense barrage. Soldiers again flew into the air, killed on instant impact. Others fell off building tops that lost their structural integrity. They fell to a gruesome, certain death.

Genaya and Heysen throttled their Drone-Speeders and zoomed off down the road. 'Thud! Thud! Thud! A quick stream of large blasts impacted the rear of Genaya's shields. Two Land-Class Vehicle-Immobilisers made their way behind Genaya and Heysen. They were firing bright red, high powered Photon-

Cannon bolts towards the Drone-Speeders.

The artillery vehicles were hovering around a metre above the ground. They were arched-shaped and about seven metres long. They had three cylindrical lights at their front, with a triangular-like, black-tinted windscreen just above the lights. They had two long, cylindrical, High-Powered Photon-Cannons poking from their sides. Furthermore, they each had a sharp, slanted plough at the front, attached to a ringed protective barricade that stretched the circumference of the vehicle. This barricade was yellow, opposed to the rest of the vehicle which was of a steel grey colour.

A strange logo was imprinted on both sides of the artillery, but Genaya was unable to distinguish what it represented. The logo was of a pointy, violet coloured horseshoe shape. It had an inner dark grey crest, with the tips of the inner crest connected to two downward slanting lines which converged at the centre of the logo. Situated here was an umbrella-like shape, only missing the inner sections of its horizontal line, with the top of the umbrella curve converging with the two slanted lines. This inner infilling was of a bright fiery red. The umbrella-shape and slanted lines, however, consisted of a rich black colour.

"They've deployed artillery, Heysen," said Genaya to Heysen over the communications. "What will we do?"

"What are they?" enquired Heysen.

"They appear to be some sort of land artillery, a VI-L I think," said Genaya.

"Okay," said Heysen before pausing to think about the next course of action.

"Well?" asked Genaya again impatiently.

Heysen looked intently at the T-junction at the end of the road. A large building stood steadfastly in front of it. "We'll render them useless," said Heysen, somewhat smugly given his appreciation for his plan.

Genaya watched on as Heysen elevated, attempting to fly above the building ahead. Genaya attempted to follow suit, hauling the controls back to elevate the ship above the building situated imminently ahead. The rear circular turbines tilted as far down as they could to give maximum upwards thrust. Genaya watched as he narrowly avoided clipping the top of the building. The turbine thrusters moved back into position swiftly and Genaya was once again alongside Heysen, now hovering above the general cityscape of Nantan. Troops from various rooftops and streets attempted firing at the Drone-Speeders, with little to no avail. Although Genaya and Heysen had their shields in place; both their speeders had less than half of their shield strength left.

Genaya heard some more heavy thuds against his speeder. Now another artillery vehicle, bearing what appeared to be a similar symbol to the one on the VI-L's side, was tracking after them in the air. This Air-Class Vehicle Immobiliser was also steel grey in colour, shaped as a trapezoidal box. It possessed sturdy metal panels giving it strong rigidity. Large cylindrical Photon-Cannons, slightly bigger than the VI-L's, were attached on either side of the VI-A, which was firing larger red bolts at the Paxian's Drone-Speeders. The Air-Cruiser had two stretched, parallelogram shaped wings. Rectangular thrusters were attached on the wings' ends, propelling the cruiser forward. Also, like the VI-L, the VI-A had three circular lights underneath its black tinted triangular windshield.

"We've got more company," said Genaya tensely.

Heysen looked at his Drone-Speeder's dashboard to see the Air-Class Vehicle Immobiliser bearing down on them.

"There's only one. If we split in directions, whoever isn't

being followed can tail behind it and take it out," said Heysen.

"Roger that," said Genaya.

Genaya's speeder veered right, while Heysen's veered left, around some of the taller suburban buildings. The VI-A tailed behind Heysen, getting closer behind him. Genaya glanced to his left. The thudding of Photon-cannon bolts was relentless. He could hear the impact of the blasts against Heysen's Drone Speeder. He knew Heysen had little time remaining. Genaya lost the two cruisers behind a series of buildings, before he found an opportunity to veer inwards and flank the VI-A from the rear. The VI-A was still pounding its Photon-Cannons into Heysen's Drone-Speeder.

Suddenly though, it stopped. Genaya unleashed hellfire on the VI-A from it's rear. The Laser Cannons tore through the cruiser with ease. A fireball of destruction and relief ballooned into the air. Genaya's Drone-Speeder narrowly avoided the fiery debris and emerged emphatically from the fading cloud of fire. The remains of the artillery were left scattered across the suburban city below. Buildings crumbled down on impact, adding to the explosion.

"Great work, Genaya," said Heysen enthusiastically over the communications.

"Thank you," said Genaya pleased.

They had reached the far outskirts of the city and were now approaching the dense hills of the rainforest. The thick, tall trees of the rainforest would make flying low a difficulty.

"We're coming up to the rainforest again. We'll have to stay low to avoid any further detection," said Heysen.

"What do you mean further detection, we nearly died," scoffed Genaya.

"We cannot afford any more ships to follow us, my shield

levels are critical and yours shouldn't be much better," said Heysen insistently.

"We inadvertently destroyed an artillery vehicle, hundreds of soldiers and left flaming rubble strewn across multiple buildings. How could they not deploy more firepower at us," Genaya scoffed further. "Besides, even if we do reach the ship and fly away, they'll notice us leave. We'll have to deal with whatever they send us on that front too."

"Yes, that's true, but for now I'm focussed on finding our ship and getting out of this place," said Heysen with frustration.

"We should be able to find our ship in these things," said Genaya assertively.

Genaya and Heysen proceeded into a large gully within the hills of the rainforest, hoping it would help lead them towards their ship. Many slanted trees, vines and other flora lay upon rockfaces and on the inclines of some of the hills.

Suddenly behind them, several red blips of light raced past them at tremendous speed. Genaya and Heysen carefully manoeuvred around them, narrowly avoiding trees and cliff faces, to their sides. Genaya looked at his dashboard to see several Cross-Fighters pursuing them. Again, another barrage from their Electron Cannons flew past. This time they struck Genaya's shield.

Five percent shield strength, they read.

Genaya breathed heavily. His lungs could barely keep up with the intensity of the predicament. He was caught off guard. Evidently, so was Heysen.

Where did these fighters come from? Genaya wondered.

"Heysen, we're nearly out of time. Have you got a plan?" asked Genaya nervously.

"Not really, but I do have one risky idea," said Heysen

hastily.

"Yeah, well, I'm willing to take it," said Genaya insistently.

"In that case, we're going to hover as close to the forest floor as we can," said Heysen with angst to Genaya's reaction.

Genaya looked downwards. The sprawls of trees and undergrowth stretched upwards. Miscellaneous objects created an uneven flying space, one that would be near suicidal upon attempt.

"You're joking, right?" said Genaya fretfully. "There's no way we'll survive down there."

"It's our only chance, Genaya. I'd rather that than death from these knuckleheads," said Heysen assuredly. "Just go with the flow, and follow me," said Heysen.

Genaya was hesitant, but upon seeing Heysen's Drone-Speeder divert down towards the rainforest floor he changed his tune and followed suit. Genaya now came up right behind Heysen, as the Cross-Fighters eagerly followed their dangerous path.

Genaya's fears were partially relieved. Two Cross-Fighters immediately succumbed to the canopying trees and broke apart. Their flaming debris littered the forest, taking down a few trees in the process. The trees then toppled downwards from the impact. Three Cross-Fighters narrowly escaped certain death. One more however, was not so lucky, crushed by the sheer size and force of one of the trees.

"It's working, Genaya," said Heysen over the communications.

"Yes, but there's still a heap more coming," said Genaya dismissively.

Genaya narrowly escaped a tree ahead of him, protruding across the gully. Veering left, then right, and left again, the pair managed to escape some of the obstacles the rainforest had left for them. Some of the Cross-Fighters weren't so successful and suffered the consequences of their misjudgements. Genaya could see Heysen veer sharply to the right and proceeded to follow right behind him, as if Heysen was towing him along.

They had entered into a gorge now. The walls were extremely high, and with night beginning to fall, the little sunlight that was left in the day was barely reaching Heysen and Genaya. A deep blue river, forged from a large cascading waterfall Genaya had just passed, ran parallel with their Drone-Speeders. The water shimmered, flickered as they flew over it. The Cross-Fighters had a similar, yet more powerful effect on the water.

More Electron Cannon fire was directed at the Drone-Speeders. Genaya's shield instantly disappeared. He was defenceless. A scratch on the side of the cockpit from an Electron Cannon bolt provided Genaya a frightening reminder of this. He turned to see Heysen copping more of a barrage. His shields appeared as if they were about to find the same fate as Genaya's.

"My shields are gone!" said Genaya frightfully to Heysen through the communications, which were now a little scratchy.

"All good. Go ahead of me. Lead the way," said Heysen unfazed.

"Me?" asked Genaya with confusion. "Are you sure?"

"Not really. Just do it, Genaya, I still have some shield strength left," pleaded Heysen.

Genaya increased his thrusters, so that he was now hovering over Heysen. The loud humming of the turbine engines vibrated across Heysen's Drone-Speeder. He felt his controls shaking in his sweaty hands. Genaya passed Heysen and was now situated ahead of him. He narrowly avoided some misguided Electron

Cannon fire in the process.

The Cross-Fighters still shrieked and buzzed behind them, a constant reminder that their escape was nearing a lethal end. Genaya then shot back up in the air and veered into a small narrow gully. Heysen followed behind, confused by the abrupt move.

"I'm going to regret letting you go ahead," Heysen muttered over the communications.

"Trust me," insisted Genaya calmly.

The gully they were travelling down led to a large rock wall, however, there was a long and small circular opening in its middle. This led to the other side of the hill. The dark pink, purple and partly dark blue sky was ahead, along with smaller distant hills. Genaya steadied the speeder. Waiting, waiting. He closed his eyes in hope. 'Shoooom!' Genaya's Drone-Speeder raced through the gap, precariously positioned inside the hole in the hill. The speeder nearly kissed the wall in all directions. A few tiny sparks indicated to him just how close he was from a painful death.

Genaya was relieved to see Heysen follow right behind him, although he was sure Heysen was completely flabbergasted at the success of his manoeuvre.

The Cross-Fighters appeared to be unaware of Genaya's ploy. Genaya's lips pursed together, a broad grin formed on his face as he looked behind him. The Cross-Fighters were intent on seeing their demise. They continued to pursue them, firing at Heysen as best they could, until Heysen went through the tiniest of gaps. Genaya's eyes lit up in delight. Heysen had escaped.

But his satisfaction did not end there. He could see that the nearest Cross-Fighters to Heysen, for a flicker of an instant, realised their folly. They all piled into the gap, exploding on impact. Their engines fell off instantaneously. The wreckage of their hulls piled up inside the narrow hole.

Genaya's face was now permanently frozen in a smile. The final four Cross-Fighters at the back had clearly witnessed the calamity and realised their ships were too big and would succumb to the same fate as their now obliterated comrades. They had flown up and over the tediously steep cliff and came over the other side of the hill. They went to flank back down into a small valley, but Genaya's secondary plan had also come to fruition. The Paxian started up their Drone-Speeders after pulling up and using the crest of the hill for cover. The four Cross-Fighters were now dead ahead in their sights.

Boom! One of the rear Cross-Fighters tore apart into a ball of flames. Its engines wept to a swift death. Then another round of Laser Cannon fire tore through another. Then a third. Their shields were no match for the ferocity of the Drone-Speeders' Laser Cannons. Voom! Voom! Voom! The pulsing of the lasers' blasts rung out beside the final Cross-Fighter. It managed to avoid all of Genaya's fire with a swift spinning and turning manoeuvre. However, Heysen then followed up Genaya's luckless attempt. The Laser blasts surged into the Cross-Fighters cabin. It too fell apart into a ball of burning wreckage.

"Your ploy was expertly executed," said Heysen excitedly over the Speeder's communications. "Waiting for the remaining Cross-Fighters to follow over the hill and strike unexpectedly. That was an Ordo level move."

Genaya felt warmed by Heysen's compliment. Rarely had he been praised for his abilities in recent times. "Thank you, Heysen."

"Anytime, Genaya," said Heysen cheerily. "Now let's get out of here and report back to the Ordo."

Heysen and Genaya circumnavigated the rainforest for a very brief period before locating their ship. They parked their Drone-Speeders in a nearby clearing, setting foot on solid ground for the first time in what felt like ages. Genaya's legs shook as they pressed firmly against the rigid surface. After their intense encounter and escape, the calming walk back to their V-craft spaceship was much needed therapy, particularly for Genaya.

As they approached their ship, the soldiers they had witnessed in what felt like forever ago, had seemingly only just found their ship. They were standing outside the front, facing the doorway.

Genaya and Heysen crept up slowly behind them, watching on as the soldiers analysed their ship.

"I can't get in, sir, the door is locked," said one Soldier.

"For goodness' sake, just open the door. Blow it off if you have too," said the captain of the two-dozen large regiment, distinguishable by his golden helmet. "I don't think they're here anyway," he said in frustration.

"Don't be so sure," said Heysen smoothly, as he and Genaya unsheathed their Plasma-Blades and engaged them.

The captain turned to this voice that had emerged from behind the clearing. The glowing suits and Plasma-Blades filled him with fear, but also of pleasure that he'd found his targets.

"By order of Premier Finkel, you are under arrest. Stand down immediately, or you will be terminated," he yelled vigorously at Heysen.

Genaya and Heysen ran forward at them now, much to the fear of the captain.

"Fire!" he screamed to his regiment in angst.

They began firing their Photon-Guns towards the Paxian, who deflected their aimless blasts away with ease. These

Corvaanian Soldiers were as clueless as the ones Genaya and Heysen encountered before. They had their Photon blasts returned to them, fatally wounding them.

Quickly, they began to fall to the ground. The captain lunged towards them in fright of their strength and skill, wielding a small dagger-like object. Heysen took care of him with ease. A simple one-two motion with his Plasma-Blade and the captain's hands were sliced off before he became impaled by the Plasma-Blade a second later. Heysen thrust back his Plasma-Blade from within the captain's chest. He watched the body fall, lifelessly onto the ground. The small regiment was taken care of. Now, they needed to board their ship.

Heysen approached the door, unlocking it with the Ordo logo from his ring. The door hatch came open and they boarded with urgency. They sat themselves down quickly in their chairs and Heysen began igniting the ship's engines. The door hatch closed, and the V-craft levitated up into the night sky. Their escape to their ship was a lucky success. Now they had to escape the planet alive. Their information was vital to the Federation. Their knowledge of what was happening would be pivotal to liberating Corvaan. Genaya understood the gravity of the situation well. They had to reach Manoma. He would not let Dreyfus' death be in vain.

Chapter 13

Genaya looked out of the V-craft, the shadows of the trees and hills lurked ominously around him. The final, faint glow of Corvaan's sun shone a deep orange, surrounded by a shrouding navy-blue night sky. The stars of systems across the galaxy twinkled through the atmosphere. Genaya now looked upon Nantan, the city where they had just pinned a miraculous escape. The red radiance of burning rubble gleamed throughout the city, a reminder of the carnage that had ensued that afternoon. The damage was high, and as a result their capture would only be more bountiful.

"We need to leave quickly, Heysen," said Genaya with a frenetic urge.

"I know, I know. This thing only goes so fast," Heysen insisted.

The ship steadied now well above the tree line, turning towards a fixed position in the atmosphere. The engines roared to life with a burst of energy. The ship began ascending above the rainforest, above Nantan and away from Corvaan.

"Company at seven o'clock," yelled Genaya, noticing the fleet of Cross-Fighters hotly pursuing them.

"Keep those Laser Cannons ready and warm. We're going to need them," said Heysen focussed.

As they burst into the upper atmosphere, the Cross-Fighters started firing at them. The gap between the V-craft and the Cross-Fighters was diminishing quickly. An onslaught of Electron

Cannon fire whizzed past the V-craft. They were now into space. As they fled, they both glanced irately at one of the moon bases orbiting nearby.

"I really don't like the look of that," said Heysen jostling with the ship as they narrowly avoided the Electron Cannon blasts.

"We've got five of them hot on our tail, but more are coming," yelled Genaya, the ship shaking with every viciously tight manoeuvre.

"I have an idea," said Heysen with brief confidence. "However, you're not going to like it."

"You're not doing anything stupid, are you?" asked Genaya with a severe degree of nervousness.

"I hope that's not the case, but we'll find out. Get ready to fire those Laser Cannons on my call," said Heysen, concentrating on the task at hand.

"But we're not even facing—" said Genaya before being instantly interrupted by a determined Heysen.

"Just trust me," he pleaded out of frustration with Genaya's questioning.

Genaya looked towards Heysen's face. The hope radiating from it gave Genaya the confidence to trust his colleague's judgement. "Okay, ready on your signal," he said calmly.

Heysen turned to Genaya. His face showing signs of happiness from Genaya's trust. "Hold on," said Heysen with tenseness.

Heysen pressed some buttons on the dashboard, and then turned the control stick lightly. The humming of the engines got louder. Heysen had put the thrusters on full throttle. They were hurtling through space, just past the orbit of Corvaan's moons. The ship began to turn. The asteroid field lay just ahead. Genaya became concerned.

What was he thinking? Is he going to get us killed? He thought to himself.

Heysen then cut off the engines by pressing a few buttons. The once roaring engines suddenly died into complete silence. They were still moving at an immense pace. Their momentum was carrying them through the vast vacuum of space. They were, however, slowly spinning around their minor turn was agonisingly long. They sat and watched as the Cross-Fighters approached them from behind, laying their Electron Cannons into the V-Craft's shields. A hundred percent shield strength was quickly diminished to eighty. Then sixty. Thirty now.

Genaya thought Heysen was insane. He was simply letting them drift through space waiting to be blown to pieces by these Cross-Fighters.

What was the point? They were better off chancing their luck and making a hopeful dash for the asteroid field in the distance, he thought to himself.

The safety, the protection the ominously floating rocks could provide them would certainly give them the cover they needed. Genaya did also realise that at such a high speed the asteroids could also provide them their swift doom.

As the shields diminished quickly to twenty percent, the ship was steadying around to face the Cross-Fighters. The Cross-Fighters Electron Cannons fired relentlessly as their engines spun around their hulls. The elegant movement of engines provided a soothing sight; not as such though for Genaya and Heysen, knowing that their demise may soon be upon them.

"Ready, Genaya," said Heysen anticipatedly.

Genaya readied himself. His body language shifted from gloomy and confused to a more focussed, at-the-ready demeanour. He watched as the cockpit was now almost facing directly at the incoming Cross-Fighters.

"Now!" yelled Heysen as Genaya kicked into action.

Genaya grasped the controls of the Laser Cannons and began to fire at the incoming Cross-Fighters. At first, the impacts were insignificant as the Cross-Fighter shields whisked the blasts away with ease. One by one they deflected away. This was only very brief; the first Cross-Fighter at the front shattered into thousands of pieces. The Laser Cannons finally wore down the Cross-Fighter's shield and breached the ship's hull. The Cross-Fighter following behind that one flew directly into the centre of the wreckage. It too, was destroyed by the impact of Laser Cannon fire, but additionally from the growing field of debris.

The three remaining Cross-Fighters now spread out a bit more, still directing their fire towards the V-craft. The red Electron Cannon blasts continued to whiz past Heysen and Genaya, each getting closer than the last. Their shield got hit again. Fifteen percent. They did not have long left. The V-craft began drifting away from their centre path. Genaya fired again, destroying the Cross-Fighter to his left. It exploded as well. Its defence capabilities were inferior to the weaponry of the V-craft.

The centre Cross-Fighter swerved to avoid the debris, only getting struck by minor shards. It swerved to its left. Then back right. However, it overcorrected, and was now within Genaya's grasp. Genaya fired again, his thumb aching with tension as it pressed firmly once again on the Laser Cannon controls. The Cross-Fighter stood no chance. The Laser Cannon blasts were rapid and cannoned into its hull, destroying it instantaneously after its shields failed.

Four down, one left. This pilot was much smarter. It directed its fire towards the V-craft, steering clear of Genaya's narrow firing line. The shields were being weakened further. Ten percent was all that remained now. The sturdy, effective shields could only take so much fire.

"Hang on, Genaya, I'll help you out," said Heysen, concentrating on his steering controls.

The right engine of the V-craft began to move downwards, rotating along the ship's hull to be positioned parallel to it, in a three o'clock position. The left engine remained in place.

"Give him hell," said Heysen eagerly.

With the right laser cannon now on a wider arc, Genaya let the Cannons do their thing once more. The first few landed hefty blows on the Cross-Fighter, before it managed to swerve out of the way. Nonetheless its shields were dealt a near lethal blow.

"I nearly got him, I need one more crack," said Genaya wishfully.

Heysen began to think further. They were now drifting around again, the Cross-Fighter was almost out of view. Then it came to him. Heysen's face lit up from his seemingly genius idea. He lowered the left engine to a nine o'clock position now, such that the ship flew with its engines and hull positioned in a seemingly horizontal line. The left engine started humming to life again, but not completely.

The V-craft stopped spinning anti-clockwise abruptly. Now, thanks to the left engine delicately powering them, they were slowing down, but spinning clockwise back towards the Cross-Fighter.

"You've got to be quick Genaya or we're goners," stressed Heysen to Genaya, who only just realised Heysen's tactic.

Genaya quickly snapped into focus once again. A highly determined look thrust itself upon his face. He fired once more at the Cross-Fighters, his thumb aching further as his enthusiasm and desire drastically increased. His hands were clammy, cramping from the vigour in which they grasped the Laser Cannon controls. The bright green bolts of the Laser Cannon shot out of the V-craft. To Genaya, they moved in slow-motion. Each bright bolt of energy moving seamlessly through the vastness of space towards the final Cross-Fighter.

Then came the satisfaction. One bolt struck. Then two. Three. Now ten. Twenty. Fifty. Boom! The last Cross-Fighter was no more. A dazzling display of destruction erupted as it split up and spread its debris in all directions. It was clearly caught unaware of Heysen's tactic; professionally drawn up, expertly executed.

Heysen and Genaya began laughing in a nervous release of energy, almost cheering. They'd got them. Even when their outlook seemed bleak, they had pulled through and survived a highly treacherous and unforgiving ordeal. Genaya's face was brighter, for the first time in a while. His joy and happiness accompanied his relief. His stresses began to vanish quicker than they had built up. Genaya released his grip from the Laser Cannon controls, his hands getting their first chance to breathe, to relax in what felt like forever.

Heysen immediately returned the engines to their V-formation. The right engine now came on again, humming to life swiftly and robustly. The ship began to accelerate again, having nearly spun back around to their original direction of motion. Heysen used their momentum and turned the V-craft around and steadied it directly towards the asteroid field.

"That was close," said Genaya to Heysen, exhaling his remaining anxieties.

"You could say that. But we were in control most of the time," said Heysen coolly.

"Don't underplay it, Heysen, we were lucky," laughed Genaya.

"Perhaps, but we made it nonetheless," smirked Heysen joyfully, glad that they had averted danger.

As the V-craft entered the asteroid field, Heysen began swerving around the variety of rocks that inhabited it. Huge ones, tiny ones, oblong ones and round ones. They were everywhere, most of them easy to navigate. Genaya began inspecting the dashboard. He witnessed some unusual movement coming from behind them. At first it was indistinguishable, but now it was evidently apparent.

"Ah, Heysen," said Genaya nervously.

"Yes?" enquired a confused Heysen.

"We've got more company," said Genaya fearfully.

"How much more," said Heysen, more concerned with the drifting rocks in front of him.

"About twenty or so," said Genaya fretfully.

Heysen waited until he was slightly clear of any asteroids before inspecting the dash screen. The rear-view screen showed the brigade of Cross-Fighters swirling towards them, navigating the rocky hazards with ease.

"Great," Heysen muttered in frustration.

The Cross-Fighters started firing their Electron Cannons towards the V-craft.

"What are we going to do now, we can't take them all down," said Genaya fearfully, his anxiety rushing back to him.

"All right, ready the Neutron missiles. On my call, deploy them," said Heysen. "Don't guide them, just arm them and drop them."

Genaya learned his lesson last time to not question Heysen's methods. He was clearly well experienced and innovative. Such skills had garnered Genaya's respect and admiration.

Genaya armed the missiles and prepared to release them on Heysen's call. The Cross-Fighters flickered behind asteroids but were coming closer by the moment. Genaya began to feel sweat seeping off of his hands. His head was very tense, much more than usual. Surely, surely, they could not fall now after all they have endured.

Heysen knew what he was doing, Genaya thought to himself.

His mind though still questioned the validity of that belief. The physical situation in front of Genaya tried to persuade him of otherwise.

The Cross-Fighters now were getting really close, within easy striking distance. Genaya's heart was thumping viciously, screaming out for Heysen to release the tension and stress that was frothing inside of him. His hand trembled now in fear.

"Now Genaya. Go!" yelled Heysen, carefully analysing the situation moment by moment.

Genaya released the Neutron Missiles without hesitation. They seemingly floated out of their holsters, drifting through the asteroid field using the momentum from the V-craft. Heysen put the V-craft's engines on full throttle, and they started rocketing away from the missiles. They zoomed over some asteroids. Then under the others. Sometimes they even flew through gaps in some of the floating rocks. The entire time they narrowly avoided the precariously positioned asteroids.

The missiles proceeded to float at speed through the asteroid field, before a brief moment of contact when they clashed and clumped into the side of a large asteroid. Within an instant, they exploded on impact. Rocks were sent hurtling in all directions. The blast radius was massive. The Cross-Fighters closest to the blast site were torn apart in seconds. Their remains scattered amongst the tsunami of debris.

Heysen and Genaya relaxed, more at ease now seeing the bright blue flash of the Neutron Bomb explosion well behind them. They knew not many Cross-Fighters would've survived that blast, and those that did would be unable to track them through the vast fields of hovering, irregularly shaped rocks. The tension was now fully released. Heysen and Genaya eased off and calmed down. They had now officially escaped Corvaan, relatively unscathed.

Chapter 14

After passing through the asteroid field and being well on their way to Manoma, the loss of Dreyfus still bore on Genaya's mind. His determination to bring the perpetrators to justice grew every agonising second. He reflected on Dreyfus and how he had died. His fury was building, but he knew such feelings of anger, such feelings of outrage, would only lead to more dangerous and consequential outcomes. It was difficult for him to emotionally quell these thoughts. So badly did he want to hurt those who hurt him, who murdered Dreyfus. Revenge was squarely on his mind, but his conscience was insisting on something else.

Your duties as a Paxian should not be meddled with by emotions, Genaya's thoughts pleaded to him. He knew his desire to be a part of the Ordo would vanish if he let his rage fuel his conquest for success. The emotionally driven conflict raging inside his head tormented him. He could not go down one path without completely rejecting the other. They were mutually exclusive.

Heysen noticed Genaya's face had filled with anger, or at least misery and grief. Genaya's head was slumped into his right hand, giving Heysen the obvious impression he was quite upset. Heysen tried to console him.

"Everything all right, Genaya?" he enquired, concerned about Genaya's wellbeing.

"I… I guess so," stuttered Genaya dismissively, drawn back into reality by Heysen's query.

"It doesn't seem like it though," said Heysen. "Being a Paxian doesn't mean you can't express how you feel."

"It's Dreyfus," said Genaya dismally.

"Oh," said Heysen, realising the folly of his question. "I know it's sad that he's gone, but if it weren't for him, we would have suffered the same fate."

"Maybe, but he shouldn't have had to die," insisted Genaya more with frustration than sadness.

Heysen paused again, concerned about Genaya's state of mind. "Genaya, I understand he was your friend. I know that loss isn't easy, I recently had to cope with Conraya's death myself. But he did what he did so you could survive, to try and rectify the situation that led to his death," Heysen pleaded.

"Why? Why did he have to die? If it wasn't for the stupid political stoush caused by Corvaan then there would have been no problem. No death," said Genaya in anger, frustrated by the situation.

"Genaya, those people controlling Corvaan are The Malum," said Heysen grievously. "Dreyfus' killer was a member of the Malum. Many more of the soldiers and government officials there are clearly Malum sympathisers. Those ideals aren't ordinary. They are not normal. They are evil. That's why Dreyfus was in a predicament. He sacrificed his life, so that such tyranny would cease to exist. So, no one else would suffer the same fate," said Heysen sincerely, hoping Genaya would understand.

Genaya removed his hand from his head and sat up. He turned to face Heysen now, more calmly, yet still frustrated with the events.

"I just feel so much rage, so much anger against them," said Genaya angrily. "I know I shouldn't. But I had no parents to grow up with, just Grandmaster Zeffiro. I lost so much before I even knew I had it. Dreyfus was a great friend. Now I don't really have many left," said Genaya, relieving his anguish.

"I know Genaya. That would be extremely hard to deal with. I cared about Dreyfus too. Even though I wasn't as close a friend as you were, it still hurts me deeply to see him go," said Heysen solemnly.

"But do you ever feel angry?" enquired Genaya earnestly. "I keep getting told that it hinders my credentials to be on the Ordo, even my credentials as a Paxian. To have such a title and not be able to express such feelings. It hurts!" said Genaya, expressing his thoughts with decreasing frustration.

"I do. We all do, I guess," said Heysen in contemplation. "It's natural to feel anger, and we don't want to suppress it. But if we let it interfere with our duties, our position, the role we have to play in society; then it is an issue. We cannot let our feelings take over us, make us hate relentlessly. It's not a Paxian quality because it's dangerous," said Heysen with seriousness.

"How so?" enquired Genaya calmly.

"It makes us something we're not," said Heysen before pausing briefly. "I do get aggrieved at some things. However, I know that if I let it consume me, I won't do my job. I cannot protect those I care for, those that depend on me for help, because I'm more focussed on my own interests."

Genaya paused and reflected on what Heysen had said. "Thanks, Heysen, that's very helpful," said Genaya earnestly.

"No worries, Genaya, I'm happy to help," said Heysen with a grin.

"What was that thing. The one that killed Dreyfus," asked Genaya with intrigue.

"What Dreyfus feared and we've slightly suspected. It was a member of the Malum," said Heysen, the words striking fear into

Genaya's mind.

"Malum? How though?" asked Genaya.

"That's what we are not sure of, but some must have escaped the battle of Vormok," said Heysen.

"Wow," expressed Genaya. "But what do they even stand for though? Do they just like to cause trouble?"

"They all hate the Federation, as Dreyfus said," said Heysen. "But all Malum are generally former Paxian, or those trained by former Paxian. Their common goal is to defeat the Federation and create the Dark Federation, a more authoritarian system," said Heysen emphasising the seriousness of the Malum's intent.

"Why do they dislike the Federation though?" further enquired Genaya.

"Because they all had a disagreement with it," said Heysen. "Like I was just saying to you about Dreyfus. The Malum let their anger, their selfishness and their hatred control them. Rule them. It made them lash out at those who they deemed were oppressing their talents, because they constantly wanted more recognition, more power. Their lust drove them to violence and eventually what they fought for lost all meaning. They became so self-consumed, so angered and so fearful that they turned evil. That's why their suits are a different colour, as well as their Plasma-Blades. The gem inside Plasma-Blades as you may know is dictated by intent, by soul. Their intent became evil, their soul shrouded in evil. As such, their Plasma-Blades glow in violet or dark grey. They customize their suits to match. It allows them to recognise who has similar values to them and who doesn't," said Heysen solemnly.

"How does a gem decide though? Who is good and who is bad?" asked Genaya fascinated by the topic.

"I'm unsure," said Heysen. "The gems used in Plasma-

Blades have been used by the Federation for millennia. It's said they were collected at the forging of the galaxy and that their power was used to protect those that needed it. The Paxian were born upon these values. The Ordo have even more special gems. These are always orange, and Ordo members suits are tailored to this of course. I've never heard of an Ordo gem changing to violet or dark grey before though. That would be something that would cause great angst. To be able to turn such a powerful gem from its true natural orange would require a soul of pure evil. A powerful soul. But as you're aware one is granted Ordo powers on the strictest of provisions for such reasons," said Heysen.

"Yes, I have witnessed that. Grandmaster Zeffiro is particularly picky on who becomes Ordo and who doesn't," said Genaya with a wry laugh.

"Yes, but it's for the betterment of the Federation. Without it, those such as the Malum could infiltrate the Federation, destroy it from within. That would be the only major threat to the Ordo itself," said Heysen gravely.

Genaya sat back in his comfy black chair with great intrigue and gazed at the infinite galaxy of stars that was displayed in front of him. This was all new information he had not learned. Such information was useful in understanding the situation at hand, as well as the underpinnings of the Paxian themselves.

Manoma was now appearing ahead in the distance. The bustle of traffic around the planet made its identity all the more obvious. Genaya turned to Heysen with one remaining question on the tip of his tongue.

"Do you think the Malum are undermining the Federation as we speak?" he asked calmly, intrigued to see what Heysen's response would be.

Heysen turned to Genaya, looking at him genuinely.

"Hard to say. With all that is happening, I'm sure they're lurking somewhere. Based on what you alluded to as we left Dohna about Corvaan tracking trade ships and the way that Corvaan was almost effortlessly taken over by the Malum, I'd say in some respects they already have. We just have to be ready to defend ourselves when they reveal themselves," said Heysen frankly.

Genaya nodded softly, contemplating Heysen's bleak outlook. He looked out the window, the city on Manoma engulfed almost all the land of the planet. The majestic sight was a spectacle to behold after an arduous journey. The layout and construction of it all continued to leave Genaya awe-struck.

"I've received a message from the Federation. When we arrive, there should be a delegation in the Ordo Chambers. We will have to wait a little as Governor Pehran and Vice-Governor Ghoni will be meeting with Grandmaster Zeffiro and Vice-Master Yaneema," said Heysen.

"Oh, what do you mean delegation?" asked Genaya curiously.

"The heads of the Federal Government, of the House of Representatives are meeting with the heads of the Paxian. It's about the conflict with Corvaan and Dohna," said Heysen.

"But we know what's going on there. We must tell them," insisted Genaya.

"I know, but don't stress. They are special guests of the emergency Ordo meeting afterwards. We can inform them then," said Heysen calmly. "Until then, upon our arrival, we will have to wait around outside the chambers with the other Ordo members."

"Easily done," said Genaya now relaxed.

The situation had become clearer to him now, in terms of

what was happening. It made more sense. The conflict was merely a rouse by the Malum to create uncertainty and division. The extent of their success, Genaya could not measure. He felt uneasy about it all.

If they had infiltrated Corvaan with such ease, who else was manipulating the Federation? he wondered.

So many questions were still unanswered. The Malum's exact intent was still unclear. To Genaya though, it didn't really matter. The Malum killed his friend, they caused this unrest. They were out to jeopardise the way of life he and so many billion others had enjoyed across the Galaxy for many years. Genaya wouldn't let them get away with it. Justice would be served.

Chapter 15

Night had fallen on Corvaan. An eery stillness suffocated Nantan, choking the life out of the once prosperous and vibrant city. Lights were still shining from buildings. From the air at least, it seemed as if life in the city was running normally. However, on the ground, the stranglehold of totalitarian authority had tightened firmly. Life at the city's core had just about ceased, flatlined. The only inkling of activity was the sizable swathe of soldiers patrolling the streets, marching through the main plaza. The buzz of VI-L artillery being mobilised and the VI-A artillery scouting above the streets being the only significantly distinguishable sounds. Citizens had been couped up, either in fear or obedience to the rule of their new government. Any resistance fighters did not dare entice themselves upon a certain death for disobedience and insolence.

Jeppora, frustrated at his failed efforts to subdue the snoopy Paxian, made his way across the plaza, passing brigade after brigade of troops. He looked around him. Most of Corvaan's troops had now been mobilised. A large open area to the far end of the plaza had been cleared for the soon-to-be-arriving reinforcements. Despite the setback, everything was still progressing as planned. He looked down at his ankle. The minor cut from the Paxian's Plasma-Blade was stinging a little, but it was barely a flesh wound. It did not prevent him from doing what he needed to do.

The suit could easily be repaired, he thought to himself.

Jeppora started ascending the white stone steps towards Corvaan's Government Building. They weren't excessively big, nor were they overly steep. For Jeppora, it was a sight for the sore eyes of a battle-weary warrior. Jeppora moved up the steps without displaying his battle fatigue. He knew what lay ahead of him. Vondur Sombria would not be impressed by his failure.

As Jeppora reached the top of the steps, he turned out to look at the Corvaanian fleet he and Sombria had assembled.

Marvellous, he thought to himself.

The open plaza was filled with soldiers. The surrounding buildings were restricted in activity. Everything on Corvaan was as he intended. Jeppora assessed the city one last time, before turning to his right and proceeding down a side corridor.

There were corridors on both sides of the Government Building, but the main entrance at the front was barricaded shut. This was to ensure all who entered the building were screened and assessed for security purposes. As Jeppora made his way down the hall and followed it left, he encountered Malum guards.

The guards wore golden, metallic armour. It was not bulky or obtrusive, and it was clear it perfectly maintained the Guards' athleticism. Their masks were also thick and gold coloured. They had black-filled eyes lots and mouth filters, allowing the soldiers to venture into uninhabitable regions. Their helmets were dark grey in colour and rounded. At the top of these helmets was a feature, resembling the Malum logo. A crested, pointy, violet coloured horseshoe shape with an inner crest also coloured in dark grey. The only thing differentiating it from the Malum logo was the absence of the slanted lines from the tips of the inner crests and the umbrella-like lining that converged with the two slanted lines. The guards were armed with specialised Photon-Guns.

Jeppora walked past them, giving them a serious look of frustration as he passed by. They stood upright, saluting to their superior. The two Plasma-Blades sheathed into Jeppora's graphite grey suit, and that unmistakable face were evidence enough of his position of authority. Jeppora turned away from them, walking ahead intently towards the main Government Chamber.

The hallway was checker-tiled in salmon and black colours, with a bright white painted ceiling. The walls were of light grey stone. Pictures of former Corvaan Premiers and Officials lined this hallway, which led towards the main chamber. Many assorted rooms of varying size existed on either side of the hallway, mainly as offices and meeting rooms. Most of them now, as Jeppora could see, were used for tactical planning, weapons storage and other relevant purposes.

More Malum Guards appeared out of one of the rooms, saluting Jeppora in a doorway as he passed them. The four Malum Guards standing by the entrance to the main Government Chamber were heavily armed. They looked fixedly at Jeppora as he made his way down the hall. They parted evenly to the sides of the hallway and also saluted him as he went by them.

Jeppora entered the main Government Chamber, where a dozen Malum Guards lined either side and knelt in unison as he arrived. Jeppora looked to the back of the chamber. A long violet rug lined its way to a menacing crystalline black throne. Jeppora looked up at the throne to see Vondur Sombria perched comfortably in it. Sombria was twiddling her fingers on one of the arm rests, contemplating recent events as Jeppora entered the chamber.

"Vondur Jeppora," said Sombria, engaging in minor pleasantries.

"Yes, Vondur Sombria," replied Jeppora in his muffled tone.

"That was a lot of commotion out there earlier," she said interrogatively. "Why was that?"

"The Corvaanian Soldiers discovered two Paxian roaming the outer streets of the city. They reported it to me," said Jeppora with conviction.

"And?" enquired Sombria, unappeased by Jeppora's vague recollection.

"The Paxian were tracked to a building, nearby one of our larger weapons ammunition stockpiles. An old Paxian outpost as it turned out. The soldiers found the Paxian with what appeared to be an unknown adversary. The Paxian killed the soldiers and made their way to the local hangar, where I ambushed them. The Paxian did escape, however..." said Jeppora calmly before being harshly interrupted by Sombria.

"Escaped? They escaped?" she asked rhetorically.

It was very clear to Jeppora that she was extremely dissatisfied by his failure.

"Vondur Sombria, I do apologise for my failure," said Jeppora calmly, withholding his frustration.

"Apologising doesn't get them back, Vondur Jeppora. Maybe Veneticus should hear of this failure. He would not be so forgiving," insisted Sombria callously.

There was a pause as Jeppora took a few moments to stomach Sombria's cold-hearted suggestion.

"What about the adversary?" followed up Sombria, relaxing herself from the irritating situation.

"I killed him, Vondur Sombria," said Jeppora with pleasure, happily mentioning his one positive point. "It appears that the local Paxian Dreyfus wasn't actually killed after all."

"Now that's better," said Sombria with much more gratitude.

"It is, but we believe he's been aiding locals. We also suspect he informed the Paxian of our operations here," said Jeppora hesitantly.

Sombria leapt up out of her chair in rage, storming towards Jeppora's position.

"WHAT?" she screamed in fury. "Let me get this straight. The soldiers identified that they were there. We let this Paxian go around undetected, all the while he snooped around and mapped our operations. Then, you allowed him to pass on that information to enemies of The Malum, WHO ESCAPED!" berated Sombria loudly.

Jeppora hunched down in fear of Sombria. She was venting her anger and breathing heavily, infuriated by the way the events had turned out.

"If I may, Vondur Sombria, I did notice that one of the Paxian who escaped was wearing an Ordo suit," said Jeppora calmly, steadfast against Sombria's outrage.

"Ordo you say?" enquired Sombria more calmly, trying to remain resolute despite plans beginning to show signs of fragility.

"Yes, Vondur Sombria, unmistakably. His Paxian suit was orange, and he was highly trained. They escaped via two Drone-Speeders. They destroyed several Cross-Fighters in the rainforest and a few artillery vehicles on their way there. We lost them in space. They detonated a sweeping explosive, making passage through the asteroid field impossible," said Jeppora calmly and resolutely.

"Do you understand the ramifications of this?" asked Sombria rhetorically to Jeppora, containing the ball of rage that had quickly pent up inside her.

Jeppora turned slightly away from Sombria now, who had positioned herself to be right up beside Jeppora.

"I do," said Jeppora coolly.

"You do, do you? Given the state of affairs I wouldn't think so," said Sombria petulantly. "I've put everything into this operation to make sure it succeeds and now some Paxian, including an Ordo member, obtained crucial information and are now probably reporting back to the Federation as we speak."

"I know that, and if it were not for Lucifer Dun's sloppiness, we would not be in this predicament, Sombria," said Jeppora.

"I agree with you there. He has done good, but his arrogance and cockiness may have cost us here," said Sombria. "But Veneticus sees him as the best there is in the galaxy, so we'll be unable to sway him on that matter."

"I do have further good news, Sombria," said Jeppora, hoping to garner Sombria's appraisal again.

"And what would that be?" dismissed Sombria as she turned away from Jeppora.

"The Battle-Bots are nearly here and are expected to arrive tomorrow morning, fresh from Vormok," said Jeppora.

Sombria turned back to face Jeppora slowly, eager to hear more of this sole positive news.

"That is good," she said in surprise.

"We have additional units available too, now six hundred thousand to be deployed alongside the Corvaanian Army. More are currently in development to be deployed to Ferra as we speak," added Jeppora with delight.

"Excellent news Jeppora, that may make things a little sweeter," said Sombria more upbeat.

"It gets better," insisted Jeppora. "Veneticus sent additional fleets of Cross-Fighters down, as well as some Battlecruisers to accommodate them. Soon we will be able to defend Corvaan against a fully-fledged army."

Sombria's eyes lit up upon Jeppora's statement.

"Excellent, but we must be prepared," said Sombria now trying to curb her satisfaction. "When the Ordo discover what we are doing here they will send their army to wage war against us. They will send many soldiers, Paxian and most likely Ordo members as well, so we best be prepared," said Sombria in a serious tone.

"Yes, Sombria," said Jeppora in agreeance. "I am departing for Vormok. Veneticus requires my presence for further training of our new Malum recruits. I will inform him of the situation here. I believe the Ordo may head to Vormok to confirm their premonitions regarding us," said Jeppora with concern.

"Okay, thank you for your update, Vondur Jeppora. It has been of much use," said Sombria pleasantly. "I'll inform Premier Finkel of these updates."

Jeppora nodded to Sombria and turned towards the chamber exit. The Malum Guards continued to stand steadfast in their statue-like positions as Jeppora exited the chamber. He exited the hallway and made his way out of the Government Building. The soldiers stood firmly in their positions, despite the darkened night dragging on. The moist, crisp tropical air filled Jeppora's lungs upon exiting the building.

Jeppora made his way towards a nearby landing pad where his Cross-Fighter was located. It was like the other Cross-Fighters, but of a much darker, near black shade of grey. It was barely visible under the covers of night's darkness. The only thing alerting Jeppora of its presence were the landing pad lights illuminating it from the ground. Jeppora entered it, and began to ignite its engines, listening on as it roared to life.

As he began to hover above the ground, he contemplated what had just unfolded. The Ordo investigating the matters on

Corvaan further, more deeply than they already had, was a certainty.

They would uncover the Malum's operations soon enough, he thought.

It would be a matter of time before they sent an invasion to Corvaan to thwart the Malum's plans. Jeppora was not entirely concerned. They were ready. To him, the Federation's weakness was their lack of awareness. By the time the Federation realised how strong the Malum had become, they would already be on the backfoot.

Chapter 16

"We have to deal with this situation immediately," said Grandmaster Zeffiro to the rest of the delegation, which involved Vice-Master Yaneema, Governor Pehran and Vice-Governor Ghoni.

The delegation was being held within the Ordo Chambers. The Governor and Vice-Governor were seated in Ordo member seats, so that they were able to easily converse with Zeffiro and Yaneema.

"I understand that Grandmaster, but we cannot create undue panic," said Governor Pehran.

Zeffiro analysed the Governor. A female human with even, short black hair. She had slanted blue eyes with thin and curved black eyebrows. Her nose was straight, and her ears were small, but pointy. Her lips were thin and faint red and she had a medium-to-dark-coloured complexion. She wore the Governor's symbolic golden robes with white-coloured inner robes underneath. A mature, near middle-aged woman, Pehran was a valiant and diplomatic leader. Highly responsible and highly regarded, Zeffiro could sense her diplomatic abilities and persona attempting to deal with the increasingly tense situation at hand.

"That may be true Governor, however, we must take this matter with the utmost of seriousness," urged Grandmaster Zeffiro.

"If I may interject, Grandmaster. How certain are we of these allegations?" said Vice-Master Ghoni in a slightly timid and polite tone.

Zeffiro now inspected Vice-Governor Ghoni. A tall, well-built alien who was of a similar figure to a human. He had a long, bald egg-shaped head. He too had a straight nose, but had two circular white eyes with fully black pupils. He had near non-existent lips, and they were coloured similarly to his complexion, a rich buttery yellow. Similarly, to Governor Pehran, Ghoni wore the Vice-Governor's robes with white inner robes, but his main robes were Kelly green in colour. Zeffiro could tell Ghoni was the weaker of the two politicians, but Ghoni was nonetheless steadfast and unyielding on certain issues of great importance.

"We have intel from some Paxian regarding the crisis between Corvaan and Dohna. There are also several trade ships that have been destroyed or are missing in the region," said Zeffiro resiliently. "Given the spate of issues I can assure you, Vice-Governor, that we do not take these issues lightly."

"I see. That is comforting to know, Grandmaster," said Vice-Governor Ghoni sincerely.

"If I may enquire, Grandmaster, how dire is the situation looking from your perspective?" asked Governor Pehran.

"Not good, not good at all. From what we can gather, one of the systems is hiding something from us," said Zeffiro warningly. "These allegations of espionage appear to be a rouse of some kind to distract us."

"From what exactly?" enquired Governor Pehran, clearly intent on finding out more information.

"Well, we're not sure on that yet," said Zeffiro slightly frustratedly. "We have reason to believe that some form of Anti-Federation group is infiltrating one of these planets. It's not every day that an Ordo member is killed whilst on investigative duties, Governor."

"I can understand that Grandmaster and we share your grief and discomfort at the news of Conraya's death. However, we do not have sufficient information to take action yet. We cannot simply intrude on planets uninvited, particularly if they have done nothing wrong," asserted Governor Pehran.

"That is a valid point, Governor. Might I ask how the House of Representatives has dealt with this matter?" enquired Zeffiro.

"Well, there is mixed debate, Zeffiro. You must understand that such uncertainty and disagreement is simply politics. And with the lack of clarity on the situation, speculation and rumours will continue to triumph reason. The members will not vote for action until they understand what is actually occurring. To them, voting on matters with no knowledge of the ramifications or their importance to the democracy we hold, would be considered highly dangerous and reckless. I, for one, agree with their sentiments," said Governor Pehran diplomatically.

"I realise your concern, Governor Pehran," said Vice-Master Yaneema. "However, I should inform you that we have taken additional investigative action."

"I see," said Governor Pehran, hoping Vice-Master Yaneema would elaborate.

Grandmaster Zeffiro turned to Vice-Master Yaneema and gave a brief nod of approval to continue.

"We have sent two Paxian, one of which is an Ordo member, to investigate both planets on a mission of diplomacy. They should be returning soon and will be at the emergency Ordo meeting following this meeting," said Yaneema confidently.

"That is good, but what exactly are they doing?" followed up Governor Pehran.

"They are inspecting both Governments for any signs of treason or malicious intent," said Yaneema.

"Well, why haven't they reported back via hologram?" persisted Governor Pehran.

"From our initial briefing on the matter, it seems that the communications in Corvaan have been knocked out, either accidentally or deliberately," said Zeffiro informatively. "Hence, they have not sent a message to us. Furthermore, it could jeopardise the mission if anyone tracked their communication. They would be a target. That's why they'll be reporting their findings at the emergency Ordo meeting."

"Very well, Zeffiro," said Governor Pehran. "It does appear you're making good progress on the matter. Although I must insist that Vice-Governor Ghoni and I, as well as the House of Representatives, will not be able to take action without a vote."

"That I am aware of Governor. That is why Yaneema and I are insisting that you and Vice-Governor Ghoni ensure no funny business occurs during these sitting times, or even out of them. The last thing we, and the Federation as a whole need, is its peace and democracy being undermined by pawns or followers of our adversaries. They could manipulate the system and interfere with our efforts, Governor," urged Zeffiro stressing the importance of the issues.

"Yes, Zeffiro, we are aware that may be an issue. I can assure you we are dealing with this responsibly and effectively. However, we cannot simply judge members of systems based of some of their decisions. They have values too and we don't want to persecute those who disagree with certain operations of the Ordo. That would be an oppression of freedom," said Pehran cautiously.

"Yes, and I agree we certainly do not want to do that. Yet, this suspicious activity seems highly coordinated, and I would not be surprised if some members of the House, or even staffers or other government officials are not in cahoots with the perpetrators behind at least some of these activities," warned Zeffiro.

"I share your sentiment, Grandmaster. Ghoni and I will continue to monitor the integrity and honesty of the House of Representatives, as well as other government officials and staffers. The last thing we need is people within the Federation committing acts of espionage to bring it to its knees," said Governor Pehran earnestly.

"Good, good. Also be wary of a mercenary by the name of Lucifer Dunn. It appears he is working for these people that are causing trouble," said Zeffiro warningly.

"A mercenary you say?" enquired Vice-Governor Ghoni.

"Yes. From what we understand he has been hired to eliminate Paxian. The man claimed to have hired him supposedly placed a bounty on each Paxian killed, at around two million Federal Units," said Zeffiro grievously.

"Interesting. Do we know who this man is?" asked Vice-Governor Ghoni.

"Not as of yet, Vice-Governor," said Zeffiro disappointingly. "One of our Paxian managed to capture Lucifer Dunn after one of these assassination attempts. This is where our information regarding him has been sourced. Yet somehow, he allowed Lucifer to escape his grasp and he has not been seen or heard of since. We do know he is still out there and it is likely that he has more targets, so we are urging you to keep an eye out for him."

"We will. I'll make sure the Head of the Manoma Guard hears about this. Their officers can remain on the lookout for him and attempt to arrest him if he is sighted," said Governor Pehran assertively.

"That may be so, but this man is highly dangerous, and is

believed to be behind at least two Paxian deaths so far. Ensure you tell the Manoma Guard that he is extremely dangerous and volatile and should be dealt with the utmost of caution," pleaded Zeffiro.

"We will, Grandmaster. Please, you take care too. And you Vice-Master Yaneema," said Governor Pehran grinning heartily at Yaneema.

"I can assure you we will, Governor," said Yaneema smiling pleasantly.

"If you wish as well, you can join the Ordo section of the House of Representatives when they meet tomorrow. Just if you wanted to observe any questionable behaviour," insisted Governor Pehran warmly.

"We shall take up that offer, Governor, thank you!" said Zeffiro happily and welcomingly. "On a different note, I think it's almost time for our Ordo meeting. If you would kindly take your seats in the guest section of the chamber, I'll head outside and inform the Ordo members that we're ready to commence," said Grandmaster Zeffiro cheerily.

Zeffiro rose up from his comforting Grandmaster's chair and made his way towards the entrance to the Ordo Chambers. This meeting would have massive ramifications, not only for the Ordo, but for the Federation. He was not sure what Heysen and Genaya had found at Corvaan or Dohna. All he did want to know was who was behind the issues plaguing the Federation. Once that was established, swift action could be taken.

Chapter 17

Genaya and Heysen exited their V-craft shuttle in the Ordo's Manoma Hangar. A long, demanding mission had been completed. Whilst Genaya found the experience beneficial, he was thankful to set foot on safer territory. The feeling was ever so delightful, and arriving at Manoma made it more special, given its constant buzz of activity. Both Heysen and Genaya entered the elevator up to the ministerial sector of the Federation building. Genaya knew a long walk to the chamber would ensue.

"I'm not sure how long this delegation will be going for, but it's very important. It is an opportunity for Grandmaster Zeffiro and Vice-Master Yaneema to convene and exchange information privately with Governor Pehran and Vice-Governor Ghoni. One of the few times the leaders of the Ordo and of the Federation get together," said Heysen informatively.

"Okay, but why would they host it right before an emergency Ordo meeting, which both the Governor and Vice-Governor were invited to?" enquired Genaya curiously.

"Simple. The delegation was due to meet today anyway. They opted to host the meeting afterwards so that they could be a part of the briefing we will soon deliver," said Heysen.

"Okay, but I have another question. Does Zeffiro know we will be attending the meeting on time?" asked Genaya with even more curiosity.

"Yes, he does. I did message Zeffiro as we were arriving at Manoma to inform him we would be back in time to attend the meeting," said Heysen earnestly.

"So how will this meeting go?" asked Genaya.

"We will take our seats. Zeffiro will introduce our guests and then open the floor to us," said Heysen.

"I see," said Genaya slightly nervously.

The elevator stopped. Its doors slid open swiftly in a horizontal direction. They'd reached their desired floor and were now pacing through the long corridors of the Federation building. Genaya was so thankful for being able to walk through the Egyptian blue corridors again. Such was the beauty in their design that they alleviated the anxieties of those that were privileged enough to walk through them.

The Federation building, particularly, was abuzz with activity from various staffers trekking through the ins and outs of the building, making their way from office to office. Some were making the most of the relaxation rooms at hand, and plenty of others were taking the opportunity to have refreshments.

"What's going on?" enquired Genaya, confused by the relentlessness and magnitude of the activity within the building.

"It's sitting day tomorrow in the House of Representatives," said Heysen, speaking with amusement as he watched staffers making their way around.

"I see. So, it's always this busy before a sitting day then?" enquired Genaya in a surprised tone.

"No. I believe that tomorrow's session will focus on the events of our meeting today," said Heysen with slight concern.

Genaya and Heysen continued to make their way around the Federation Building before reaching the Ordo Chambers. The entrance to the chambers was locked, and Genaya could now see that the doors guarding the chambers were dual, horizontally sliding, automatic doors. They too, were coloured in Egyptian blue, but had two oval shaped, indented panels in middle which were of a frosted orange colour.

Outside of the doors were several members of the Ordo, awaiting confirmation that the emergency meeting was ready to begin. Most of them did not pay any attention to the fact that Heysen and Genaya had just arrived back from their mission, particularly given that they would reveal what they had found in a short matter of time. Nonetheless, there were a few 'Hellos' and 'Ah, you're backs!'. One in particular though, drew inordinate amounts of Genaya's attention.

"Heysen, Genaya, you're back!" said the delighted and pleasant voice.

Genaya turned slightly to his left to see Xevo, speaking to both of them. She approached the two Paxian and hugged them. Her actions left Heysen, but particularly Genaya, quite flustered.

"It's good to see you again too," said Heysen, a little surprised at Xevo's overly warm greeting.

"I was worried about you guys. We all were. The way things have unfolded, all the speculation about what is happening. I was unsure if you would make it back," said Xevo, relieved to see her colleagues again.

"I'm glad to see you too," said Genaya smiling awkwardly, still flustered by Xevo's welcoming embrace.

Heysen could not help but draw a grin and hide his laughter at Genaya's response. Genaya noticed this and gave Heysen a disconcerted and displeased look, to which Heysen abruptly stopped grinning and pretended to act professionally.

"I'm off to get some refreshments, I'll be back in a few moments," said Heysen cheerily, sensing Genaya's embarrassment around Xevo.

Genaya looked at Heysen with a slightly daunted look as

Heysen went into a nearby room. Genaya turned to Xevo now, anxious about the encounter. His hands trembled slightly, shaking almost. They became clammy and soon he was starting to sweat all over. His legs received a surge of adrenaline through them. They too, began to jitter and tremble with nervousness. His mouth was dry, its moisture sucked away by the tension in his body.

"Ah, are you okay, Genaya?" asked Xevo concerned.

Unbeknownst to Genaya, he'd been standing there awkwardly for several moments, without exhaling a single word.

"Oh, yeah," blurted Genaya in angst, "I was just... thinking."

"About?" enquired Xevo in soft laughter, bemused by Genaya's daydreaming.

"Stuff," said Genaya slowly, unsure of where he was going with the conversation. "Nothing much really?

"I see," said Xevo unconvinced.

"So how did you end up in the Ordo?" asked Genaya politely, though hastily attempting to switch the subject of their conversation.

"Thank you for asking, Genaya," said Xevo with delighted surprise at Genaya's interest. "I've only been on the Ordo for a few months. The position only became available after a more senior Ordo member retired," said Xevo proudly.

Genaya, half listening to the conversation, was distracted by Xevo's comforting and charismatic voice. Her jaw seemed to move with elegance, back and forth with aesthetic precision. And her eyes. Genaya watched them sparkle and dance with glamour, their majestic allure tugging firmly on Genaya's heart. His eyes were magnetised to their movements, their grace. Never had Genaya felt so compelled by another's physical features.

"Oh, I see," said Genaya pretending he wasn't on cloud nine. "Where are you from?"

Xevo laughed a little at Genaya's frail attempts to cover his embarrassment. "I'm from Yontour. I was a Paxian there for six years before… this," said Xevo slightly nervously.

"Really, Yontour?" asked Genaya in disbelief.

"Yes. I know it's quite cold there, but it's good," said Xevo. "What about you? Although I have heard a lot about you already," said Xevo before being shocked by Genaya's fearful expression. "I mean, Zeffiro has mentioned you a few times," said Xevo, unsure if her words relaxed Genaya.

"Wait, Zeffiro talks about me?" enquired Genaya surprised.

"Well, yes. And some other Paxian. Only because you were his mentee. He explained many things about you, including how skilful you are," said Xevo, trying to contain her awkwardness.

"Oh, yeah. Zeffiro worries a lot about my emotions though for some reason," said Genaya, now more confident in socialising with Xevo.

"Well, I don't know the situation completely, but from what I have seen and heard, he is partly right. You do seem to let friendships and relations with others or situations affect your ability to carry your duties. It can hinder your performance," said Xevo, trying not to be too critiquing of Genaya.

"I know, and I'm trying, but I can't help it. I've never really had 'family'," said Genaya. "All I can really remember was Zeffiro looking after me and then training me. He seemed to believe in me, but I'm not convinced he was wholehearted. I think he fears me for some reason," said Genaya, sceptical of Zeffiro.

Xevo simply laughed at Genaya's suggestion. "Ah Genaya. You are quite funny," said Xevo amused.

Genaya was now unsure how to respond. He was happy that Xevo found him humorous, yet struggled to withhold his conviction on Zeffiro.

"I'm serious though, he seems to berate me too much," insisted Genaya calmly.

"Oh, well. I wouldn't quite say that. Zeffiro is the Grandmaster for a reason. He's the most rational, skilful Paxian there is in the galaxy. Why would he have a grudge against you?" asked Xevo, unsure as to why Genaya seemed so critical of Zeffiro.

"I'm not entirely sure, but it just seems as if he pesters me over minor things. I'm never perfect to him. I think it may have to do with my mother," said Genaya speculatively.

"Your mother? But why would that affect Zeffiro?" asked a confused Xevo.

"My mother was Zeffiro's mentor. She trained Zeffiro up to be Grandmaster, and as I've been told stood down to Vice-Master so that Zeffiro could be Grandmaster," said Genaya passionately.

"But why would Zeffiro dislike your mother for doing that?" asked Xevo.

"He wouldn't. I think it has to do with the fact that he enjoyed my mother's company, and he may be disappointed that I'm not fulfilling her standards," said a slightly deflated Genaya.

"But then Zeffiro would be letting his emotions interfere?" asked a highly confused Xevo.

"Perhaps, but that's partly why I find it so frustrating when he says it to me," said Genaya politely in defence.

"Well, maybe. Well, maybe, but I wouldn't dwell on it. That would create fear and hatred. We cannot allow that to fester within us. We would be betraying our Paxian duties," asserted Xevo. "I think it would be best for you to not worry about Zeffiro and focus on your betterment, Genaya. You're pretty good anyway from what I hear, but we all can improve in some way."

Genaya paused to absorb Xevo's compelling point.

Had he thought about it too much? Overanalysed it all. Villainised Zeffiro to defend his weaknesses? He wondered.

Genaya dismissed those thoughts now, aware of their illegitimacy.

"Why did you become a Paxian?" enquired Genaya, changing topic to avoid further embarrassment.

"Because my mother was. She wasn't Ordo, but she was quite skilled," said Xevo proudly.

"Well, that's good. And your father?" asked Genaya once more.

"He was a Paxian for a bit too, but became an assistant for the Yontour member in the House of Representatives after he met my mother and I was born," said Xevo.

"Oh, that would've been stressful," said Genaya sincerely.

"It was, but he got through it. He wanted me to have the best chance I could," said Xevo.

Genaya went to speak before Xevo interrupted him quickly. "Anyway, I'm going to get refreshments before I head in. It was nice to finally talk to you, Genaya," said Xevo warmly as she left with a smile.

Genaya couldn't help himself. His eyes followed Xevo's every move. They were locked on with her gracefulness until they stumbled upon Heysen standing to Genaya's left. His eyes were watching Genaya's, intently analysing his conversation with Xevo. Genaya rolled his eyes at Heysen. Genaya rolled his eyes at Heysen. He waited for Xevo to be out of earshot before approaching Heysen slowly.

"You do realise that's a little rude," said Genaya annoyed by

Heysen's surveillance of him.

"Perhaps. You know, Genaya, I did find it interesting that you happily revealed to Xevo your fullest beliefs as to why you reckon Grandmaster Zeffiro is disgruntled at you," said Heysen slightly sarcastically.

"And?" asked a bemused Genaya.

"I understand it's important to speak out about issues and your feelings sometimes, but you really only just met Xevo. You haven't even told me about that in full," said Heysen.

"I guess so. I just felt so comfortable around her," said Genaya.

"That you certainly were," smirked an amused Heysen. "Be careful, Genaya. You said you were trying to curtail your emotions more, to ensure you perform better and don't become swayed by them."

"Yes, and?" enquired Genaya slightly irritated by Heysen's reference.

"I'm just saying, The Ordo does not see too kindly to Paxian with professional duties having unprofessional relationships. It can hinder their performances," said Heysen sincerely.

Genaya's pleasant mood dissipated. He was now disgruntled that he would simply have to remain friends with Xevo. Despite these feelings, Genaya knew it was for the best. He now fully understood that, as difficult as it may emotionally be, his long term wishes of becoming an Ordo member was his highest priority. He could not let anything interfere with that.

"Now, as we head in, I should remind you that this is a highly professional environment. It should also give you a glimpse into the life of an Ordo member, albeit in more strenuous than usual times," said Heysen. "The Governor or Vice-Governor may ask you questions. However, no one aside from the Governor, Vice-

Governor, Grandmaster or Vice-Master speaks out of turn."

"Well, then it should be fun," smirked Genaya sarcastically.

"Ah, see now you're getting into the spirit of it," laughed Heysen.

Genaya and Heysen continued to smile jovially about the situation. Genaya sensed an increased connection between him and Heysen. Words and feelings were comfortably shared between the two. Heysen was to him almost a role model.

Their joking was abruptly interrupted when the sound of the large doors being unlocked rung out. The doors then gracefully opened up, revealing Grandmaster Zeffiro. He stood at the entrance, in front of the pinkish-orange evening light that pierced its way through the top of the Ordo Chambers. His figure seemed welcoming, yet at the same time serious.

Genaya looked up to see Grandmaster Zeffiro looking upon the Ordo members, expectant and eager to begin their emergency meeting. Zeffiro paused briefly before resoundingly stating, "The delegation has finished. I now invite you all in for an extremely important emergency meeting. If you will please take your seats, swiftly, we will begin."

As the members began entering the chambers, Genaya felt his nervousness rise. This was the most formal meeting of his life. He thought about the possibility of stuttering in front of the Governor, of misleading them, accidentally saying something wrong.

Genaya felt this tension rise, until the calming left hand of Heysen was placed firmly on his shoulders. Heysen noticed Genaya's trepidations rise. This was all new to him. Genaya felt grateful and expressed a smile of endearment towards Heysen as he led Genaya into the chambers. Even if he did do wrong, Heysen had his back.

Chapter 18

"The emergency meeting of the Ordo is now officially in session," said Grandmaster Zeffiro with seriousness.

Genaya watched Zeffiro look intently at the semi-circle of Ordo members seated around him. Vice-Master Yaneema was situated to his left. Grandmaster Zeffiro then turned and gestured to the two guests situated to his right.

"We are honoured to have Governor Pehran and Vice-Governor Ghoni in attendance to the meeting. They are here to report back to the House of Representatives tomorrow once we are all briefed on the situation between Corvaan and Dohna," said Zeffiro. "Now, Heysen, what information did you and Genaya manage to find from your journey?"

Genaya looked at Heysen as Zeffiro mentioned their names. Heysen was poised and seemed as confident as he could be. However, Genaya noticed his arm twitch as he stood to speak. His chest moved faster, inhaling and exhaling at more than the usual rate. Genaya could tell Heysen was worried about informing Grandmaster Zeffiro of the news. Regardless though, he remained steadfast and buried his trepidations under a highly professional façade.

"I should start with Dohna, Grandmaster Zeffiro," said Heysen calmly. "As we arrived, the Dohnan guards within the Dohnan Government Building were on an extremely heightened alert. They were watchful for any foreigners entering their building; however, this was through fear of attack."

“What do you mean fear of attack?” enquired Zeffiro curiously.

“They seemed worried about us interfering with their home, but when they found out who we were we managed to have a meeting with Premier Sphixter,” said Heysen resolutely. “Premier Sphixter claimed adamantly that all this commotion between them and Corvaan was not through their doing. He also mentioned that Lucifer Dunn attempted to assassinate their Paxian. We did not see them though, as Premier Sphixter claimed they were being secured in a safe, undisclosed place.”

As Heysen paused, allowing the information to sink in, Genaya watched the facial expressions of Yaneema, Zeffiro, Governor Pehran and Vice-Governor Ghoni draw increasing confusion and concern.

“In addition to all this, we have found out that Dohna has not received many trade ships since the escalation of tension initiated. From what we could gather, these ships were signalled towards Corvaan for some reason and destroyed. We believe some of them to be the trade ships Genaya witnessed when he first investigated Corvaan,” said Heysen, attempting to remain calm in light of the anxiety and concern that was gushing through Zeffiro’s face.

“Are you suggesting that Corvaan has been deliberately misguiding trade ships into their region, just to destroy them?” enquired a baffled Zeffiro.

“Yes, well kind of. They did so with a purpose. What is most concerning is most of these ships were headed for Dohna or passing through there, and somehow were lured into Corvaan. Someone within the Federation must have of known their movements and schedules and aided in the demise of these trade ships,” said Heysen as murmurs and looks of shock were now painted on all the members within the chamber.

"Silence, please," said Zeffiro loudly and in frustration. "Are you absolutely certain that Corvaan has lured these ships in. Such an allegation must be supported with a high degree of evidence, Heysen," said Zeffiro, somewhat in disbelief of what Heysen was saying.

"Both Genaya and I are certain, and our venture to Corvaan deepens the seriousness of the situation," said Heysen as the disbelief in the chamber grew. "Genaya's claim that there is an inability to send and receive signals in the region was correct. We tried and failed, but somehow Corvaan must have sent one to direct these ships into the area," said Heysen. "Additionally, upon arrival, we noticed several structures, possibly bases, had been set up on the moons orbiting Corvaan. The size and shape of these structures indicates that they may be building some form of shield generator, forming a perimeter around the planet," said Heysen to faces of absolute astonishment.

Genaya's attention was squarely drawn to Zeffiro, wriggling uncomfortably in his chair upon hearing this news. Zeffiro's fears may have been confirmed.

"When we arrived, we landed within the rainforest and encountered many Corvaanian Guards patrolling the city. We did manage to make contact with Dreyfus," said Heysen as Yaneema and Zeffiro's faces shot up in hope.

"Dreyfus? Dreyfus is still alive?" inquired a surprised Yaneema.

Heysen turned to Genaya, both expressing dismal looks, before Heysen struggled to churn out the words, "He…was!"

All the tension within the chamber dissipated instantly and was replaced by a concentrated dose of sorrow.

"Before his death, he informed us about the situation.

Premier Finkel is suspected of treason against the Federation. They had troops scattered everywhere, artillery and the like. We barely escaped alive," said a slightly troubled Heysen.

"Who killed Dreyfus?" asked a highly concerned and slightly defeated Zeffiro.

"We saw his face, a patterned blend of icy grey and fiery red," said Heysen more calmly and professionally now. "He wore a suit like a Paxian's, but different. The fatal blow to Dreyfus was delivered by one of this individual's two grey coloured Plasma-Blades," said Heysen, his words freezing Zeffiro.

Genaya could see that Zeffiro was greatly perturbed by Heysen words.

"Grandmaster Zeffiro, if I may, I believe this individual was from Vormok. But more concerningly it was confirmed to us that the perpetrators controlling Corvaan are the Malum. They have returned," said Heysen.

All chamber members were now uneasy about Heysen's findings but were curious to find out more information. Genaya had not seen such widespread shock before in his life.

"The fact that we were chased out of Corvaan by a fleet of Cross-Fighters was a strong indicator, but some of the artillery vehicles they had were bearing a strange logo. We suspect it was the Crest of the Malum," said Heysen concluding his findings.

As Heysen sat down, Genaya watched on as Zeffiro and Yaneema looked at each other, clueless as to what to do. Genaya then looked towards Xevo, who appeared to be deeply concerned with the new developments.

"Member Heysen," said Governor Pehran, trying to make sense of the damning information. "Are you positive on this. If we inform the House of Representatives on such a matter, we may have to take extraordinarily decisive action. Possibly war."

“I understand that, Governor, and I can sympathise with you for the predicament you are in. However, with all due respect, I fear that if we don’t act soon the Malum may succeed in infiltrating the Federation,” said Heysen, now voicing his concerns.

“I am deeply worried about the potential for war,” said Governor Pehran gravely. “The Federation had not had one in over twenty years. The House of Representatives, as well as the general public, would be distasteful towards another war, even if it were necessary.

“Governor Pehran, if I may, we must decide upon what our next course of action will be,” said an adamant Zeffiro.

Governor Pehran paused for a moment, thinking hard about the entire situation. “Well, what do you suggest we do, Grandmaster?” she asked politely.

“I’m not entirely certain on that yet, Governor. This situation is perched precariously. If we make a move too late, or even a wrong one, we may risk the stability of the Federation,” warned Zeffiro.

“I agree. We are stuck in a situation where both an overreaction and an underreaction may cause terrible and detrimental harm to the foundations that this Federation was built upon. Yet also, if we do nothing, the Malum will continue to fester and eventually destroy the Federation one way or another. This next move we make will be vital. It must be executed to perfection. Any failure now and we risk the liberty, peace and security of everyone in the galaxy, not just ourselves,” stressed Vice-Master Yaneema.

“I understand your points Grandmaster Zeffiro and Vice-Master Yaneema, but I must remind you that any decision we make will have to be put forward to the House as a motion and passed by a majority. I do not think many systems will unanimously vote for galactic war unless it's happening at their doorstep," insisted Governor Pehran.

Zeffiro appeared displeased by Governor Pehran's comments even though Genaya could see that he recognised their validity.

"I see that that could be a potential issue, but if we delay any necessary changes we will be at a significant loss," said Zeffiro.

"Are you suggesting I enact the Federation army without consent of the House?" enquired a flabbergasted Governor Pehran.

"No, of course not, and the Ordo does not interfere with Federation Government matters. All I'm saying, and most here would agree, is that if we do not do something soon, we may be well and truly on the back foot before a war even breaks out," said Zeffiro with concern. "I'm afraid, Governor, that any action we take won't stop another war, it's inevitable. But if we make the right call now, we can put ourselves in the best position to win it when it comes."

Governor Pehran appeared deeply concerned by the situation. "How do I persuade the House of Representatives, of which there are thousands of representatives, to commit to this?" enquired Governor Pehran, clueless as to how to rectify the situation.

"I'm not sure, Governor," said Vice-Master Yaneema sincerely. "I must remind you as well that, despite Zeffiro's highly valid points, The Ordo cannot declare war on systems, and Paxian do not fight wars by themselves. We're Peacekeepers. That has been our role since the foundations of the Federation were laid and so it must remain. Ultimately, you have the call," said Yaneema cautioning Pehran.

The faces of those present in the room looked deeply puzzled. Genaya was astonished at the predicament. The Federation's hand was forced. Take action now and incite fear amongst the people, whilst watching the democratic system teeter precariously, or do nothing and risk the destruction of the Federation from within. The chamber fell silent. No one knew exactly what to do.

"This situation is unnerving. There is no right answer, but there are many wrong ones," warned Vice-Master Yaneema.

"We must be careful too," warned Zeffiro. "Even though we may not want to, the Federation and the House of Representatives must know of these developments. They may cause unrest and fear, but openness and transparency are our allies. Without it, we cannot achieve anything without acting deceitfully and corruptly. With any luck, we may weed out those who conspire against us."

"I agree," stated Governor Pehran affirmatively. "If we wait, our hidden adversaries only grow stronger, whilst we grow weaker. The sooner we try and oust this enemy, the better chance we have at defeating it."

"How do we deal with it though?" asked an unsure Zeffiro. "We may uncover more than we bargained for. The Malum may be much stronger than we anticipated. Remaining vigilant and aware of the situation will be crucial," said Zeffiro.

"Ahh, Grandmaster Zeffiro," interjected a slightly diffident Vice-Governor Ghoni.

All the eyes focused on him now, curious as to what he had to say.

"Given the House of Representatives will take a while to sort out their differences of opinion, perhaps we should look at what ways the Ordo can legally help reduce the threat and find out more information," he said hesitantly.

"Ah, excellent point, Vice-Governor Ghoni," exclaimed Zeffiro, enthusiastic of the idea. "We should do more interrogative investigations; however, they must coincide with military action," cautioned Zeffiro.

"Perhaps though, whilst the House of Representatives decide, we should send some Ordo members to Vormok to investigate the situation," said Ghoni more assuredly.

"I see. That will be advantageous, but risky. Vormok is outside of our jurisdiction too," pondered an indecisive Zeffiro.

"The mission should be brief; intelligence is our only option. If we encounter an army we will be in trouble, but knowing of their operations would be tremendously useful," said an assertive Yaneema.

"But who would we send on such a mission, we only have nine Ordo members left," stressed Zeffiro.

"Heysen and Genaya did outstandingly on the last mission. I cannot see why they would not be a perfect fit for this one," said Vice-Governor Ghoni.

Genaya could see that Zeffiro appeared vexed by Vice-Governor Ghoni's suggestion, but Governor Pehran stole Zeffiro's fleeting moment to object to the idea.

"Vice-Governor Ghoni is correct, they have done very well thus far. Given what they already know about the Malum, they would be well suited for this mission," said Governor Pehran adamantly.

Zeffiro looked on with disappointment at the Governor's backing of Vice-Governor Ghoni's suggestion, believing it was not the correct one. "All that may be true Governor, but I cannot allow Genaya to embark on this mission. He is not on the Ordo and is not ready to be on it," said Zeffiro stubbornly.

Genaya felt disappointed by Zeffiro's remarks. He could not

fathom that despite his efforts to prove himself on Corvaan with Heysen, Zeffiro still did not see kindly to him. Zeffiro still lacked the belief in him that he was ready. Genaya turned to Heysen, who was also in shock at Zeffiro's statement.

"With all due respect Zeffiro, Genaya has been useful. I do believe he would continue to be helpful on this mission. Genaya's skills have developed a fair amount, and a mission such as this one will only bolster his abilities," confirmed Heysen steadfastly.

Genaya felt disheartened by Zeffiro, who sat on his chair groaning about the possibility of allowing Genaya to embark on a second Ordo mission. Genaya's heart continued to sink further and further with each agonisingly long second.

How could Zeffiro believe that he could jeopardise the operation, that he personally would prevent the Ordo from gaining an upper hand on the Malum, Genaya thought to himself.

His emotions were still uncontrolled. However, he did not believe it would interfere with his job.

"I appreciate your honesty, Heysen," said Zeffiro politely. "However, I simply cannot allow it. Genaya is a risk and his safety, as well as your own would be threatened."

Genaya turned to Heysen, who was looking at Zeffiro, baffled by the allegations.

"I understand your reasoning, Grandmaster, but I implore you to understand that whilst Genaya's emotions are still uncontrolled, he is learning to manage them well," said Heysen calmly.

Zeffiro appeared perplexed by the idea now. Genaya was hopeful that Heysen's words may have convinced Zeffiro to have a change of heart. Yet, at the same time it seemed Zeffiro's gut feeling was screaming at him to prevent Genaya from going. Zeffiro was trapped in two minds.

"Zeffiro, I understand you feel he may not be ready. But at the moment our hands are tied. No one is really ready for what is about to occur. I believe letting Genaya go will help prepare him. That, alone, is vital to our success," said Vice-Master Yaneema.

Genaya waited anticipatedly as Zeffiro considered Yaneema's words, and after a brief pause, he caved in to the mounting pressure.

"All right!" he exclaimed, "Genaya may go with Heysen to investigate Vormok. But I must stress Heysen, in doing so you accept full responsibility for his safety and wellbeing," insisted Zeffiro.

"I understand," said Heysen, now more relaxed due to Zeffiro's acceptance.

"It's settled then. Heysen and Genaya will investigate the Malum operations in Vormok whilst Governor Pehran and Vice-Governor Ghoni will attempt to pass legislation for the deployment of the Federation Army," announced Zeffiro. "This meeting has now concluded."

Upon that statement, the Ordo members began to rise and make their way out of the Ordo Chambers as the last light of the day snuck through the chamber windows. Genaya was nervous, yet happy that he had another opportunity to prove himself to Grandmaster Zeffiro. Excitement channelled through his veins; his legs filled with adrenaline. Genaya got up out of his chair as a smirk developed on his face. He saw Xevo leaving, waving goodbye to him. Genaya waved back. Governor Pehran and Vice-Governor Ghoni left; leaving Genaya, Heysen, Zeffiro and Yaneema inside the chambers.

Genaya waited for Heysen, however, Heysen was standing still, facing Zeffiro and Yaneema who were conversing about the details of the meeting. As the pair finished their discussion,

Yaneema began to leave whilst Zeffiro paced towards the outer wall of the chamber, facing the city.

"Heysen, are you coming?" enquired a confused Genaya.

"Just wait for me outside a moment, Genaya. I'll only be a second," said Heysen to Genaya, as Genaya found himself leaving behind Vice-Master Yaneema. The last thing he saw was the stern look on Heysen's face staring intently in Zeffiro's direction.

Chapter 19

Heysen waited for Genaya to leave the room and for the chamber doors to slide shut before conversing with Zeffiro. Zeffiro was clearly aware of Heysen's presence. However, he seemed to be more interested in gazing out the chamber window at the bustling city before him.

"May I ask you a question, Grandmaster Zeffiro?" queried Heysen politely and calmly.

"What's troubling you, Heysen?" asked Zeffiro, genuinely concerned for Heysen.

"It's Genaya!" said Heysen, making Zeffiro turn with keen interest.

"What about him? Has he been performing okay?" asked Zeffiro with induced panic.

"Yes, he's been relatively fine," said Heysen reassuringly to Zeffiro. "It's to do with your treatment of him."

Zeffiro's eyebrows raised up like an elevator in complete astonishment at Heysen's statement. "What about it?" replied Zeffiro slightly defensively.

"I don't want to gloss over it too much, but Genaya mentioned that you seem to be prejudiced against him. I initially dismissed it, but I was observing you in the meeting just then and I couldn't help but notice that Genaya was correct," said Heysen steadfastly and calmly.

"Prejudiced? Me? What else has he told you?" asked Zeffiro in disbelief at the allegations.

"Look! Grandmaster Zeffiro, I don't know much about your past with Genaya, but his claims that you are harsh on him were evident for everyone to see. There is no valid reason why he should not go on this mission," pleaded Heysen.

"Why are you supporting Genaya?" asked Zeffiro with great intrigue.

"I'm not, necessarily. Your claims against him are valid that he does let his emotions get in the way of him performing his duties. For a Paxian, that's very dangerous, and I understand that. However, your prejudice against him could be argued as unfair and unjustified as well. It's causing you to let your emotions become too involved and interfere with your duties," insisted Heysen, hoping Zeffiro would recognise his point.

"I know," said a deflated Zeffiro, stunning Heysen.

"You… you know?" stuttered Heysen, in bewilderment at Zeffiro's claim.

"Of course, I know. I've tried to be as inconspicuous as I could about it for years, but it's getting harder as he improves," said Zeffiro.

"I agree that Genaya is one of the more skilled Paxian that I've ever seen. But why have you been so harsh on him? He hasn't done much wrong?" asked Heysen.

"Well, it's partly to make him strive to be better. But it's also partly because I fear for his wellbeing," said Zeffiro earnestly.

"If you care for him, why do you continue to berate him?" asked Heysen confused.

"I'm worried about him. He reminds me of one of my former apprentices," said Zeffiro with disquiet.

Heysen was frozen still, astonished by Zeffiro's revelations.

"However, you can never tell him this. Genaya would be outraged. It may affect his abilities. Now, with the Malum around, he may turn in anger," warned Zeffiro.

Heysen stood and nodded in agreeance. "I can assure you, Zeffiro, I won't," said Heysen sincerely, fully aware of the ramifications. "But who was this apprentice?" asked Heysen with great interest.

"I do not wish to tell you who it was, but it was over twenty years ago," said Zeffiro. "He was my mentee and he longed to be on the Ordo, just like Genaya. He persisted and persisted, and I reluctantly gave in to him, foolishly," remarked Zeffiro with disappointment at himself. "Not long after being on the Ordo, he requested to be Vice-Master, under my wing as Grandmaster. I blatantly refused, unwavering in my decision. The position was already taken, and he was certainly not ready for the role, yet he persisted. His greed for power drove him until eventually I forced him out of the Ordo, and he was dismissed as a Paxian. I never saw him again," said Zeffiro disheartened.

Heysen stood statue still, remaining astonished at Zeffiro's revelations. "Wow, that would've been very hard for you," said Heysen, consoling Zeffiro.

"I know I'm being harsh. Although I do not want to repeat the same mistakes with Genaya," said Zeffiro.

"I understand, Grandmaster," said Heysen consolingly.

Zeffiro turned to look out over the city once more, the deep blue to purple clouds mesmerising Zeffiro and calming him down. "I know I have let emotions interfere, but in this instance it's for the betterment of Genaya, The Ordo and Paxian in general," said Zeffiro somewhat resolutely.

"Thank you, Grandmaster," said Heysen, highly satisfied with Zeffiro's responses.

"Anytime, Heysen," said Zeffiro.

Zeffiro paused for a bit as Heysen made his way to the

chamber doors. "Be careful, Heysen," cautioned Zeffiro, looking over the city as Heysen was exiting the chamber. "These are now dangerous times. I need you and Genaya back safely," said Zeffiro serenely.

Heysen watched Zeffiro turn to face him. Heysen nodded in reply, acknowledging Zeffiro's request. As Heysen began to make his way out of the Ordo Chambers, the significance of his upcoming mission with Genaya started to sink in. The Federation would no longer be the same. Given the Malum had returned, no one was truly safe. The threat clearly extended throughout the galaxy. Heysen knew that what he and Genaya found on Corvaan was the tip of the iceberg. The next systems to succumb to the Malum would help reveal their intentions.

Chapter 20

Vondur Jeppora paced his way down a long fiery path towards a large, cylindrically shaped structure of metallic design. Its windows were frosted grey, and the building was wide but not overly tall. The pathway itself was of stone, and was lined on either side by searing hot, flowing magma. The magma was orange with hints of red in colour, and was running calmly along the path, away from the building.

Vormok was a darkened planet. Blackish grey clouds hung around the air. The hot glow of red magma was absorbed by them, giving them a red tinge. The planet had lakes of lava, and some lava geysers were situated throughout the settlement of Vormok, but there was not much activity there.

Jeppora paced down the main path, intent on seeing Vondur Veneticus. The path widened at the entrance to this building, where six Malum Guards stood. They were evenly situated on either side in full, gold-coloured, metallic armour. Like always, they saluted Jeppora as he made his way past them, as if he were some form of godly being.

The door of the main entrance to this building slid upwards at Jeppora's presence, as he began to navigate its passageways. The entryway was darkened. Bright red lights were the only things lighting his way. Two suits of armour greeted him, albeit hollow and for decorative measures. Jeppora turned right and paced down a hallway, which then veered left and lead towards another entrance. This doorway was guarded by dozens of

Malum Guards, lined down the sides of the hallway leading to its entrance. They too saluted Jeppora in unison as he proceeded past them.

Jeppora entered a special chamber. It was not exceedingly large in size, but not too small either. It consisted of an inner and outer octagon, the outer one being twice the size of the inner one. The inner octagon was sunken, with steps on all but the far side from the main entrance. On this side, a large throne, coloured in black and blotted red stood intimidatingly. The inner octagon had black, cylindrical stone pillars on the inner four points of the octagon, which supported the chamber ceiling. The floor of this building was tiled in an iron grey. The chamber had no windows and was lit solely by hot red coloured lamps of an unknown source that were spread across the chamber.

Jeppora made his way from the entrance, down the steps and onto the sunken octagon. Here, lying large and boldly in the tiles, was the Malum logo. Jeppora knelt on the logo, bowing his head to the seemingly powerful figure on the throne in front of him.

This figure was clad in a lightweight and highly mobile suit; however, it did not appear as such. It was similar to a Paxian suit, but with many advancements. Its charcoal grey colour stood out, giving off an extremely threatening intent. In addition, the figure wore a large, horned helmet. This helmet had a soft yet thick neck brace coloured in charcoal grey. The mask attached to the helmet was gold plated and had thick black coverings. It also had a thick black mouth covering to allow the figure to see out of the mask and breathe out of it whilst still providing those areas with adequate protection. The face mask itself was shaped and designed to appear menacing; a face lacking mercy. The helmet had a curved neck guard stretching off the helmet to just below the neck brace. It too, was charcoal grey and had thick curved lines running around its circumference in a slightly darker grey colour. The helmet was charcoal grey and shell-like in structure and was slightly thicker at the top. It had two ear-like ornaments protruding from its side, both containing the Malum logo.

"I have come, Vondur Veneticus," said Jeppora looking up towards the throne.

"Excellent, Jeppora," said Veneticus in a deep, malevolent, but praising tone. "I am pleased with the progress we are making. It must continue."

"Vondur, if I may add, we have been watched," said Jeppora hesitantly and in an anxious tone.

Veneticus was motionless, seemingly pausing to comprehend Jeppora's words. "What do you mean, watched?" enquired Veneticus slowly, yet calmly.

"Vondur, two Paxian made landfall on Corvaan and escaped," said Jeppora hesitantly.

"I see," said Veneticus softly, but slightly agitatedly.

"What should we do, Vondur?" asked Jeppora.

Veneticus' head tilted slightly, finally displaying to Jeppora that the ominous figure of Veneticus was indeed motionable. "Vondur Jeppora, have the Battle-Bots arrived on Corvaan?" asked Veneticus.

"Yes, Vondur," said Jeppora affirmatively. "They arrived shortly after I left Corvaan. Vondur Sombria informed me of their successful arrival and deployment."

"Then nothing more needs to be done. Our plan is in operation," said Veneticus pleasantly. "Soon, Corvaan and the rest of the Trade Intermediate will be under our control. The Federation will be crippled with their lack of supplies and then, we will strike," exclaimed Veneticus maliciously.

"Wonderful, Vondur Veneticus, however, one of the Paxian

was an Ordo member. I suspect that they would know of our presence now," said Jeppora cautiously upbeat.

"Never fear Vondur Jeppora, they would have known eventually," said Veneticus smoothly.

"If they know of our operations, they might come here to investigate," insisted Jeppora.

"I've taken care of that issue, Jeppora," said Veneticus, slightly frustrated by Jeppora's lack of faith. "We are moving base to Normona. A headquarters has already been constructed as well as a Battle-Bot factory three times as large as all the ones here combined. In addition, a huge star-base is being set up, and satellites and permanent anti-spacecraft artillery are being stationed along the planet to ensure no one intrudes on our plans."

"Vondur, how have we been able to afford all of this?" said a confused Jeppora.

"It has all been funded by Corvaan's government budget, in exchange for future repayment and a prime seat in the new Dark Federation," said Veneticus wickedly. "Soon, we will be unstoppable."

"Vondur, this is all going exceptionally well. But how do we plan to subdue the Federation in the meantime?" asked Jeppora.

"The Federation is naive, Jeppora. That old fool Zeffiro is still Grandmaster, and Governor Pehran will not easily cave in to the proposition of war," said Veneticus darkly. "They are discarded, whether they recognise it or not. The folly of their democracy lies in their erroneous belief that they have freedom. Power is true freedom. You and I and Sombria will soon demonstrate to the galaxy what true freedom really looks like."

Jeppora's face lit up at Veneticus' words. Such bold ambition was paying off for the Malum, and soon they would be able to exude their growing power on the rest of the galaxy. All the time they'd spent lying in hiding was paying off.

"Jeppora, I need you to train the final group of Malum Trainees, get them battle-ready as fully-fledged Malum. We may have to deploy them to Corvaan under Sombria's guard. I believe the Federation will eventually attack. I do not wish to waste the entirety of our elite forces on an expendable cause," said Veneticus indifferently.

"As you wish, Vondur, but what of our relocations to Normona?" asked Jeppora.

"You shall remain here, Jeppora. Our base here is now mostly desolate. I want you to spy on any Ordo that come here. Destroy them if you must, but if you are outnumbered, leave," said Veneticus warningly.

"I shall not fail you, Vondur," said Jeppora.

"I know you won't," said Veneticus graciously.

Jeppora rose from his knelt position, acknowledging Veneticus as he turned and exited the chamber. Jeppora went down the hall but turned right down the corridor towards a training area. He thought about what Veneticus had said to him, about how they would take over the galaxy. Veneticus' gambit with Corvaan would pay off, and soon they would control the Trade Intermediate. Jeppora also considered how he would ambush any Ordo that would arrive. If they sent multiple members, he may not be able to fight them.

Jeppora turned his fixations away to Corvaan. The Malum being sent there would help bolster their already significantly large forces. The Battle-Bots would surely deal with the pitiful forces of the Federation. They were designed to do away with them. Jeppora did realise, however, that the success of Corvaan could be a turning point in the beginnings of this war. Success would prove decisive, but as Veneticus had illustrated to him, failure would be merely a minor setback in their ploy.

Chapter 21

Grandmaster Zeffiro and Vice-Master Yaneema made their way down a wide, arched hallway towards the House of Representatives chamber. The hallway was the same standard Egyptian blue colour of most other hallways within the Federation Building. However, this hallway had a long, wide golden rug stretching its entire length. The ceiling was extremely high, roughly three to four times higher than the other hallways in the building. Crystalline, glass chandeliers hung from the ceiling, reflecting their warm, bright orange colour across the hallway. They were designed in an intricate spiral pattern with an opening at their centre, allowing light to filter down through this opening uninterrupted.

"This will hopefully go as planned," said Zeffiro to Yaneema as they paced down the hallway.

"I would want that to be so," said Yaneema in a wary tone. "If the motions fail to pass the House today, the Federation will be at severe risk of Malum attack. That is something unfathomable," expressed Yaneema with great worry,

"Never stress, Yaneema. I have faith that Governor Pehran should be able to use her rhetoric to our advantage. The Bavokka Confederation will almost certainly vote to support our cause. It's whether members of the Trade Intermediate follow suit, given any conflict will be on their doorstep," said Zeffiro.

"Perhaps that is true, Zeffiro. We must be wary. Our adversaries may be lurking from within. They may inadvertently reveal themselves to us today," said Yaneema intently.

"Indeed," said Zeffiro jubilantly. "But the vote will only provide us indication, not assurance."

Zeffiro and Yaneema made their way towards an automatic glass door. The door was split, having two sides. The door was translucent, with the Federation Logo squarely in its centre. The doors moved apart horizontally as Zeffiro and Yaneema approached. As Zeffiro and Yaneema passed through the door, they made their way through a large arched opening and onto a spacious open balcony. Here they were nestled perfectly, positioned centre-top on one side of the House of Representatives Chamber.

The chamber of the House of Representatives was shaped in the form of an inversed square-based pyramidical frustum. On each of its four walls were other smaller, more rectangular balconies. Each of these balconies were allocated for a member of each planetary system within the Federation. Hundreds of these balconies were evenly distributed across the chamber on all sides.

In the centre of the chamber was a circular pedestal shaped like a bowl. This pedestal rested upon a trigonal pyramid-shaped support at the centre of the chamber floor and rose one-fifth up the chamber in height. No balconies were below this level, as the only thing that was there was the Federation Logo painted on all four faces.

The chamber as a whole was royal blue in colour, with the podium at the chamber's centre being gold. The Ordo balcony was coloured orange. Many of the balconies were a whitish grey colour, and clearly were able to illuminate. The chamber ceiling, as well as the chamber floor and sections of the chamber walls, had white lights to illuminate the chamber evenly.

Zeffiro and Yaneema sat down in their plush, comfy seats as they looked over the chamber. Members of almost all the planets of the Federation were in attendance for this meeting. The members were a diverse mix of aliens and humans, of many different shapes and colours.

As the murmurs of chatter grew between sitting members and their aides, Governor Pehran and Vice-Governor Ghoni made their way out from a small opening on the ground level of the chamber, opposite Zeffiro and Yaneema's position. A form of hovercraft was transporting them across the chamber floor to the Speaker's Podium at the centre. As they disembarked the hovercraft, they walked into the glass support of the podium. Inside this support was a small, circular step. As Governor Pehran and Vice-Governor Ghoni made their way with ease onto this step alongside the Adjudicator, it quickly revealed itself to be an elevator.

As the elevator reached the peak of its incline, the trio gracefully rose up onto the podium. It was clear to Zeffiro now that the Governor was wearing her golden robes, whilst Vice-Governor Ghoni was wearing his kelly green robes. The Adjudicator wore thick white robes, with some royal blue stripes along his sleeves. The Adjudicator was an alien of sky-blue skin, with long thin arms and was of a standard humanoid stature. He had wide black eyes, a very straight face and two small holes for a nose. His mouth was wide, and he had a very round and bald head.

"Members of the Galactic Federation," proclaimed Governor Pehran with great emphasis and pride. Her voice was processed through a sound amplifier and rung throughout the chamber. "This emergency meeting is in regard to the increasingly dangerous situation unfolding in Corvaan. After conversing with the Ordo and undergoing an exchange of intelligence, we have been made aware of a severe and significant threat to the Federation."

Zeffiro continued looking on as the chamber echoed in deafening silence at the words. The chamber was rattled by Governor Pehran's revelations.

"Corvaan is under control of the Malum," said Pehran solemnly as hushed murmurs continued to reverberate around the chamber.

"Silence, please!" said the Adjudicator in a deep voice, standing up to allow Governor Pehran to continue speaking.

"Thank you," said Governor Pehran to the Adjudicator softly. "We have been informed that like Corvaan, other planets may have been, or are in the process of being infiltrated by the Malum forces and their sympathisers. I must warn you all that this is of great risk to our peace and sovereignty. A lack of action on the matter will only hinder our ability to remove this threat. In order to preserve and protect our freedom, we must make sacrifices. That is why today, I'm enacting a motion known as the Corvaan Liberation Act. It is an emergency motion which enables the Federal Government to mobilise our galactic forces and take aim at any systems that are currently being, or at risk of being, besieged by and set upon from Malum forces. The first of such places will be Corvaan," declared Governor Pehran.

A bright, but small yellow light pinged from one of the balconies to Pehran's right.

"The House recognises the member for Togara," said The Adjudicator.

Zeffiro directed his attention to the Togara representatives' balcony. The balcony light then switched from yellow to green and the member began to speak.

"Governor Pehran, with all due respect. How can we be ensured that what you're saying is true? Are we certain that this is not some form of excuse from Dohna to invade Corvaan?" enquired the member for Togara, a short male human with short, parted black hair, a round face, brown eyes and a slightly pointed nose.

The light for the platform switched off as the member finished his statement.

"I thank the member of Togara for his question," said Pehran formally, "Our intelligence from the Ordo indicates the Dohnans have been victims of the Malum. We are unsure of their strategies as of yet, but we do not want to wait until they are revealed. By then a full-scale war may be inevitable."

Murmurs continued to ring out amongst the chamber but stopped at the realisation that Governor Pehran had not sat down.

"I now move the motion forward to the House of Representatives. A vote will decide whether the motion is passed. I ask all member nations to vote reasonably and fairly. Your vote will be displayed to the rest of the chamber under the Openness and Transparency Act. As always, green light means you voted yes, red means you voted no. The voting may now commence."

At the conclusion of the Governor's statement, podium lights automatically shot up in green and red. These lights were scattered, as nearly half of the members were still deliberating the motion with their aides. One by one, they slowly lit up in green or red. When more than half of the votes were cast, a large projection shot down from the centre of the chamber ceiling, nearly stretching to the Speaker's Podium and displaying figures to all four faces of the chamber.

Zeffiro looked over at the large holographic projection facing his side of the chamber, before once more glancing towards the Speaker's Podium. The Governor was watching a much smaller projection of the same image from the podium. Displayed on the projection were the real-time figures of the voting. Zeffiro looked back to the larger projection to check in on the voting. Sixty-three percent yes, twenty-eight percent voted no, whilst nine percent were still undecided.

"Do not worry yet, Zeffiro," said Vice-Master Yaneema reassuringly. "There are still nine percent undecided. We are only two percent of votes away from a majority volume."

Zeffiro gave Yaneema a look of optimism before glancing back at the screen and watching the numbers tick over as the amount of balconies lighting up continued. Seven percent were left undecided, the votes swinging the way of the no's. Zeffiro could see Pehran growing slightly worried. Whilst they only needed two more percent of votes, a swing to the no's would prevent them from being able to forcefully fight against the Malum.

More balconies continued to illuminate, but this time in a reassuring green colour. The motion now had seventy percent support, with thirty percent disapproval. No one else was left undecided in the chamber, as all the balconies were lit up. Zeffiro's face widened in pleasure as a broad grin broke out. He looked down towards Governor Pehran, who also had a smile strung across her face.

"The Motion carries seventy percent yes, thirty percent no," declared Governor Pehran with delight. "The Corvaan Liberation Act is now enacted. A Federation army will be deployed to Corvaan within the coming days. Once we have more information and the battle has begun, we will hold a follow-up meeting of the House of Representatives. Until then, I wish you all well. Be safe!"

Upon concluding her statement some minor cheers and jeers arose from the crowd. However, they were relatively insignificant. Governor Pehran, Vice-Governor Ghoni and the Adjudicator now began descending down the podium's elevator. As they reached the bottom they stepped off and made their way away from the podium and into the Hovercraft, which took them out of the building whilst the rest of the members of the House of Representatives vacated the chamber.

Zeffiro and Yaneema rose from their chairs and proceeded away from the Ordo balcony.

"That was intriguing," said Zeffiro suspiciously.

"Indeed," said Yaneema, echoing Zeffiro's sentiment. "I believed it would achieve support, but not so much opposition."

"Well from what I was able to gather a large section of the Trade Intermediate disapproved the motion," said Zeffiro. "Whilst that's not surprising they're quite large numbers. I know we'd say that they would not want war on their doorstep or us interfering with their trade business, but I fear at least some of those members had more sinister ulterior motives," said Zeffiro warningly.

"Agreed, we must be wary. Those states are the ones now most at risk of Malum control," stressed Yaneema. "The balance of the Federation depends on us getting on top of the Malum immediately."

"Then we must monitor these states vigorously for any suspicious activity," stated Zeffiro adamantly. "None shall be allowed to nurture hate and destruction from the eyes of peace."

"Aside from them though I was relatively pleased. Of course, when we get a copy of the voting script, we must cross-examine all the no votes to ensure nothing undue is occurring. Even some of the yes votes will need inspecting for malice intent.

We can never be too safe," urged Yaneema.

Yaneema and Zeffiro reached a T-junction in the hallway and turned to face each other as they were both soon to travel in opposite directions.

"Stay safe," said Zeffiro earnestly to Yaneema smiling.

"You too, my old friend," responded Yaneema with a small grin.

"I'll let you know of the war situation when Governor Pehran outlines the details soon," said Zeffiro, as Yaneema turned to walk down the hallway to the right.

"Please do! The liberation of Corvaan cannot afford to fail," cautioned Yaneema.

Zeffiro watched Yaneema begin making his way down the left hallway. Things within the Federation were becoming murky and unclear. The first hurdle had passed. Now, The battle of Corvaan would ensue. The result of this battle had major consequences. Not just for the war between the Malum and the Federation, but the political landscape of the galaxy for years to come.

Chapter 22

"How far away is Vormok?" enquired Genaya frustratedly.

The duo was flying at speed in their V-craft across the galaxy towards Vormok. Stars whizzed by them as blurred lights. The various colours of the universe were on full display.

"It's on the outer edges of the galaxy, Genaya," said Heysen slightly annoyed by Genaya's continuous impatience. "No one said it was close."

"Well, I must say, the Malum are quite smart," said Genaya with some admiration.

"How so?" enquired Heysen intrigued.

"Setting up operations out of the Federation's reach," said Genaya, surprised by Heysen's querying on the matter. "It's clear that they have deliberately waited many years before restarting operations. No one would have bothered to monitor Vormok after a while. Especially given that it is beyond Federation jurisdiction. It was a matter of simply waiting for complacency to kick in, which it certainly did."

"Yes, it appears that that is the case," said Heysen reluctantly. "Are you not frightened by their gradual infiltration?"

"Very much so, Heysen," said Genaya with worry. "My fear is that with a scheme so elaborate and expertly pulled off, they have done other things. Such a big, crucial plan for them appears to be succeeding with ease. My fear is that they have done more than we can comprehend because for some reason we are naive."

"Naive, you say?" said Heysen in a scrutinising tone. "I must warn you Genaya, that would be quite an unpopular opinion amongst other Paxian and Federation Officials."

"I know it's controversial, but it's true!" stressed Genaya defensively. "If they have done what we feared and infiltrated the Federation, we've allowed our freedoms to be compromised because we foolishly let our guard down. Complacency is very dangerous."

Heysen looked at Genaya curiously, processing his comments. "Well, I must say Genaya you do make a good point," he said hesitantly. "Whilst I agree with that sentiment, I would not go around saying it to Grandmaster Zeffiro and Governor Pehran. They may not see it so favourably."

"Governor Pehran has been an excellent Governor. No, I'd say if it's anyone being naive it's Grandmaster Zeffiro. Although Vice-Governor Ghoni is a bit submissive too," said Genaya speculatively.

Heysen started laughing. "Grandmaster Zeffiro? Naive?" Heysen remarked with surprise. "Grandmaster Zeffiro has been the most level-headed Paxian I have ever known. He is not one for complacency or naivety."

"But Zeffiro has been in charge of the Ordo since the Malum were defeated. Is it not his responsibility to help maintain peace?" asked Genaya perplexed by Heysen's disagreement.

"You must stop these fixations; they cloud your thinking, Genaya. If Zeffiro were complacent, he would not give you such a hard time, am I right?"

Genaya looked defeatedly at Heysen. "I guess you are right," said Genaya in a frustrated tone.

"Ah Genaya, you have much to learn about politics," said Heysen with a smirk. "Most large-scale decisions require the backing of the House. If they do not fully support a motion, it does not pass. That is clearly what happened with the Malum twenty years ago."

"Well, that is silly," said Genaya disapproving of the fact.

"That is democracy, Genaya, whether we like it or not," said Heysen more seriously. "Hindsight is a wonderful thing. I'm sure if those members knew of the Malum's presence now they would have voted otherwise," reassured Heysen.

Genaya just continued to look frustratedly at his feet as he sat in his relaxing black chair. "How much further until we reach this deathly planet anyway?" Genaya asked.

"It sits in the Perigo Nebula," said Heysen. "A very dangerous place."

"And why is that?" asked Genaya.

"Well, aside from the Malum, the nebula itself is a mix of thick colourful dust and very large chunks of rock that just float around it," said Heysen with warning. "Vormok itself is situated somewhere in the denser regions of the nebula. We will have to cloak ourselves as we will not be able to determine whether enemies are nearby or not."

"That's wonderful. So, I'm assuming we're not shooting any Cross-Fighters this time?" asked Genaya with slight annoyance.

"No, keep your fingers on the trigger. They could be anywhere. When we land, have your Plasma-Blade at the ready as well. We may have company. But for the love of goodness try to remain incognito," stressed Heysen as Genaya rolled his eyes with jest at Heysen's trepidations.

As they approached the Perigo Nebula, Genaya could now distinguish thick dust clouds of emerald green, scarlet red and navy blue. The nebula sprawled across in front of them in an ominous ball of mystery.

"No wonder they chose to hide away in here. No one could possibly tell if anyone was in here," said Genaya laughingly.

"It makes sense though. The Vormokans have resided in here for millennia. It is only the past few centuries that they allowed the Malum to call it home too," said Heysen.

"Who are the Vormokans?" asked Genaya with confusion.

"The Malum Warrior who killed Dreyfus. I suspect he is a Vormokan," said Heysen with conviction. "I've never properly seen one, but from what I have read and heard about them, he fits the description. They're known for their red skin with grey patterning, which our Malum adversary possessed."

Genaya pondered Heysen's theory with great interest. "How are they as fighters?" he asked.

"Generally, very good, although, as you saw they have four arms so that is a bit of an advantage. The one we saw though was highly skilled," advised Heysen.

The ship continued towards the thick Perigo Nebula until it made contact with the outer dust of the cloud. The colours of the nebula were mesmerising; structures and pillars of clouds within the nebula rose up and dazzled Heysen and Genaya by their beauty. Such artistry by the universe was magnetising to many, and its allure was impossible to turn away from.

Heysen, who was paying more attention though to their path, managed to swerve to avoid a huge chunk of rock that appeared out of nowhere from the thick veiling of the nebula cloud. The ship's alarm began to ring out. Errrr! Errrr!

"What is it?" asked Genaya now alert with fear.

"The ship's instruments, they've gone haywire," said Heysen slightly panicked. "They're messing up. We have no bearings."

"What do you mean the instruments are playing up, that

doesn't just happen?" said Genaya in disbelief.

"I think some of the dust from the nebula has gotten entrenched in the engines and the sensors, causing them to play up. I'll try and divert energy to the filters to see if that will de-clog the dust," said Heysen reassuringly.

Heysen decreased the engines before adjusting some of the controls on the dashboard. Suddenly, the alarms stopped. The engines were now free of dust, and the sensor's bearings were back to normal.

"Knew it would work," said Heysen elatedly. "I'll decrease some of the power to the filters, but we're going to have to keep some if we want to make it through this place. That means we're on reduced engine output," said Heysen alerting Genaya to the new issue.

"How reduced?" asked Genaya.

"About twenty percent, we won't be out of here in a hurry," said Heysen. "Make sure you're at the ready to fire at anything that comes our way. We'll need it now more than ever."

The V-craft continued humming through the nebula. Heysen avoided the large pieces of rock that appeared out of the thick dust clouds with relative ease. Soon, they approached a clearing deep within the nebula. There, at the centre of this clearing, was a small but deathly looking planet. It was covered in a deep red coloured glow, with streaky jet-black clouds circling its perimeter.

"We're here," said Heysen ominously.

The V-craft slowed down as it entered the atmosphere. After a very brief assessment of the terrain, Heysen landed on a landing pad just away from a cluster of large structures. As the ship gracefully landed, Heysen and Genaya got out of their chairs and unsheathed their Plasma-Blades, engaging them to ready for any encounter. Their suits illuminated the relatively dark V-craft cabin until the door hatch gracefully sprung open and they emerged onto the mysterious planet of Vormok.

Genaya began scouting the area, wary of potential danger. The planet was very rocky and rough. Black and brown igneous stone was seemingly the sole surface of the planet. The only rivers on the planet were of lava, seeping their way snake-like through crevasses in the landscape. There were a series of structures ahead of Genaya and Heysen. These buildings were of various shapes and sizes and were all located within close proximity to each other.

"Eyes open Genaya, there may be Malum anywhere. We must be alert for any ambush," warned Heysen in a hushed tone.

Genaya looked around, before slinking away to cover behind a building. Heysen soon followed and they crept around the series of buildings until they reached an opening in the middle. Here, they could see a long pathway leading towards a tall building. The path was met either side by a thin moat of freshly erupting magma oozing along with searing heat.

Genaya looked up at the cylindrical building, metallic in design. Its frosted windows contradicted the burning of the land below, but it stood eerily in front of Genaya, as if it were about to torture him.

The most discernible thing about the situation, however, was the lack of living presence. The planet was devoid of activity. Not a soul could be found, although this was much to Genaya and Heysen's liking. The planet appeared to be completely desolate.

"What's happened here?" asked Genaya with great uncertainty.

"They were expecting us," said Heysen disappointedly.

"That doesn't make sense, they could fight us easily.

Besides, why would they abandon their main base just because they expected us to show up?" enquired Genaya.

"It wouldn't matter to them. They clearly felt that their operations here were compromised. In regard to your other point, I feel it may be part of their plan," said Heysen now with perplexment. "But they haven't tried to cover anything up?"

"Maybe they're not worried if we find anything," suggested Genaya.

"Hmmm perhaps, but maybe they want us to find something?" said Heysen with intrigue. "It could also be a trap."

Genaya glanced towards Heysen with angst before scouring the area again. "What's that over there?" said Genaya softly, pointing towards a large warehouse-like building in the distance.

"It appears to be a factory of some kind," said Heysen with curiosity. "We should investigate!"

Heysen and Genaya moved towards the factory tactically, seeking cover from the open spaces where possible. They constantly turned their heads around to ensure no one was following them.

As they approached the factory, its features became more discernible. It was the size of a massive hangar. The factory doors were automatic, however, appeared fixed in the open position. The factory was made of steel and was painted in dark grey. Within the building, rows of production lines were evident, but abandoned. The machinery ceased to move. Any evidence of what had been produced in it could not be found from the factory's exterior.

Heysen and Genaya, after carefully surveying the area, proceeded inside to inspect.

"Oh my!" said Heysen in awe of the structure.

"Indeed, Heysen," said Genaya with shock. "What was

going on here?"

"Clearly a mass manufacturing operation, but of what?" pondered Heysen.

Genaya walked towards a section of the factory. A tall and hidden figure was lurking behind some factory machinery. It remained unmoved. As Genaya approached it, he could discern its features more easily.

It was standing on a pedestal adjacent to one of the production line stations. "Perhaps they were making this!" said Genaya with unease.

Heysen quickly made his way over to Genaya to inspect his finding. Genaya could see Heysen's face erupt with concern at the finding.

"It appears to be a modern version of a Battle-Bot," said Heysen with grave certainty.

Genaya looked at Heysen with confusion over the name, but Heysen was quick to clarify.

"Battle-Bots were what the Malum used as a source of troops. It saved them having to sacrifice their followers or themselves for battle. They were feebly designed though, but in numbers they could be effective. These Battle-Bots, however, seem more sophisticated and more powerful."

Genaya looked at the Battle-Bot prototype more closely now. They were taller than standard human height and had broad, metal plated shoulders. They had two arms, the right bigger and thicker than the other. The right arm was fitted with a Photon-Cannon, whilst the left hand consisted of a long, sharp metallic blade. The body thinned out towards the legs, and the Malum logo was crested onto the front plate. As the body thinned, it joined into the conjoined legs. The legs were in a sharp U-shape and appeared long. They were coloured a fiery red, whilst the rest of the Battle-Bot's body was of a deep grey colour. The head was a relatively small semi-circle at the centre of the shoulders. A wide, thin and oval-shaped eye sat at the centre of the head, coloured in deep violet.

"Is that its eye?" asked Genaya.

"Yes, but when it's activated it illuminates," said Heysen.

"Where are the rest of them?" asked Genaya perplexed.

"Not sure, but no matter where they are it means trouble for the Federation," said Heysen concerned. "If there are more factories like this, they could have produced hundreds of thousands of them. And if that is the case, the Federation could come under significant threat."

"They don't appear to have been gone long it seems," said Genaya. "Most of the equipment seems freshly used, it hasn't withered from abandonment at all."

Genaya and Heysen stopped inspecting the machinery. Something was behind them. They were alerted by the harsh, crisp voice that shot towards them from near the factory entrance.

"You two are a glutton for punishment," said Jeppora with a wicked look on his face.

Heysen and Genaya whizzed around and faced Jeppora, engaging their Plasma-Blades swiftly. Jeppora already had his two Plasma-Blades engaged and at the ready, their dark grey glow illuminating off the harsh black rock of the ground below him.

"Who are you?" asked Genaya, now angered by his presence.

"I am Vondur Jeppora," said Jeppora in a powerful tone. "Malum conqueror and soon, Ordo exterminator."

"I don't think so," rebutted Heysen distastefully.

"You killed Dreyfus!" yelled Genaya in anger.

“Oh, was he your friend?” asked Jeppora rhetorically, mocking Genaya’s pain. “If I’d known that, I would have made him suffer more,” quipped Jeppora snidely.

Genaya yelled and charged towards Jeppora in fury. Jeppora’s lure had worked to perfection.

“Genaya! NO!” yelled Heysen in disbelief of his comrade’s recklessness.

Genaya slashed at Jeppora with fury. Their Plasma-Blades buzzed with every hit. Jeppora expertly wielded his upper and lower Plasma-Blades to instantly gain the upper hand. Genaya quickly fell into a vulnerable position. He was dealt a flurry of attacks. One. Two. Snap! Genaya’s Plasma-Blade was split down the middle, his magnetiser no longer working. Genaya wielded the two severed ends of the Plasma-Blade like knives.

Heysen came to intervene. His assistance now stopped Jeppora’s attack. Jeppora wrestled fiercely against the two. Despite his efforts, Heysen dominated him, grazing the midriff of Jeppora. Jeppora winced at the slight cut but used his Electromagnetic Boots to propel himself upwards. Jeppora flipped before facing both Genaya and Heysen from the rear of the factory.

From there the slashing continued. Left. Right. Up. Down. Left and right. The attacks from Genaya and Heysen were relentless. Jeppora though, skilfully deflected the strikes. Genaya continued to slash with rage and passion. Heysen followed with a swift attack, splitting Jeppora’s upper Plasma-Blade into two ends. This only hindered Heysen though. Jeppora slashed his left side at Heysen, slightly cutting his face. The follow up strike was blocked. They were at a stalemate.

Jeppora looked around, feeling the pressure from the Paxian mount. The contest of dark grey and orange light sparkled in

Genaya's eyes. The Plasma-Blades gave off an electrifying buzz.

"You lose, Paxian," said Jeppora, nearly exhausted from tussling his Plasma-Blade against Heysen's.

"What makes you think that?" asked Heysen, hiding his pain as his cheek bled slightly.

"This!" exclaimed Jeppora confidently.

Jeppora released tension from his Plasma-Blade quickly, before quickly attacking again. The shift on momentum put Heysen off balance. Jeppora kicked Heysen away right as the momentum shifted. It was a brutal blow. Genaya could only watch it send Heysen back several metres. Heysen's impact onto the hard surface echoed through the factory.

Genaya, still feeling a rush of adrenaline and vengeance, thrust himself at Jeppora again. Slashes flew in all directions. Jeppora dodged and blocked them quickly with expertise. Precision strikes from Jeppora knocked Genaya off balance and he moved backwards. Jeppora though was wise enough to resist attempting a fatal blow and retreated.

Jeppora used his Electromagnetic Boots to escape the two Paxian, flying onto some scaffolding on the upper level of the factory. Once up there, he turned his back on the Paxian and began to run.

After recovering quickly, Heysen and Genaya gave hot pursuit. They used their Electromagnetic Boots to join Jeppora on the scaffolding, following close behind. Jeppora slashed his split upper Plasma-Blade at some support beams, and the scaffolding began to fall. Heysen and Genaya leapt across the void successfully, using their boots to propel them towards a safer ledge. They slipped and stuttered but held position. The delay though lost them crucial ground on Jeppora.

Jeppora then leapt out of a window and out of the factory,

much to Heysen and Genaya's surprise. The glass shattered and rained down on the ground below. Jeppora used his boots to guide him down gracefully.

A specially designed Cross-Fighter, mixed with violet and near black colours, was positioned not far ahead. As Genaya and Heysen jumped through the broken windowpane, they could see Jeppora making his way to the Cross-Fighter. Genaya and Heysen landed gracefully on the ground with the aid of their boots, but by the time they steadied, Jeppora had just entered the Cross-Fighter. Genaya quickly realised the folly of their pursuit.

"Quick, Genaya, back into the factory!" yelled Heysen with haste.

Genaya with a frightened look turned and ran as fast as he could back towards the factory. Jeppora had barely gotten his Cross-Fighter to lift off the ground before he started firing its Electron Cannons. He moved the ship to face Genaya and Heysen, the bolts narrowly missing both of them. As they entered the entrance to the factory, Jeppora began hovering much more steadily, moving towards their position.

Electron Cannon fire burst through the factory walls and Heysen and Genaya took cover to their left behind one of the now empty, large molten metal pots situated near the production line. Roofing and other debris cascaded down as Jeppora hailed fire upon the factory. Part of the structure came tumbling down, but Genaya and Heysen were protected by the rigidity and sturdiness of the large metal pot.

As the barrage ended and that section of the factory ceased collapsing, Heysen and Genaya ran to the nearest entrance to gage what Jeppora was doing. They watched on as his Cross-Fighter took off into the dense, thick reddish-black clouds of Vormok. Clearly, Jeppora's mission of intimidation was complete. Now alert to the situation going on, Heysen and Genaya started sprinting back to their V-craft, which luckily was untouched.

"We need to alert the Ordo of this situation immediately," said Heysen with conviction as they approached the V-craft.

"Indeed, this matter is quite out of hand now," said Genaya, exhausted from their brutal encounter.

"I reckon those Battle-Bots have been deployed to Corvaan. That's what the Corvaanian Soldiers would've been expecting," said Heysen with conviction.

"It must be, but how many did they send do you reckon?" asked Genaya.

"Too many most likely," said Heysen ominously.

The V-craft doors thrust open and Genaya and Heysen leapt aboard. As they settled in and took off away from Vormok, Genaya used the hologram receiver to dial a call to Grandmaster Zeffiro. The information he and Heysen were about to deliver would be indisputable. The Malum operations were in full swing. War was on the horizon.

Chapter 23

"We must act now, and we must do so carefully," said Heysen, appearing as a hologram within the Ordo Chambers.

"What have you found?" asked Grandmaster Zeffiro, sitting alongside Vice-Master Yaneema and the rest of the Ordo panel.

"I'm afraid Vormok was empty, but what was left behind painted a daunting picture, Grandmaster," said Heysen solemnly. "They're much further advanced in their rebuild than we thought."

"How dire is it, Heysen?" asked Yaneema optimistically.

"I fear their forces on Corvaan will be highly advanced," said Heysen fearfully. "They have been manufacturing Battle-Bots again, however, these ones seem much more sophisticated than the ones I've heard about from the past wars."

"Battle-Bots you say?" asked Yaneema delicately with surprise.

"Yes, we saw a prototype design of one. Their factories were abandoned. They knew we were coming," said Heysen regrettably.

"How could they know that you were coming?" asked Grandmaster Zeffiro sceptically.

"I don't know how, but they did," said Heysen. "They had abandoned the entire planet, not a soul in sight. They must have moved elsewhere, but they were expecting us. We encountered the same Malum we saw on Corvaan. He ambushed us. He is extremely skilful and goes by the name of Vondur Jeppora."

"Vondur?" queried Zeffiro with concern. "You encountered a Vondur?"

"What is the concern with Vondur?" asked Heysen with confusion.

"Vondur is a Malum title. It's their ancient term for Lord. Only three Malum at any time can be Vondur," said Yaneema. "To encounter one is a rarity, but they are extremely dangerous."

"Well, this figure was intimidating. He had red, grey patterned skin. I'm adamant he is Vormokan," said Heysen.

"From that description, most likely," said Zeffiro concerned about the matter. "Do you know if he was the Supreme Malum?"

"I'm not sure, given he was on Corvaan I would not be convinced he is," said Heysen.

"We must be wary, there are two others, with many more Malum out there as well," said Zeffiro warningly. "It is likely there's another on Corvaan, but it may not be the Supreme Malum. When Governor Pehran convenes with us shortly, we shall inform her of this update and request additional forces be sent to Corvaan. This is a battle we cannot afford to lose."

"I agree with you, Grandmaster Zeffiro. From what Genaya and I witnessed on Corvaan, and now here, I fear the Malum have sent a massive force to defend Corvaan. Given the scale of things though, they may be planning additional attacks on other systems."

"Heysen is right. We are entirely focussed on Corvaan. If we are to stay in touch with the Malum's advancements, we must be wary of their next targets. I fear a devious strategy may be at play," said Yaneema in a cautious tone.

"Very correct you are, Vice-Master Yaneema. Things appear to be spiralling out of control at the moment. More than we can willingly handle," said Zeffiro thoughtfully. Is there anything else we should know?"

"Not much else, Grandmaster. The Battle-Bot factory was empty and from what I can gather, Corvaan will be heavily defended. We will need to send a lot of fire-power to take them down," said Heysen.

"Very well, we'll convene with Governor Pehran on the matter," said Zeffiro. "Thank you for your information. Now, we need you back here as soon as you can. Our attack on Corvaan will not be too far away."

The hologram message ended as Zeffiro turned off the call. At the instant in which he did so, the wide Ordo Chambers doors slid open smoothly. Governor Pehran and Vice-Governor Ghoni paced intently through the doors and towards the guest's seats of the Ordo Chambers.

"Grandmaster Zeffiro, Vice-Master Yaneema, fellow Ordo members," said Pehran formally.

"Ah, Governor Pehran, Vice-Governor Ghoni, how good to see you," said Zeffiro pleased. "Have you any update on the battle?"

"Yes, we have, we've been deliberating with members of many systems since the motion was passed," said Governor Pehran. "Many were questioning the legitimacy of the deal, while others were questioning how hard we should attack."

"In regard to that last point, is there a decision?" enquired Zeffiro.

"Not fully as of yet. At the moment, we were considering twenty-five million Federation Soldiers, plus a hundred thousand space fighters and additional Battlecruisers. Along with some Paxian reinforcements, that should be able to manage the Corvaanian Army," said Pehran assuredly.

"I fear that may not be sufficient," said Zeffiro.

Governor Pehran looked at Zeffiro as if he was mocking her. "What do you mean it may not be sufficient, that is nearly five percent of our army?" enquired Pehran confused.

"We have just had word from Genaya and Heysen, they encountered a Vondur on Vormok," said Zeffiro. "Furthermore, they discovered a Battle-Bot factory, capable of producing countless volumes of Malum troops. There are possibly more of these factories across the galaxy too!"

Pehran looked at Zeffiro stunned, still in disbelief at what he was saying.

"Are you saying that they've been building a monstrous army under our noses?" asked Pehran.

"Apparently so. Since no one thought the Malum existed, no one bothered to check, especially given that Vormok is dangerous and well outside of our jurisdiction as a Federation," said Zeffiro.

"Well then what shall we do?" asked Pehran with confusion.

"We recommend sending at least double the forces you outlined," said Zeffiro steadfastly.

"What?" asked Pehran in disbelief.

"We must send these forces or Corvaan will be lost," urged Zeffiro.

"You want me to sacrifice nearly one tenth of our entire Federation Army just for Corvaan?" enquired Pehran in sheer bafflement. "It may be important, but it is only one system in tens of thousands."

"Governor Pehran is correct," said Vice-Governor Ghoni slightly timidly, afraid of interrupting. "We should not throw all our eggs into one basket. This seems like a bit of an overreaction."

"It may seem like that, Vice-Governor Ghoni," said Yaneema. "However, that is not the case I can assure you. This situation requires a proportionate volume of soldiers at the ready. A loss here could be catastrophic; not just tactically, but for confidence in the Federation. We must show our allies, as well as our adversaries, that we are not to be reckoned with. Only then will our situation have the opportunity to improve," said Vice-Master Yaneema intelligently.

Everyone within the chamber paused at Yaneema's statement, contemplating its validity. After a brief moment of thinking, everyone agreed with the sentiment. Zeffiro grew delighted by their quick acceptance of the matter.

"Vice-Governor Ghoni and I may be wrong here," said Pehran admittedly. "We shall try and send more forces, but maybe not as many ground troops. We can spare more space fleets I guess, but we best hope we win."

"Do not fear, Governor, I will send three Ordo members into the battle initially, as well as many Paxian from low-risk systems to ensure our security and integrity remains. This way we have trained combatants to slow and stop the Malum if they appear," said Zeffiro confidently.

"Excellent, although I fear at the end of this war, we will need to source additional soldiers from somewhere," stressed Pehran,

"I may be able to assist with that too, Governor," said Zeffiro. "But it will have to wait until after the battle. Now, we need to prepare our strategy."

"Agreed, Vice-Governor Ghoni and I shall inform the House of the situation. From there, we will prepare our tactics and ready our forces," said Pehran confidently.

"Wonderful, we will debrief Heysen and Genaya on the situation when they arrive. They may be able to assist with tactics too," said Zeffiro.

"Good, anyway we have a hectic schedule, we shall meet early tomorrow morning," said Pehran slightly hastily. "Thank you!"

Governor Pehran and Vice-Governor Ghoni exited the Ordo Chambers swiftly to attend other matters. As the members vacated the Ordo Chambers, Zeffiro contemplated Yaneema's words and Heysen's information. If what Heysen said was correct, Yaneema's words were even truer. The Federation had to be successful on Corvaan. Not just for the freedom of those on Corvaan, but to prevent the spreading of the disease that was the Malum.

Chapter 24

Jeppora exited his Cross-Fighter, stepping foot onto the landing pad. He was now back on Corvaan, and he was pleased with what he saw. Scores of Battle-Bots accompanied Corvaanian Soldiers in patrols. Many were there to greet him as he arrived.

"Welcome back Vondur Jeppora," said one of the violet-coloured Battle-Bot commanders in a high robotic voice. "Vondur Sombria requests your presence in the Government Chambers."

"I'll head there right away," he said to the Battle-Bot.

Jeppora paced his way from the landing pad towards the Corvaanian Government Building. As he approached it, thousands more soldiers and vehicles lined the plaza at the front of the Government Building, whilst several Battlecruisers were situated in the skies above Corvaan and circling the planet's space territory. Jeppora was escorted by some of the Battle-Bots inside the chambers, as they proceeded down the right corridor of the Government Building. The Battle-Bots followed in double-file right behind Jeppora, as he passed by the Malum guards who remained seemingly unmoved since Jeppora last saw them. As he expected, they saluted him as he passed.

Jeppora entered the main chamber again, and Sombria was seated upright on her throne, looking directly at Jeppora as he entered. The Battle-Bots stopped at the entrance, maintaining their formation.

"Good to see you're back, Vondur Jeppora," said a delighted

Sombria.

"Vondur Sombria, good to see you as well. How have our plans been going?" enquired Jeppora.

"I was about to ask you the same question," said Sombria with a hint of humour. "We've received Vondur Veneticus's forces as you can tell. We have sufficient ground troops to fend off even large-scale Federation invasions. Furthermore, our Energy Shield Generators are up and running on all three moons. They'll have to take them out before reaching us. I've sent one Battlecruiser with Cross-Fighters to scout ahead of the shield to alert of any attempted invasion. They shall help diminish any pitifully attempted attacks on this planet."

"Excellent, Sombria, and what about the Battle-Bots?" asked Jeppora, pleased by the updates.

"They are far more sophisticated and intelligent than before," she said with a wicked smile. "Veneticus has outdone himself there. What of your expedition should we note?"

"The Paxian," said Jeppora now annoyed.

"What about them?" asked Sombria with slight concern.

"They were on Vormok, they were investigating us," said Jeppora with slight worry.

"And what happened to them?" asked Sombria curiously.

"I ambushed them. As far as I was aware I trapped them in the rubble of the factory, but I reckon they would've made it out," said Jeppora unconvinced.

"And what else about them, who are they?" asked Sombria.

"One is definitely an Ordo member. His orange suit is easily distinguishable, but his abilities are exceptional. The other is a very highly trained Paxian. I'm unsure of where he's from, but he is youthful and has a gold streak through his brown hair. It's tied in a bun. He was, though, deeply upset that I'd slain his friend. He seemed emotionally weak."

"Do you think we could exploit that?" asked Sombria with excitement.

"Perhaps, but I believe it would take time. We would have to wear him down first, but that is our last concern at the moment. I believe they'll send a large force in the coming days. We must be ready!" stressed Jeppora.

"Agreed, what has Veneticus said about our operations?" asked Sombria.

"He is pleased by our progress and is unfazed by the threat of the Federation. He says we are too well established to be wiped out now. Any success will further boost our rightful claims as supreme rulers of the galaxy," said Jeppora delightedly.

"Excellent, and what of our new base on Normona?" queried Sombria with anticipation.

"It's completed. It is state of the art and the Battle-Bot factory there is many times larger and more sophisticated than on Vormok. There are at least two more under construction. Soon, our stronghold will be complete, and we will be unstoppable. Our attacks on other members of the Trade Intermediate will ensue soon. Once they are conquered, we will control the galaxy, whether in power or not," said Jeppora with delight.

"Excellent, and I hope those Malum you were training are up to standard," said Sombria.

"They are, but Veneticus did not wish to send our best. We have many more up and coming fighters, but they will stay on Normona. Only a handful of current members have joined us here. The rest have been deployed on other missions that will aid our conquest, both on Normona and across the galaxy," said Jeppora.

"Perfect," said Sombria wickedly. "Also, Veneticus

informed me that Lucifer Dunn has been hired for additional work across the Trade Intermediate, both on Paxian and members of the House who are unwilling to accept our bargains."

"Lucifer Dunn? How could Veneticus accept him again after his failings?" enquired Jeppora in angered disbelief.

"He trusts that he will get the job done. Additionally, Veneticus has been using the weapons' manufacturing plant to customise a suit for him, aiding his missions. I do not know of anything else, but I'm keen to see what Veneticus has devised for him."

"I hope he does not throw away an opportunity by doing so," stated Jeppora sarcastically.

"Veneticus is extremely wise, and seldom makes a poor, ill-informed judgement. I trust that he knows what he is doing," said Sombria.

"I can only hope so," said Jeppora. "Also, I'll need to get one of my Plasma-Blades fixed, it was split at its centre."

"Commander!" yelled Sombria viciously in a shrieking tone.

A Malum Soldier came forward and knelt before Sombria.

"Yes, Vondur!" said the obedient Soldier.

"Send Vondur Jeppora's Plasma-Blade to be fixed urgently. Ensure it is in Jeppora's quarters by tomorrow morning or there will be consequences," barked Sombria.

"Yes, Vondur," said the Soldier, as he rose up and collected the two Plasma-Blade ends from Jeppora's hands and marched out of the chamber.

Sombria then got up out of her throne and lent over towards her side table. Sombria picked up her helmet and placed it gently on her head. Jeppora looked at the menacing helmet, luring his eyes with its hints of violet.

"The Battle of Corvaan is nearly upon us, Jeppora," said

Sombria in a slightly muffled voice from the helmet. “Ensure you and the rest of the Malum are prepared for attack at any moment. We will not lose.”

“Yes, Vondur,” said Jeppora, before he paced out of the chamber alongside Sombria. The Guards saluted them as they exited. The Battle-Bots at the chamber entrance parted to allow both Vondur’s to vacate the chamber, before proceeding behind the two.

Jeppora felt the tenseness of the situation through his legs. They were eager, brimming with energy. War was soon to be upon them. The Malum army was ready. The only uncertainty was in regard to the Federation Fleet. The strength of their forces would help determine the fate of the Battle of Corvaan.

Chapter 25

"Are we ready to begin?" asked Grandmaster Zeffiro.

The Ordo were gathered inside the Ordo Chambers one final time before the Battle of Corvaan. This meeting was Ordo members only, despite Genaya's presence. Governor Pehran and Vice-Governor Ghoni were not in attendance. Genaya felt privileged to be accepted into such a meeting, however, understood the seriousness of the formalities.

"Good," said Zeffiro, given there were no objections. "I've been briefed about the battle plan from Governor Pehran and Vice-Governor Ghoni, who for obvious reasons are unable to attend today's emergency meeting. The basic strategy is to corral their fleets and squeeze them in," he said, as he pointed to a holographic outlay of Corvaan and Nantan. "We're expecting a few obstacles, so listen up. We'll send as many cruisers as we can towards the centre. From there, as many H-craft as we can muster will take out their Cross-Fighters, providing a pathway for our Troop Carriers and artillery to make landfall. From there we have several objectives. Firstly, to clear out any Corvaanian Soldiers and Battle-bots that stand between you and your objectives. Secondly, we must target the Nantan commerce building. Three troop regiments will storm the building to prevent the Malum fleeing with any extra Federal Units. Thirdly, the Government Building. We believe a Vondur or Vondurs are using this structure as a haven. Send Paxian as well as troops in there to clear out any threats. It is likely that there will be Malum Guards there too, so use extreme caution. Of course, any ground artillery must be taken out quickly, hopefully by our spacecraft. Otherwise, troops won't be able to land."

Zeffiro paused while he contemplated his next words. "If we do not execute the landing phase right, we will lose time and more importantly lose many soldiers along the way," stressed Zeffiro with great importance. "Any questions so far?"

"Yes, how many of us are headed to the battle?" asked Hetana-Cia curiously.

"For security and liability reasons, we have decided to stick with initial plans of only sending three Ordo members, who have been pre-selected, but over one hundred other Paxian will join you," said Zeffiro.

"And who are those members?" asked Xevo intriguingly.

"Well, Vice-Master Yaneema, along with myself, Governor Pehran and Vice-Master Yaneema, have all decided that the three members to take part will be you Xevo, Heysen and… Genaya," said Zeffiro, hesitating before announcing Genaya's name.

Genaya looked up in complete shock at the announcement. He was in complete disbelief that he was selected. He had only ever dreamt of being on an Ordo mission, let alone being a part of something as major as this.

"Me?" asked Genaya astonished.

"Yes, Genaya, you were selected," said Zeffiro more accepting of the matter.

"Me? Really?" enquired Genaya, still baffled by the decision.

"Well, you and Heysen have gained a lot of knowledge on the situation. We felt you would be handy, despite the fact you're not quite Ordo yet. Also, Heysen has mentioned you are improving in controlling your emotions. So, I'm giving you a chance to prove yourself to me and to show that you have changed," said Zeffiro earnestly.

Genaya was elated by the decision and looked over towards Heysen with glee. Heysen returned the exchange with a large grin, appearing happy that his protégé had been rewarded for his endeavours to improve.

"Now given that this is a battle and technically, whilst not yet official, we are in war, you will all be given titles," said Yaneema with seriousness. "Heysen shall be named General Jogja and Xevo will be General Normone. Given that you, Genaya, are not quite Ordo yet, you will have a lesser ranking, but will be known as Major Dorsolo. These titles are solely for the purposes of commanding troops on the ground," said Yaneema informatively. "The rest of you will remain here where we shall monitor the situation."

"Also, on that note you will each be given a specialised Ordo H-craft. They'll be waiting in the hangars when the fleet departs for Corvaan," said Zeffiro. "Some time shortly, an alarm will blare out across the Federation Building. That will signal you to head to your H-craft. You will link up with the Federation Fleet as you depart as they should already be mobilised. Aside from that, good luck! The fate on Corvaan depends on you."

As Zeffiro concluded, the members rose up and vacated the chambers. Genaya rose up, his knees continuing to tremble from excitement. He could not believe that he was selected to fight as an Ordo representative. His happiness only grew as Xevo came over to congratulate him as they exited the Ordo Chambers.

"How good is that?" said Xevo in a delighted manner. "You're representing the Ordo in an official manner."

Genaya watched on as Heysen deliberately went down the opposite corridor to that of Genaya and Xevo, grinning at Genaya whilst doing so.

"Oh, yeah, it's awesome. I'm still a tad surprised Zeffiro allowed it," said Genaya.

"I know you have premonitions about Zeffiro's treatment of you, but surely this signals that he is not motivated by emotions. He does not willingly send people to fight battles whom he does not believe are capable of performing their duties," she said pleasantly.

Genaya could not divert his gaze as he walked, her lips moved so elegantly, so mesmerizingly. They danced up and down much to Genaya's delight. Her walk was so professional too, and her eyes dazzled him into an inescapable trance. He was lost deep in Xevo's soul.

"I guess you were right, Xevo, I was quite over the top with it," said Genaya in a smooth tone.

Genaya could sense Xevo felt similarly about him. She would not divert her gaze of him and continued to look adorably towards him. Her lips tremored at the movement of his mouth and her smile grew brighter with every word he spoke.

"You're funny, Genaya, I still don't quite understand you," smiled Xevo.

"Well, that's because you don't know me too well," smirked Genaya, much to the love of Xevo.

"Fair enough, but you're different to most other Paxian," said Xevo.

"How so?" laughed Genaya awkwardly, embarrassed by Xevo's appreciation of him.

"I'm not sure, there's just something about you," said Xevo with surety.

Both Genaya and Xevo looked admiringly at each other for a small period of time, before they were interrupted.

Whoop! Whoop! A siren was blaring across the Federation building. Lights flashed coercively with the noise. Genaya's eyes widened with alert. His adrenaline kicked in. He was somewhat caught off guard by the immediacy of the alarm, anticipating it to go off a little while later.

"It's the alarm, we better get to the hangar!" said Xevo in shock.

"I'll meet you there, I have to grab my Plasma-Blade from the armoury. It was being repaired," said Genaya frantically.

"All good, hurry though!" said Xevo.

The two ran in separate directions, Genaya darted down a small right corridor to collect his Plasma-Blade, whilst Xevo followed the hallway down towards the Ordo hangar.

Once Genaya had retrieved his Plasma-Blade, he made his way through the Federation Building's corridors and down the hangar elevator. As he entered the main platform, he was met by both Heysen and Xevo, who were both waiting patiently for his arrival.

"About time, Genaya. How long does it take to make it to the armoury?" enquired Heysen half-jokingly.

"Longer than I thought," said Genaya half seriously.

"Well, no matter, hurry up and get in. We have to leave now," said Heysen, directing Genaya towards the three H-craft sitting ahead of them on their level of the hangar.

Heysen handed him an Ordo ring to lock and unlock the H-craft.

"Here, you'll need this," said Heysen.

Genaya looked at the ring with amazement. The Ordo logo was impeccably crafted, and the orange and gold colour of the ring was a spectacle.

"Thanks, Heysen!" said Genaya as he gracefully slid it onto

the middle finger of his left glove.

"C'mon now, we have to leave, or we'll be behind the fleet, and we can't have that," stressed Heysen, as Genaya now made his way towards the H-craft. "You too, Xevo, we've got to go."

"What are you looking at me for, I arrived here even before you did," she said jokingly, much to Genaya and Heysen's amusement.

Genaya analysed the H-craft, it was different from the ones he saw previously. The design was still the same, but these ships were of a royal blue colour. Genaya placed his left hand out to the ships side sensor. An ever so soft 'beep!' could be heard and the hatch to the H-craft unlocked and sprung open. Genaya hopped in. The cockpit was not overly large and was located at the centre of the ship.

The cabin interior was darkened but had more than adequate lighting on its ceiling. The dashboard controls spanned the width of the cabin interior. There were two seats in the ship, but it was evident to Genaya that only one person was required to operate it. Both seats had the capability of handling the thrusters and the Laser Cannons. The windshield was large and curved, stretching the width of the dashboard. There was also a small storage compartment on the far side.

Genaya nestled into the cockpit chair and ignited the engines. The H-craft hummed and buzzed as the engines fired up. Pssshh! The gas compressors under the H-craft were now propelling the ship into a levitational state. Genaya looked up ahead of him, eager for action. The Ordo Hangar doors came open, and the bright daylight of Manoma shone between the buildings, bursting into the hangar.

Genaya looked on as Heysen and Xevo thrust their H-craft off in a flash, zooming through the opening and out of the hangar.

Genaya went to accelerate the H-craft, before speeding like a missile out of the hangar and narrowly avoiding a nearby building as he pulled up towards the sky. The H-crafts were clearly very zippy spacecraft. He negated the busy Manoma traffic and made his way quickly to the outer atmosphere, alongside Heysen and Xevo.

Genaya tailed behind Heysen and Xevo in a V-formation as they exited Manoma's atmosphere. The spectacle of Manoma grew fainter as the emptiness of space grew larger. The only absurdity was that space now wasn't so empty.

Genaya looked around his H-craft. For as far as he could see, fleet after fleet of ships were stationed outside of Manoma. Sturdy and monstrous Federation Battlecruisers were a menacing sight, even for Genaya. These hardy Battlecruisers were shaped in a simplistic, rectangular box design with slanted faces at the cruiser's front and rear. A smaller, thinner rectangular box protruded upwards from each Battlecruiser's centre. This section of the Battlecruiser was discernible as the command centre. The rear section of this command centre appeared lower in height than the main section of the ship, as the battle cruiser was slightly slanted. The command centre, as well as the body of the rest of the command centres were of a general royal blue colour.

Furthermore, several Laser Cannons were mounted on the sides of the Battlecruisers, and other anti-spacecraft turrets were scattered across each of the cruisers to ensure they were protected from enemy fire. Scores of H-craft accommodated each Battlecruiser, like a swarm of insects protecting a nest.

Smaller Troop Carriers filled in the gaps. They were of an extended U-shape design, and light grey in colour. The top section of the carrier protruded over the sides of the main body, where tiny cylindrical thruster engines were located.

Judging by the volume of them, Genaya estimated there must have been thousands of troops on those carriers alone. He was still in awe of what he was witnessing.

"We've sure got one hell of a fleet," said Genaya emphatically over the communications.

"Agree with that Major Dorsolo, looking very potent," said Xevo admittedly.

"Do you have to use that name Xevo?" asked Genaya jokingly.

"That's General Normone to you, Major," laughed Heysen.

"Sorry, General Jogja, wasn't aware of the formalities," laughed Genaya.

"All good. Major Dorsolo, just keeping you aware," said Heysen laughingly. "Now, let's go liberate Corvaan!"

Genaya, Heysen and Xevo were now at the front of the Federation Fleet, guiding the scores of forces towards the inevitability of conflict. The magnitude of the resources at their disposal had incredibly boosted moral. The fleet travelled cohesively together, in one big unit. The major test it faced; would be how it handled the scores of Malum forces awaiting their uninvited arrival on Corvaan.

Chapter 26

The Federation Fleet emerged through the worst of the asteroid field surrounding Corvaan. The majority of forces approached Corvaan from the thinnest section of the asteroid field to minimise damage. However, many still approached the planet via the more perilous sections of the asteroid field to ensure the battle plans were upheld.

The sight of Corvaan was becoming clearer in the distance for Genaya. They were nearly there. It felt like a while ago since he first investigated the planet. He could not conceive that such a short time later he would be back a third time, let alone for war.

Genaya's focus grew sharp as small, indiscernible objects were beginning to appear just outside of Corvaan. They grew bigger as the fleet approached them.

"General Jogja, this is Lieutenant Paxley of the Ganhar Battlecruiser. Do you copy?" asked the Lieutenant over the communications, audible to all three representatives of the Ordo.

"Lieutenant Paxley, this is General Heysen Jogja of the Ordo. I do copy, what is your status?" asked Heysen in a professional tone.

"General Jogja, the Ganhar has picked up several signals from a Deep Range Sonar scan. We're detecting multiple Cross-Fighters heading our way, perhaps one or two of their Battlecruisers, but there's a lot of them," stressed the Lieutenant.

"No worries, Lieutenant Paxley, inform the H-craft at the front we have company. Their main objective is to protect the

Troop Carriers. The Battlecruisers can defend themselves. Get them in defensive formation. We'll also want a couple of additional H-craft squadrons to negotiate the threat," said Heysen calmly. "Let them know we've got company."

"As you wish, General," said the Lieutenant before ending his signal.

"Xevo, Genaya, get ready!" urged Heysen.

"Will do, Heysen," said both Genaya and Xevo.

A stream of light came from a large distance away. Electron Cannon blasts propelled through, crashing into small, isolated asteroids, rupturing them into thousands of tiny harmless pieces. The small rocks ricocheted off Genaya's H-craft as merely a brief distraction, posing no threat.

The Cross-Fighters now came roaring in. Hundreds of them descending on the fleet in an attacking formation. Rays of light; of searing red from the Cross-Fighters and of sharp crisp blue from the H-craft, flew through the void of space in opposite directions. Many shields from both sides were hit. Two Cross-Fighters exploded, destroyed from the excessive impacts of the H-craft Laser Cannons. The Cross-Fighters descended into the Federation Fleet's formation, attempting to disrupt the structure of their attack. H-craft diverted to defend some of the ships. Light from the Laser Cannons continued to fly from both sides. Many Laser Cannon bolts made impact with their intended targets.

It did not take long for the relatively small Cross-Fighter fleet to be diminished. A quick assessment from Genaya counted only a handful that were left. Although Genaya also discovered that they had caused catastrophic damage to two Troop Carriers. Somewhat intelligently, knowing they were soon to be blown into smithereens, the remaining Cross-Fighters kamikazed into the two weakened Troop Carriers, causing a bright flash of death and destruction. Genaya's head sunk in despair as the mangled, fiery wreckage of the Cross-Fighters and Troop Carriers drifted away lifelessly.

"Dammit!" yelled Heysen. "We need to do a better job than that, we need all the troops we can get."

"Two Troop Carriers lost, General Jogja," said Lieutenant Paxley over the communications.

"We need to protect them better. Our ground troops are vital," said Heysen in reply.

"At least, we still have plenty of H-craft left, only about a dozen of them were destroyed," said Genaya optimistically to Heysen over the communications.

"That is some slight good news, but they were deliberately targeting the Troop Carriers. We must be mindful," stressed Heysen.

The fleet continued its progression towards Corvaan, eventually making their way through the last of the asteroid field. The fleet that took the longer path to Corvaan could be seen emerging outside from the depths of the asteroid field, on the opposite side of the planet. Almost all of the Federation's forces deployed to Corvaan were converging on the planet.

It was growing increasingly apparent to Genaya that the Malum were well equipped to fight for the planet themselves. Several Malum Battlecruisers as well as thousands of Cross-Fighters were awaiting the arrival of the Federation Fleet.

Genaya could see that the Malum Battlecruisers were much different in design than Federation ones. They had a small, but flat frontage, and were designed in a stretched hexagonal shape. Two curved lines spanned the length of Malum Battlecruiser's body, however, also stretched upwards. This gave the Battlecruisers plenty of room to accommodate hangars. The

Battlecruiser's Command Centre was located at the front and at their highest point. Its main deck window was trapezoid-shaped; however, the lower edge was curved inwards. Whilst the overall design of the Battlecruisers was different, the Malum Battlecruisers also possessed a range of artillery and guns to combat against both large and small enemy vessels.

Genaya did notice something peculiar about their positioning though. At first, he could not put his finger on what seemed off. But after a brief analysis of the situation, he soon realised what his eyes smartly detected. Along with the Cross-Fighters, the Battlecruisers all appeared to be within the wide orbit of Corvaan's three moons.

"Heysen?" asked Genaya nervously over the communications.

"Yes Genaya," responded Heysen, unsure of Genaya's query.

"Why is their fleet converged all together within the orbit of Corvaan's moons?" asked Genaya.

Heysen paused, contemplating Genaya's point. "Do you think that? No, they couldn't have. Could they?" said Heysen, baffled by what he was contemplating.

Heysen, then turned on communications to the Ganhar Battlecruiser. "This is General Jogja. Cease our advance! Cease our advance!" he yelled.

"Yes, General," responded Lieutenant Paxley.

There was a long pause before the ships stopped their advancements towards Corvaan. The entire Federation Fleet was stationary in the open area of space, as if it was physically frozen in its position.

"What are you doing, Heysen?" enquired Xevo, slightly concerned by Heysen's actions.

“Saving us from imminent destruction,” said Heysen coolly.

A signal now came through the communications from Lieutenant Paxley. “In all due respect, General Heysen, may I ask your reasoning for this strategy?” she asked.

“It’s not a strategy, Lieutenant. They are cordoned behind the orbit of Corvaan’s moons for a reason. They have shield generators on those moons. The reason why they haven’t even bothered to fire is because they know it’s there. We need to take it out,” said Heysen calmly.

“Yes, General. How do you plan on going about it?” asked Lieutenant Paxley.

“Send three squadrons of H-craft to each moon, we need to take out the generators. They cannot stop us, as doing so would only aid our cause,” said Heysen.

“Are you certain there is a shield there?” asked Paxley.

Heysen didn’t respond. Two monstrous fleets of forces were separated by a void of space. Genaya grew concerned. It appeared the stand-off would last, until three blasts from Heysen’s H-craft’s Laser Cannons barrelled towards the Malum Fleet. The Malum were unwavering in their response. Their nonchalance seemed as if they were taunting the Federation.

Genaya watched on as the beams travelled seemingly in slow motion towards the Malum Fleet, only to be stopped abruptly by an invisible wall. The section of the Energy Shield lit up as the Laser Cannon bolts barely scratched the shield’s defences.

There was an additional pause, before H-craft squadrons directed themselves and their fire towards Corvaan’s three moons. The Federation’s Fleet slowly advanced towards the Energy Shield’s perimeter with anticipation. The squadrons fired at the bases and rallied again. Then came a fatal blow. Genaya’s eyes widened with excitement at the unfolding action. The

Energy Shield generator on Corvaan's moon C-2 was destroyed, and a gap in the seemingly intangible fence had been formed.

The Malum Fleet hesitated their attack no longer, concentrating their fire on the Federation's Fleet. Swarms of Cross-Fighters flooded from the gap in the Energy Shield, as if a dam wall had broken. Fire began between the two forces and a fully-fledged war had begun.

The Energy Shield Generators on Corvaan's other two moons were quickly blown to pieces, leaving the planet exposed. Cross-Fighters and H-craft were being destroyed left, right and centre; amidst the rapid barrage of Laser Cannons, Electron Cannons and a wide variety of missiles. Even the Battlecruisers were engaging in warfare, especially given their shield defences were barely being penetrated by the smaller spacecraft. Yet, their damage output towards their adversaries was great.

Many ships succumbed to the early round of fighting, but the Federation's tactics were paying off. Scores of H-craft and Federation Battlecruisers tightly escorted the majority of Troop Carriers towards Corvaan's atmosphere. Only a select handful were the unfortunate beneficiaries of the Malum's ruthless attacks.

Genaya could feel the tenseness of the situation gripping him all over. His blood was pumping. His legs' skin itching for more activity. As the first phase of the battle had been successful for the Federation, Genaya knew a more difficult phase was about to begin. The landfall of troops on Corvaan was just the start of things to come.

Chapter 27

"Vondur! There's too many of them! They will breach the Energy Shield in no time—" said one of the Corvaanian Guards before being choked by Vondur Sombria's outstretched hand.

Jeppora was briefing Sombria on the battle status alongside a handful of the remaining Corvaanian Military Representatives.

"You are pathetic!" she said wickedly, before tossing the lifeless corpse away from her in disgust. "Jeppora, how are we looking?" asked Sombria nervously and angrily.

"Not good, Vondur Sombria. The Federation figured out we had an Energy Shield in place and are at present attempting to destroy the generators," said Jeppora looking directly at Sombria's helmet, unfazed by Sombria's ruthlessness.

"Why aren't we stopping them?" asked Sombria in frustration.

"Our fleet cannot attack them yet, that would only aid them, Sombria. Our very small outer fleet of Cross-Fighters were destroyed, but did manage to destroy two of their Troop Carriers," said Jeppora.

"Veneticus has really bitten off more than he can chew here," Sombria muttered to Jeppora. "Are the Battle-Bots in place?" she queried hastily.

"Yes, Sombria. Premier Finkel has ensured they are ready for any ground assault," said Jeppora confidently.

"She is an excellent ally," said Sombria with pleasure. "Make sure there is sufficient artillery and that they drive any landing Federation troops to the south side. That should allow us to pick them off easily."

"Sombria, I must warn you the Federation have delivered a substantial fleet, both of ground troops and H-craft. We may need to deploy some Malum Soldiers onto the battlefield to help ensure our victory," hinted Jeppora.

"Hmmm," pondered Sombria. "Perhaps you are right. We do need to safeguard. Send two groups out to assist the Battle-Bots and the Corvaanian Soldiers. I'll order the rest of the Malum stationed here as well as ourselves out into battle if the necessary time comes," said Sombria.

"I hope it doesn't come to that," said Jeppora with concern.

"It very well may, Jeppora," said Sombria warningly. "Expect your Ordo adversaries to be there too."

"I'll exterminate them once and for all," said Jeppora angrily.

"Settle, Vondur Jeppora," said Sombria more calmly. "If such a time comes, then the battle is lost. I will signal an escape and we shall join Veneticus on Normona."

"What of Corvaan?" asked Jeppora with some distaste.

"As much as I do not wish to lose Corvaan, the war has just begun. Whilst the Federation continues its worthless attempt to liberate this besieged planet, we continue to win. The more time they waste here the stronger we get elsewhere. Don't get me wrong, I'll sacrifice every last Corvaanian Soldier for this planet. But it's not the end if we lose, Jeppora, let me assure you. Veneticus' plans go way beyond what he has outlined."

Jeppora grinned widely at Sombria's remarks, to which she responded likewise. Now aware of Corvaan's purpose, Jeppora became less concerned with the outcome of the battle, but was determined to ensure the Federation's fleet suffered as much as it could. Hatred gushed through his arteries, filled his lungs and tightened his nerves. The Federation pests needed to be eradicated.

A Battle-Bot entered the Government Chamber abruptly, informing Sombria and Jeppora of the updated status of the battle.

"Vondur's!" it said in its robotically programmed voice. "The Energy Shield Generators have been destroyed. Our forces are now engaging with the enemy. They have begun to breach Corvaanian territory. Landfall is estimated to occur shortly."

Jeppora and Sombria exchanged looks of deep concern at the sudden development of the situation.

"Get those Malum in position, join them if you have to. Our primary goal is to deplete their forces as much as we can. If a victory can be salvaged, then all the better. Hurry!" stressed Sombria.

Jeppora acknowledged Sombria's words and fled out of the chamber. He could now hear some of the battle occurring. The battle was coming too close and too fast for Jeppora's liking. More time was needed to deploy the Malum warriors.

Chapter 28

Genaya thrust his controls vigorously left, narrowly avoiding Electron Cannon fire from a Cross-Fighter. Genaya's H-craft was weaving between Battlecruisers, as well as other H-craft and Cross-Fighters. It was a mess to navigate through. So many obstacles, so much debris, so much risk. This was unlike anything Genaya had ever dealt with before. It was a massive battle and at a monstrously large scale. No amount of flying experience could help anyone deal with the situation completely. Genaya knew that in order to survive he had to be adaptable.

Genaya saw a Federation Battlecruiser straight ahead and sensed an opportunity. He veered as far left of it as he could, before quickly looping around the Battlecruiser's Command Centre and firing towards the oncoming Cross-Fighter at will. It stood little chance. Within an instant of impact from Genaya's barrage, it tore apart into flaming pieces. They scratched against the Battlecruiser with insignificant threat and were deflected away.

It did not take long for Genaya to fall in hot pursuit of a Cross-Fighter that was tailing Heysen's H-craft. It was relentless in its assault and Heysen's H-craft shield had been drastically weakened. After a quick barrage from his H-craft's Laser Cannons, Genaya ensured the Cross-Fighter suffered the same fate as the one that pestered him. The Cross-Fighter entered a fiery tailspin, before smacking against the side of a Malum Battlecruiser.

"Got you covered, Heysen. You owe me one," said Genaya coolly.

"Thanks, Genaya, but don't get too boastful about saving my skin. I'll repay you somehow," laughed Heysen.

The Federation Fleet was now on the verge of Corvaan's atmosphere. The Battlecruisers remained a safe distance away. Now, it was up to the scores of H-craft squadrons to escort the Troop Carriers to Nantan safely. Genaya grew nervous. Phase two of the ground assault operation was underway. The Troop Carriers that were nestled behind the Battlecruisers now emerged speedily from their hideaway, bursting through space and into Corvaan's atmosphere with a cloak of H-craft thickly protecting them.

"Genaya, Xevo, this is our chance to aid troops onto the ground," said Heysen commandingly over the communications. "We need to assist them as best as we can. Take out whatever Cross-Fighters or ground artillery we can to ensure we get sufficient troops into Nantan. Once that is done, us and other Paxian will try and join them. All understood?"

"Yes, Heysen," they both said swiftly in reply.

"Excellent, time to take out these sorry Malum forces," said Heysen slightly cockily.

The three Ordo H-craft tagged behind a group of Troop Carriers and their escorts deep into Corvaan's atmosphere. The sky was bright, it was mid-afternoon in Nantan. Genaya was amazed. The peace and beauty of the serene rainforest was juxtaposed by the harsh, unrelenting attack of the Malum. As they grew closer to Nantan, they were met by an almighty assault from artillery as well as Battle-Bots firing into the air. The thick coating of H-craft around the Troop Carriers was quickly diminishing from the Malum's heavy attack.

“Genaya, take out those VI-L’s and VI-A’s, otherwise we’ll never make it,” said Heysen stressfully.

“Can do,” said Genaya in reply as he diverted his attention to the swarm of troops on the ground.

“Xevo, watch those Cross-Fighters. They’re circling back towards us,” said Heysen.

“Will do, Heysen,” she said as she pulled away from the fleet.

Genaya focussed his sights on a large volume of Battle-Bot troops and VI-L artillery located in Nantan’s open plaza. Genaya opened fire on them, relatively free of threat as they had diverted their attention squarely on the approaching Troop Carriers.

The Laser Cannon blasts from Genaya’s H-craft carved a path on destruction, tearing through Battle-Bots and some Corvaanian Soldiers with ease. Two VI-Ls were destroyed and Genaya now diverted some of the Malum’s fire towards him. His H-craft’s shield strength only dropped marginally from the Malum’s response. Given the success of his previous attack run, he turned and went back again.

This time he targeted more VI-Ls located in the inner suburbs of Nantan. One by one they were destroyed; debris was sent flying everywhere. Buildings were damaged instantly. The battle was already leaving a sour mark on the once prosperous city.

Genaya could tell he was now seen as a major threat by the Malum. Two VI-As were now flying behind him, pursuing him with relentless intent. They opened fire on Genaya, their Photon-Cannon bolts narrowly missing him. Then, he got hit. Twice. His shields suffered catastrophic damage and were now inoperable. He was exposed.

Genaya weaved left, then right. He attempted to use the

rainforest as cover. Through a valley gap, over some hills and even around rock pillars. But it was of no avail. In fact, he had attracted even more attention. Four VI-As pursued behind him. In addition to this, five Cross-Fighters joined the chase, hellbent on annihilating Genaya. Despite the increasing inevitability of his doom, Genaya continued his evasive attempts.

Bracing for certain death, Genaya's hopes suddenly lifted. Amongst the red fire of the Malum craft, some blue coloured bolts appeared to whiz past his ship.

"Xevo!" he muttered to himself.

Behind the VI-A artillery vessels and Cross-Fighters targeting Genaya's ship, was Xevo, taking down as many ships as she could. Genaya quickly pulled up and looped around. The VI-A crafts were unable to repeat the manoeuvre and were caught unawares. The one that did attempt to replicate it smashed into a hill and was destroyed on impact in a ball of flames. The last remaining Cross-Fighter in pursuit of Genaya almost managed to execute the manoeuvre, but was expertly gunned down by Xevo.

With the Cross-Fighters now out of the way, Xevo and Genaya flew alongside each other, with the seemingly easy and simple task of destroying the VI-A artillery vessels. Swiftly they were all eliminated, and a trail of wreckage was carved from their defeat at the hands of Genaya and Xevo.

"Now, you owe me one," smirked Xevo over the communications.

"Is that so?" smirked Genaya in reply.

"Let it be known that your death was certain without my assistance," said Xevo smugly.

"I had them fine," wryly remarked Genaya, fully aware that that was not the case.

Their brief exchange was promptly interrupted by Heysen

desperately attempting to communicate to them.

"Hey, you two! If you're finished debating who the best pilot is, I need plenty of assistance back here stat," said Heysen with urgency.

"No worries, Heysen, we're almost there now," said Genaya as both he and Xevo exited the rainforest and remerged on the outskirts of Nantan.

The initial volume of Troop Carriers attempting to make landfall had been depleted to three. The rest of them lay obliterated across the cityscape.

"Genaya, there are some VI-Ls in the desired landing zone. You and Xevo need to take them out. Our ground assault is going too slow. We're losing too many of them," said Heysen.

"No worries, Heysen, I'm already onto it," said Genaya, eyeing off the pestering threat.

Genaya rose up into the air before descending on a somewhat steep attacking angle. His descent positioned him perfectly to maximise the carnage on the three VI-L artillery vehicles evidently causing havoc. Pressing his thumbs firmly into the Laser Cannon triggers until they ached, Genaya drove an inescapable surplus of fire into the artillery, destroying them, all the while avoiding the imminent return fire of the Malum's forces.

"Good stuff, Genaya, now we have a window. We just need to protect them as they attempt to land," said Heysen.

"Roger that, Heysen, but we've got bogeys incoming," said Genaya worriedly.

"Let's give them hell then," said Heysen calmly.

The two paired up to attack the incoming Cross-Fighters whilst Xevo remained to assist the Troop Carrier landfall. Heysen and Genaya veered away from each other before wheeling back in and opening fire on the Cross-Fighters. They were swiftly taken care of and destroyed.

Suddenly, there was a bang. Genaya heard it easily yet was unsure as to exactly what it was. His system controls were ringing alerts into his ears. His hands trembled fearfully. A burning red glow reflected into the cockpit. At that instant Genaya knew what had happened. The back right engine was fully ablaze. Genaya heaved at the steering, begging for it to work. But it was no use. The ship veered right. Its altitude gradually lowering. Genaya hoped that he would be lucky. He hoped that he would be okay. The ship's alerts continued to echo. It was constant reminder of the inevitable impact with the ground.

The ship passed a building. It then passed over a small tower. He was coming over the northern outskirts of Nantan. The rainforest was just ahead. Genaya feared he would not make it. Genaya was fretful, unsure whether crashing in the rainforest or in the city was safest. He wondered if any landing was safe.

What would be a worse outcome? he wondered. *Was he just going to die?*

He did not wish to think that all his efforts were in vain. His communications were no longer working. The ship grazed the side of a building, speeding up its painfully long descent. Genaya knew that a level landing was his best hope of survival.

A plume of black smoke trailed behind him. Even if he did survive, company would not be far away. Some Corvaanian Soldiers were watching as his H-craft went down. Genaya watched on as they began to converge towards his position. He narrowly directed the H-craft in between a wide road as it coarsely kissed the pavement. Sparks sprung everywhere. The second engine caught fire now, just before Genaya managed to turn off the thrusters. A trail of debris was left behind. The H-craft turned and bumped its way into a tree, before splitting into two sides, one now almost completely mangled and destroyed.

The Corvaanian Soldiers arrived, assessing the scene. Genaya knew he had to exit the H-craft cockpit soon, or he would be dead. The Soldiers continued to look towards his H-craft. Genaya could see the full extent of the two main sections of the ship splitting up. One section was damaged, the other destroyed. The Soldiers appeared dubious of his survival. Even Genaya could not believe he had survived.

Just as the soldiers were convinced that Genaya was dead, the windscreen of the H-craft burst open. A bright yellow light protruded from it and sent glass flying away. Erupting from the remains of the H-craft was a bloodied and bruised warrior, wielding two ends of an engaged Plasma-Blade. Genaya hopped out and stood in front of the remains of his H-craft and magnetised his Plasma-Blade ends together. He was not going to give up now. He had soldiers to eradicate.

Chapter 29

A strike to the head. A lusty blow to the chest. A searing slice through the torso. One by one, Genaya felled his enemies. Corvaanian Soldiers fell down like dominoes at Genaya's relentlessness. He could not be stopped. The plasma beams at the ends of Genaya's Plasma-Blade buzzed with purpose, with intent. They seared through flesh as if it were nothing, as if it ceased to exist. Its molten scars were permanently inflicted on the dead it left behind.

Genaya was now clear: the Corvaanian Soldiers present had been eliminated. He knew though that more were coming. He had to find safe territory. Genaya used his Electromagnetic Boots to leap up onto a building to get a view of his surroundings.

The battle was now in full flight aerially. Cross-Fighters and VI-As littered the skies, attempting to thwart the H-craft and Troop Carrier invasion. For what Genaya could see, the battle was evenly poised. After watching the intense action unfold, Genaya once again searched for the Troop Carriers. There was now only one Troop Carrier left in the sky. Genaya was hopeful that the other Troop Carriers had made safe landfall.

Genaya's observations were interrupted abruptly by the fire of Photon-Guns. The red bolts zipped upwards past his head. Genaya scoured below him to see where they came from. However, he could not distinguish any Corvaanian Soldiers present. The fire was from an unknown source.

Genaya used his boots to gracefully leap off the building and onto the street below. There were some canopies on both sides of the street, and small dark alleys were embedded within the dense packing of buildings.

The shooter or shooters were likely hiding, but may have left, Genaya thought to himself.

Genaya spun around. There was noise. A hard noise. Something firm, rigid. It clattered on the stone pavement of Nantan's city streets. What it was, Genaya was unsure of. It lurked behind an alley.

Genaya stood defensively, anticipating a surprise attack. As Genaya cordoned around and got a view of the alley, he noticed two tall and bulky figures, shadowed by the afternoon sun. The only discernible feature was a sole violet eye on their heads.

As they noticed his presence, they opened fire on Genaya aggressively. The sun's shadow no longer disguised them, and Genaya's confident guess was proven correct. Two Battle-Bots were onto Genaya. It did not take long though for Genaya to deflect their Photon-Gun blasts away from him and slice through their sturdy chests. The metal seared as the Battle-Bots instantly powered down and fell in a heap.

Genaya's peace was only brief, as further disruption ensued. More Battle-Bots, this time nearly twenty, were marching down the street to converge on his position. Their initial fire was rapid and intensely focussed. Genaya spun his Plasma-Blade around in a twirl, deflecting as many blasts as he could. He managed to disable nearly half of the Battle-Bots, but the rest were unscathed and continued their approach.

Genaya panicked. *Surely, he could not fall here*, he pondered.

The deathly clanking of their feet on the pavement was interrupted. Two dashing orange lights were Genaya's saving grace. Xevo was slicing through the Battle-Bots from behind. Genaya did not hesitate to join in. He slashed at them, left then right.

Genaya quickly became swarmed by two particularly relentless Battle-Bots. He slashed at one, splitting it into two pieces. The second one, however, swiped its left arm at Genaya. The Battle-Bot's blade did not pierce Genaya, but its arm still forcefully pushed into Genaya and knocked him to the ground. His Plasma-Blade was simultaneously struck away from him across the street.

Genaya felt fear gushing through him now. At that moment, in the face of death and despair, Genaya sensed everything again. The searing pain of a cut on his cheek. The thumping soreness of his bruised ribs, and the growing fatigue of his legs. The fear he felt at that moment caused Genaya to surge with adrenaline.

Genaya looked up, slightly distracted, to see the Battle-Bot wielding its bladed arm high above Genaya, preparing to thrust it deep into his gut. Genaya rolled to his right as the blade struck the ground with a screeching thud. Genaya looked up for Xevo. She was just defeating the last of her Battle-Bots. Genaya knew that if he could just last a little longer, he'd survive.

Genaya used his boots to thrust him away from the Battle-Bot slightly. As it moved towards him, Genaya spun around on the ground to now be facing the Battle-Bot. He then used his boots again, sending him through the Battle-Bot's legs, head first. He was teasing it.

The Battle-bot turned around to Genaya. It now opted for a more reassuring measure. The Battle-Bot pointed its other arm towards Genaya, raring to fire as many Photon-Gun blasts as it took to eliminate him. Just as it fastened its arm in position, a bright orange flash zipped past Genaya's eyeline, and drove itself straight into the Battle-Bot. Genaya watched as the Battle-Bot lifelessly collapsed onto the ground, and its violet eye shut off. He turned around to see Xevo, who had just speared her Plasma-Blade straight into the Battle-Bot's chest, saving Genaya's life.

Genaya got up slowly. The pair exchanging looks of shock and surprise at what they had just encountered. They slowly walked towards each other, before they paused. They looked deeply into each other's eyes, before coming together for a deep, strong embrace. Genaya felt the raw emotion gushing through his chest and tingles pulsating on his cheeks. The comfort of hugging Xevo felt so exhilarating and comforting. It felt better than almost anything else he'd ever experienced. Genaya looked deep into Xevo's eyes, and she did likewise, both smiling brightly at each other.

"We should probably go grab our Plasma-Blades," said Xevo awkwardly.

"We should," said Genaya hastily and awkwardly. They quickly separated and retrieved their weapons.

"We need to find Heysen," said Genaya with concern.

"He landed a short time ago. He shouldn't be far away," said Xevo with slight confusion.

"I'm not," interrupted Heysen with a huge grin on his face.

"Where did you come from?" asked Genaya.

"I landed about three blocks over there," said Heysen pointing in the direction he'd just appeared from. "We've got our first troops on the ground."

"We do?" asked Genaya delightfully surprised.

"Indeed, we have about twelve-thousand soldiers at present on the ground, but they won't last long if we don't help them. This place is swarming with Battle-Bots. The Federation is about to send the rest of the Troop Carriers in. We just need to hold off the Malum until then," said Heysen.

"Good, we best get moving," said Xevo eagerly.

Genaya was still grasping the intensity and ferocity of the battle. No matter what happened, he could not stop. To do so would almost ensure death. The Federation was in a prime position to force back the Malum forces on Corvaan. Genaya was not prepared to let that advantage slip, and he knew Heysen and Xevo felt the same. The battle was teetering on a precipice. Genaya was going to ensure it teetered in the Federation's favour.

Chapter 30

Genaya, Xevo and Heysen made their way across the city, swiping away any threats that tried to impede their mission. They rose over a hill before making their way to a clear region of the city. Here, the situation was evident. Battle-Bots, as well as some Corvaanian Soldiers, were attacking the two Troop Carriers which had landed at the centre of this clearing. Surrounding them were the Federation Soldiers.

The Federation Soldiers were wearing light, but sturdy white and royal blue body-armour, with shoulder plates to protect the soldiers. The soldiers also wore peculiarly shaped helmets. They were flat on top but were smooth and in a bucket shape. The soldiers' helmets grew wider at the cheeks, before slowly pointing back inwards until it reached above their collarbone level. From here, the helmets moved back up towards the mouth, leaving a trapezoidal-shaped outline. The neck was protected by a white lightweight guard.

The helmet also contained a rectangular breathing filter at the mouth, whilst two circular filters were located on both sides around the cheek. A thin white strip went around the helmet at its centre, with two black slanted lines directed away from the face on both sides. There was also a large rectangular, black tinted eye shield, with the Federation Logo located above and centre of this eye shield. The rest of the helmet was royal blue in colour, except for the cheek guards, which were kelly green in colour.

The Federation Soldiers appeared to be under severe threat.

The Battle-Bots were relentlessly converging on their position. The three Paxian ran down the hill and attacked them from behind, deflecting away the blasts that came their way with their Plasma-Blades. Soon, they had diverted the attention of the small group of Malum forces, and the Federation Soldiers seized the opportunity. They mounted a few High Intensity Photon-Guns in a semi-circular perimeter and opened fire on the now-under-threat Malum forces. The Corvaanian Soldiers and the Battle-Bots were felled quickly and in a short amount of time the Federation Soldiers, along with the three Paxian had avoided the imminent threat.

Genaya watched on as the aerial battle continued above. The sound of Electron Cannon and Laser Cannon fire zapping through the air propagated across the city. More Troop Carriers were approaching. Six were coming to land on their position, four more across the other side of town, and three more to the south of the Corvaanian Government Building. Genaya watched as all but one touched down. The one that was destroyed shattered into thousands of pieces and fell hard to the ground like hail in the distance.

As the ships opened, hundreds of troops emerged, ready to attack. Genaya knew the Malum would be worried, as that was only the second wave of Federation troops. There were two more phases coming, both significantly larger than the previous phases. As the soldiers landed and started progressing inwards towards the centre of Nantan, the volume of Malum forces increased. Battle-Bots were everywhere now, the Corvaanian Soldiers were few and far between. Photon-Gun fire was fast and hard. The blasts zipped across the battlefield by their thousands, wreaking havoc with every impact.

More Troop Carriers were landing elsewhere. Many were

making it to the ground. The Malum artillery was quickly being destroyed, almost as soon as they drew the attention of the H-craft pilots. With that threat neutralised periodically, the Federation Fleets had a golden chance to bolster their ground assault. Genaya could feel the battle tipping in their favour.

Just as he was beginning to consider the prospect of victory, the Malum were quick to confirm his premonitions. They themselves had joined the battle. Figures of various shapes, sizes and species were waving around Plasma-Blades, glowing in bright violet and deep dark grey. The Malum were slicing their way through the unsuspecting Federation Soldiers. Suddenly, Genaya felt that they were on the back foot once again.

"Genaya, Xevo, we have to take them out," said Heysen with worry. "If we don't, we'll lose too many ground soldiers. Genaya, you take the three on the left. Xevo, you take the right. I'll eliminate the ones in the centre of the street."

Both Paxian acknowledged Heysen's request and went straight into their mission. They seamlessly carved a path through the surrounding Battle-Bots and engaged the semi-experienced Malum. Their skills were not sufficiently up to the standard of the three Ordo representatives. As such, they were dealt with fiercely and with expert precision. The Malum put up a slight fight, only due to their defensive skills with their Plasma-Blades. Aside from that, they posed only a moderate threat to the well-trained Paxian and were defeated with ease, falling to the ground after little resistance.

With the Malum temporarily dealt with, the Federation Fleet moved closer to the centre of Nantan. Genaya noticed that the battle was looking increasing like an invasion. Troop Carriers were landing now all across the city. The Malum's Cross-Fighters were having their work cut out for them by the Federation H-craft in the air. The battle was slipping through the Malum's fingers. The new troops merged with the old ones, and within a small space of time, a substantial force of Federation Soldiers were approaching Nantan's open plaza. Whilst that section of the city was still a stronghold for the Malum, the fact that these forces were approaching from several directions of the city left them corralled and under severe threat.

Genaya also noticed the increased presence of Paxian soldiers, from various systems across the galaxy. With their inclusion into the battle, the ground assault progressed further.

Genaya noticed a familiar face amongst the Paxian inclusions. Genaya quickly realised it was his friend Ange Kah-Sa from Befuno.

"Funny seeing you here," said Ange, surprising Genaya as he turned around to see her in her illuminated blue Paxian armour, wielding her blue coloured Plasma-Blade.

"Ange!" said Genaya with delight. "So good to see you, it feels like it's been quite a long time."

"It feels like it," said Ange as she swiped her Plasma-Blade across at some of the Battle-Bots on the edge of the Plaza.

"How have you been?" asked Genaya as he flicked his Plasma-Blade left then right, taking out two Battle-Bots.

"Good since you've been on Ordo business," said Ange laughing, whilst taking out a Battle-Bot in front of her.

"Very funny," laughed Genaya as he continued to fend off the Battle-Bot onslaught.

The plaza was now filled with Battle-Bots and Federation Soldiers, with some Malum and Paxian embedded within the skirmish. Genaya turned to his right to see Heysen valiantly fighting off a swarm of Battle-Bots, approaching the battleline as a wave. Heysen cleared out the group of Battle-Bots before performing an unusual, but highly effective manoeuvre. Heysen demagnetised his Plasma-Blade into its two ends. He then speared one end through three closely grouped Battle-Bots, searing it through them, before remagnetising the Plasma-Blade, sending the speared end soaring back through the Battle-Bots and into the centre of Heysen's Plasma-Blade.

"Where'd you learn that?" asked Genaya impressed.

"It takes a lot of practice," responded Heysen with a smile. "If you're not careful you'll end up stabbing yourself."

"Genaya, I need a hand," called out Ange's voice suddenly, across from where Genaya and Heysen were positioned.

Genaya turned to see Ange being surrounded by Battle-Bots, swinging their sharp bladed arms dangerously close to Ange. Genaya sprinted in, slashing one Battle-Bot that attempted to impede him. A hard swipe through the chest was all that was required. He then leapt onto the collapsing Battle-Bot. He used it as a springboard. Launching high into the air, Genaya flicked his wrists, wielding the Plasma-Blade with expertise. Up. Down. A swing to the left, before returning the stroke right. In no time, he'd cleared the Battle-Bots up with ease. After saving Ange, Genaya smiled towards her, thankful she was still alive.

"Thanks, Genaya," she said, relieving her stress.

Suddenly Genaya's smile was ripped viciously from his face by the dark grey blade that had penetrated through Ange's ribs. The bright light zapped and hummed as it made contact with the flesh. Ange's eyes lit up. She was frozen still. Her body was resting on the very weapon that had just sliced through her soft flesh. The Plasma-Blade was swung to Genaya's left. Ange's body fell straight off it. Her green blood spattered across the ground. It simmered on contact with the plasma beam of her murderer's Plasma-Blade.

"NOOOOOOO!" yelled Genaya in extreme grief and outrage. He was shattered. His heart had sunk. His body felt numb.

Not again, he thought to himself. He could not fathom losing another friend to the Malum.

As Ange's body was tossed carelessly to ground, Genaya looked up and saw the most infuriating, dislikeable pair of eyes he'd ever laid witness to. The menacing yellow eyes of Jeppora stared back into Genaya's sole. Genaya knew Jeppora wasn't finished yet, he had business to take care of.

Sadness and sorrow drowned Genaya's face and body language. Genaya's anger was tearing through his skin. His frustration was clenching at his muscles. He seemed on the verge of exploding, both into tears and into a raging burst of emotional release. And yet, he still contained it. Despite the overwhelming emotional conflict in Genaya's mind, he stood steadfastly against it. He remained poised to honour the ways of the Paxian and fulfil his duties.

"You're a monster," yelled Genaya in anger towards Jeppora, whilst physically remaining calm.

Jeppora looked at Genaya with malicious intent, unresponsive to his remarks. Genaya sensed that Jeppora was aware of his emotions and how conflicted he could become. Genaya promised himself he would contain his emotions to ensure Jeppora could not use his anger and outrage against him.

Jeppora slowly moved towards Genaya, wielding both of his Plasma-Blades intimidatingly. Genaya stayed put, unmoved by Jeppora's attempted aggravation and lack of care. Genaya could see that this was starting to frustrate Jeppora, who now amongst the ongoing battle, ran in between two Battle-Bots that crossed the path between him and Genaya and launched a flurry of attacks.

Up. Down. A low right swipe. A low left swipe. Genaya defended them easily, albeit though being slightly off balance due to Jeppora's forceful strokes. Jeppora then followed up. Swinging his upper Plasma-Blade down diagonally to his right. The lower one was swung horizontally around Genaya's legs. Genaya swiftly parried both attacks.

Both Genaya and Jeppora continued parrying and swiping each other with quick, merciless arrays of attacks. Jeppora finally caught Genaya off balance. His first slash was parried by Genaya. The second though, was angled horizontally towards Genaya's chest. For a split second, Genaya anticipated the glowing blade searing through his flesh.

Bzzzzzzz! Genaya's eyes lit up by the sight of a bright orange blade parrying a potentially lethal blow. Heysen had come to save him.

Together, the two Ordo representatives wielded their Plasma-Blades in a flurry of attacks on Jeppora. Jeppora initially handled them well, using his two Plasma-Blades to his advantage. However, in a short space of time Jeppora quickly became overwhelmed and knocked off balance to the ground. Unlike Jeppora, Genaya and Heysen did not attempt to deliver a fatal blow. They instead opted to hold Jeppora down.

The moment of victory did not last long as a rich violet Plasma-Blade waved itself in front of both Heysen and Genaya. They stood back in surprise, which allowed Jeppora to recover onto his feet. The mysterious figure that had just confronted them appeared more malicious and menacing than Jeppora.

It wore an illuminated, violet coloured suit that was accompanied by a helmet. The helmet was violet, and chrome coloured, perfectly curved in structure. It was shaped like an evenly sized bucket but curved to suit a human head. This part of the helmet was chrome coloured, but the facial section of the helmet was indented, of a condensed trapezoidal shape. It had clear glass-like slit at the top to see through, split by a thin portion of the chrome helmet. The section below this slit was of a deep, dark purple.

Genaya and Heysen locked eyes onto the figure, staring at it with concern. Vondur Sombria was now on the battlefield, taking matters into her own hands.

Chapter 31

Vondur Sombria waged a brief, yet relentless battle against the two representatives from the Ordo. Her skills with the Plasma-Blade were almost incomparable. Such ferocity, such precision, such power. She was relentless. Genaya and Heysen were constantly parrying her attacks. Jeppora double teamed them, trying desperately to lay a fatal blow. Genaya and Heysen were on the backfoot, bearing the brunt of a physical barrage.

Their fortunes received a lucky turn. The Battle-Bot forces were being surged back, and the Federation Soldiers were mounting a forceful attack well into the Nantan Plaza. The Malum forces were forced to retreat, which did not bode well for Sombria and Jeppora on their aggressive advance.

Jeppora was shot in the leg by a Federation Soldier, causing him to fall to the ground. Sombria used this diversion to flee within the Malum frontline and seek refuge amongst the clump of Battle-Bots actively defending the Corvaanian Government Building.

Genaya looked around for Sombria. She could not be seen. The Battle-Bots continued to be pushed back, allowing Genaya to get closer to view the Government Building. Still, he could not see her.

"Genaya!" yelled Xevo across from him.

Genaya turned to see Xevo pointing at a violet-coloured figure absconding from the battle up the Government Building steps. She was clearly aware of what Genaya was looking for.

“Thanks, I’ll need a pathway though,” yelled Genaya back across to her.

Xevo responded by ushering a couple of Federation Soldier Squadrons towards a weakened corner of the Battle-Bot frontline. They swamped that position with immediacy, allowing Genaya to make a quick dash through the temporary opening. He deflected a few Photon-Gun bolts and tore down one Battle-Bot that stood in his way, before he broke past their line and reached the Government Building. Genaya came around the right corner of the building and proceeded up the Government Building’s steps and down the right corridor that Sombria appeared to take.

Genaya travelled deeper into the corridor, before turning down a hallway to his left. Bmm! A noise. Faint, but discernible. A boot on stone.

It was surely her, Genaya thought.

Genaya entered the hallway slowly. He crept in, making as little sound as possible. Click! Click! These sounds were more high-pitched. Two steps. A turn perhaps. Genaya paused, holding his Plasma-Blade squarely in front of him. The bright yellow light shone down the hallway, where a darkened figure stood, feet firmly apart. Genaya watched the figure intently. It just stood there. It made no sound. But it was looking straight at him. He could sense it.

Bzzzz! A bright violet light shot out from the left of the figure. Bzzzz! Now another bright violet light. This time, to the right of the figure. There was a thin metallic gap in between the two lights. Sombria had engaged her Plasma-Blade.

Her helmet was glowing in the light of her Plasma-Blade. Her suit, though, helped illuminate the darkened hallway. Bshhhhhh!

Another sound! But what was it? Genaya wondered.

Two bright violet beams of light shot up from Sombria's upper arms. Bshh! Genaya was astounded that they were attached to Sombria's Malum suit. He'd never seen that before.

A second blade engaged on each arm, located slightly below the first ones, before a third one was engaged. Three Photo-Blades protruded from each of Sombria's upper arms glowing in the same colour of her suit: violet.

"You're quite relentless," she said wickedly to Genaya. "Do you ever give up?"

"Not when I'm stopping cowards like you," said Genaya angrily in response.

"Me? Coward?" scoffed Sombria. "My goodness boy, you really don't know your place, do you?"

"You're wasting your time. You've lost. The Malum will never win," said Genaya with confidence.

"You're also clearly quite naive," said Sombria maliciously. "This battle may be lost, but it means nothing for the Malum."

"Nothing? Your stranglehold over Corvaan is coming to end," laughed Genaya.

"Corvaan is very little in our grand scheme. It's merely a pawn in the puzzle," smiled Sombria wickedly. "The only losers here are the Federation, and your pathetic friends you call Paxian."

"They are more noble than you will ever be," said Genaya defiantly.

"Foolish kid," retorted Sombria. "If only you knew what true power felt like, what it was like to control so much about the galaxy. No one ever cares about you. They use you until you can no longer benefit them. Then you're discarded like vermin. The Malum offer more than such a pitiful way of life. They offer real power. One day, if you wise up enough to it, you'll understand your folly."

"The Malum are cold hearted, selfish people. They only worry for themselves. You left your friend behind because you are a coward. Now he'll face his justice. The Federation won't stand for it," quipped Genaya.

"The Federation is more corrupt than you know," said Sombria in a deep, evil tone. "Not only for themselves, but for us. Our allies are everywhere. If they were not, we would have ceased to exist over twenty years ago."

Genaya paused, staring furiously into Sombria's eyes. She responded with a sharp, wicked smile.

"Tell me, what is your name?" asked Sombria.

"Genaya," he responded.

"Genaya? Genaya Dorsolo, perhaps?" asked Sombria with intrigue.

"Yes. And?" asked Genaya sceptically in reply.

"My, my, this is a privilege. Son of the great Paxian warrior Delisi Dorsolo," responded Sombria with a somewhat vindictive delight. "And yet, here you are. Whilst you fight with your Ordo friends, you still possess the feeble yellow light of a straightforward Paxian. You must be weak."

"I'm proud to be a Paxian," responded Genaya. "You feebly underestimate my strength."

"No, Genaya! You underestimate mine. I'm not a Vondur for nothing," responded Sombria calmly.

Sombria then ran towards Genaya wielding her Plasma-Blade at head-height. Genaya stood defensively in defiance to her advance. Sombria swiped at Genaya. Left. Up. Then parried a quick attack from Genaya. She slashed at Genaya. Then again. She flicked her Plasma-Blade left. Genaya blocked again. This time, Genaya responded. He swiped his Plasma-Blade across

Sombria's forearm. Her wrist split open from the searing Plasma beam. Blood trickled slowly down her Malum suit. She was injured partially, but not badly.

She followed up again. One. Two. Three. Her strokes were relentless. But Genaya had good temperament. He blocked them all successively. Sombria slashed at him. Genaya parried again. Genaya then forcefully thrust her Plasma-Blade away from him and slashed at her head. Dung! The contact was fierce. His Plasma-Blade scorched her helmet. The contact was so forceful, it split into three pieces. They fell onto the stone ground, clunking as they made contact.

Genaya and Sombria paused for a brief moment, stunned by what had just occurred. Genaya looked at Sombria's face for the first time. Her dark black hair and grey eyes revealed how truly evil and soulless she was. Her lips were black with death. Genaya could sense the anger in Sombria's face. Clearly, she was extremely infuriated that she was been shown up by a younger Paxian who was not even of Ordo standard.

Sombria turned viciously to Genaya. Her breathing became heavy. She screamed at him in anger, charging towards Genaya once again. Her attacks came even faster, more fiercely. Genaya was taken aback. Such sudden aggression was unexpected. Her power seemed to grow the more furious she was. She relentlessly slashed at Genaya. Up. Down. Across. Genaya had to constantly parry. There was no chance for an attacking blow.

Sombria knocked Genaya off balance, before stabbing her Plasma-Blade firmly into Genaya's left leg. Genaya yelped loudly in pain. The burning of his charred flesh pulsated throughout his body. It was torture. Sombria then wielded her Plasma-Blade just above Genaya's chest. She paused, mocking Genaya with how weak he was at that moment. How powerless he was to save himself.

"You are surprisingly talented, young Genaya," said Sombria. "Veneticus would be proud of your skill. Your fighting style is slightly reminiscent of his. Of course, he is much more powerful than you. If you were fighting him right now, you'd already be dead."

Sombria was abruptly interrupted by the clashing of Plasma-Blades. Heysen's glowing orange blade knocked back Sombria's.

"Lucky then, aren't we?" replied Heysen with a serious smirk.

Genaya looked at Heysen with relief, but Heysen was intently focussed on Sombria. She had become more enraged. She slashed at Heysen, but he parried with precision. Sombria automatically knew this Ordo member was highly skilled with the Plasma-Blade by his demeanour and speed with the weapon.

"And who might you be?" enquired Sombria angrily, pushing firmly against Heysen's Plasma-Blade with her own.

"Heysen Jogja, and you?" replied Heysen in a mocking tone.

"Your worst nightmare," said Sombria wickedly in a cold tone.

Up. Down. Up. Across. Sombria sent a flurry of attacks towards Heysen. He responded to them with expertise. The pair duelled down the hallway. One by one, they fended off each other's attacks. They were an even match.

Boom! A loud explosion ripped through the wall to the right of the corridor. Federation Land Artillery had blasted a hole into the Corvaanian Government Building. The daylight poured in now. Stone bricks were strewn across the hallway. The other wall of the corridor was left scratched and chipped.

Genaya could see the battle being waged outside now. The Federation Forces were firmly in control. Nonetheless, Photon-

Gun blasts continued to be fired from both sides. Their sound was more audible now that the wall was obliterated.

Heysen and Sombria re-engaged their duel. They both contested each other, meandering around debris piles on the corridor floor. The corridor ceiling started creaking. Stones began trickling down to the floor. Heysen gained the upper hand on Sombria. However, as he kicked Sombria down, he was forced backwards by the collapsing ceiling. The pile of stone now separated the hallway into two parts. Heysen tried to get around, but it was no use. Sombria had escaped. Genaya lay on the ground, wounded badly in the leg. Blood continued to flow out onto the stone of the corridor.

"Are you okay, Genaya?" asked Heysen.

"I got stabbed in the leg," replied Genaya sarcastically whilst still in pain.

"Yes, but how bad is it?" responded Heysen.

"I can't really move my leg, it hurts too much," said Genaya in pain.

"I'll get you a medic in a second," said Heysen. "You did well today, Genaya. You remained composed. I didn't think you had it in you."

"Neither did I," replied Genaya.

"You put a good effort in there too, she is very powerful," said Heysen gesturing towards the rubble of stone.

"She is a Vondur," said Genaya.

"Yes, I'm not surprised by that," said Heysen. "We captured the other Vondur though, Jeppora. He's been arrested, he'll be sent back to Manoma to await trial."

"Good, he can pay for his crimes," said Genaya with a sense of catharsis.

"We won, Corvaan has been liberated," said Heysen.

"Excellent," responded Genaya.

Genaya looked back out to the city of Nantan. Corvaanian locals started to emerge from their long-term hibernation. The ruthless and unforgiving Malum were being cleared away. Now they were able to enjoy themselves once again. Cheers arose from across the city from the people of Nantan, their harmonic sounds carried to the ears of the Federation Soldiers. The citizens were audibly extremely grateful.

Genaya looked out over the sun as it began to set on the tropical planet. The trail of destruction was large. The price of battle was heavy. They had triumphed over the Malum forces.

But at what cost? he wondered.

Genaya feared the words of Sombria. If what she said was true, the war had just begun.

Chapter 32

Sombria arrived on Normona. It was located in the outer regions of the galaxy and bordered on Federation territory. The planet was valleyed, and grasslands were scattered across it. In one of the plains lay a large settlement, now the home base of the Malum. At its centre was a monstrously large fortified structure that was strewn with landing pads. The building was capable of housing many of the facilities the Malum required. Adjacent to this building was a new, huge state of the art Battle-Bot factory, already in full production.

Sombria flew her Cross-Fighter past this building and landed on one of the inner landing pads. She made her way through the building and into a large, darkened throne room. This room was long and had arches on its right where clear windows let in natural light. A mural of the Malum's ideal Dark Federation was marked on the left wall of the throne room. This wall also had fire lamps hanging on its side, the flames dancing from the draught in the room.

A large violet and black rug lined its way to the far end of the throne room. There, was where Veneticus sat, in the very same throne as he did on Vormok. Sombria also noticed that adjacent to him, standing idly, was Lucifer Dunn.

"Vondur Veneticus," said Sombria looking intently at the mask on Veneticus' face. Her words gained Veneticus' attention.

"Vondur Sombria," said Veneticus pleasantly. "You've returned. I believe you've met Lucifer Dunn, if you recall?"

Sombria looked scornfully towards a neutral looking Lucifer Dunn. His pink skin appeared smoother than normal.

"I do," replied Sombria.

"What happened on Corvaan?" asked Veneticus with more intent.

"We were overrun, Vondur. There were too many Federation Forces. We depleted them a bit, but they have taken Corvaan back," she said in a slightly worried tone.

"I see," said Veneticus in a calm, but neutral tone. "I was hoping for better news, but I suspected such events transpired. Tell me though, where is Vondur Jeppora?"

Sombria stuttered initially, afraid of Veneticus' response. "He… he was… captured," she said. "Jeppora… is currently arrested. The Federation have him now."

Veneticus remained unmoving. His menacing looking helmet filled Sombria with unease. Veneticus then moved his hands to his head. Slowly, he lifted off his helmet to reveal his face. Sombria could see Veneticus was of middle age, and as such his face was partially wrinkled. His eyes were round and cold blue in colour. His hair was short of length, but deep black in colour. His skin complexion was olive, and his lips were a pale, heartless red. Most notably, Veneticus had a deep, long scar striking up his left cheek.

"It seems we lost more on Corvaan than we bargained for," said Veneticus, now concerned. "If they make him talk, our plans will be sprung. That would severely hinder us."

"Do you think we should kill him?" asked Sombria coldly, yet in surprise to Veneticus.

"No!" responded Veneticus dismissively. "Jeppora is a Vondur. He is an asset to the Malum and our ambitions. They won't be able to get much out of him. He is very loyal."

"Then what will we do?" asked Sombria.

"Leave that to me, I'll sort it out," said Veneticus calmly. "Our friends at the Federation should be able to help us hatch Jeppora's escape. But it may take a while. They won't kill him, Sombria. They are too proud to stoop to those levels."

Sombria caught Veneticus' eyes. He was looking at her deeply with intrigue. She could see he sensed something was different with her. Something was unusual. This inquisitive behaviour caused Sombria to tremble slightly in angst. Suddenly, swallowing became difficult. She was paralysed by fear.

"Where is your helmet, Vondur Sombria?" asked Veneticus with great interest.

Sombria stuttered before piecing together a relatively calm sentence. "It was… broken," she said slightly anxiously.

Veneticus looked perplexingly towards Sombria. "Broken? How?" he queried.

"It was struck by a Plasma-Blade," said Sombria now more confidently.

"The same Paxian again?" asked Veneticus, frustrated by Sombria's ineptitude against seemingly inferior foes.

"Yes, Vondur. They are highly skilled, and persistent," she said adamantly with anger.

"I see," said Veneticus in disbelief, giving little credibility to Sombria's claims. "Perhaps your continued excuses are why you continually fail?"

"I assure you, Vondur, that is not the case, however, I do have information regarding them," said Sombria, now engaging Veneticus further.

"I'm listening," said Veneticus, turning eagerly to see what Sombria had to say.

"The Ordo member is Heysen Jogja," said Sombria with

quiet excitement. “The other Paxian, however, will interest you greatly.

His name is Genaya,” said Sombria as Veneticus’ eyes lit up in surprise.

“Genaya Dorsolo?” asked Veneticus eagerly.

“The very same,” said Sombria in a wicked pleasantness.

Veneticus was left stunned and fell back into his black throne chair. He appeared baffled. He turned his head towards Sombria with a wide smile and stated softly, “So, he’s alive.”

Chapter 33

"Genaya!" said Xevo with delight. "You're okay!"

Genaya watched on as Xevo approached him. He was lying down on a bed in the Federation Building's medical room back on Manoma. His left leg was casted up as he healed from the stab wound inflicted by Vondur Sombria.

"Xevo!" said Genaya with delight as she came and sat beside him. "So good to see you."

"It's so good to see you too," said Xevo pleasantly. "I was hoping you were okay. Heysen told me you put up an awesome fight."

Genaya smirked at Xevo hearing those words. "Did he now?" asked Genaya rhetorically, knowing Heysen's devious motivations.

"You took on a Vondur, that in itself is something to be proud of, Genaya," said Xevo.

"True, true. I'm a little shocked about it all though," said Genaya honestly. "I cannot believe it happened, that I survived. And that we won."

"We did, our mission was complete," said Xevo.

"Not quite. The Battle of Corvaan may go to the Federation. But the war against the Malum has only just begun. Heysen will inform Grandmaster Zeffiro of these findings shortly," said Genaya with seriousness.

"Well for now anyway, the Federation is on top," said Xevo, now realising Genaya was morally deflated. "What's wrong,

Genaya?"

Genaya paused to contemplate his approach but looked worryingly towards Xevo. "Us," he said softly and politely.

"What do you mean?" asked Xevo, taken aback by Genaya's claim.

"I know you have feelings for me, Xevo, I have them for you too," said Genaya disappointed at the situation. "But The Ordo doesn't see Paxian-to-Paxian relationships too kindly.

"Oh, yeah," said Xevo, realising where Genaya was going.

"I like you a lot, but my whole life I've strived to follow in my mother's footsteps, to be as brave she was. I want to be Grandmaster one day like her," said Genaya earnestly and considerately. "However, I fear that engaging in a relationship with you may jeopardise my chances of even being selected on the Ordo. I've come so far in such a short amount of time. Before all this, I was still a bit immature, reckless. But after seeing how serious being an Ordo member really is, I cannot go back to my old ways. I feel like a better Paxian through Heysen's guidance, closer to my ultimate goal. I want you, but sometimes we all have to make necessary sacrifices to achieve our goals," said Genaya solemnly.

Xevo turned to Genaya, disheartened by his words, yet accepting of their meaning. "I understand," she said with sadness. "I knew a relationship between us would make your dreams unobtainable, and that's not fair on you."

"Thanks for understanding, Xevo," said Genaya genuinely.

"No problem, Genaya," replied Xevo happily. "We can still be friends."

"Of course, Xevo, nothing can stop that," said Genaya, now with a smile.

Xevo came in to hug Genaya on the bed. Her embrace still

filled his heart with peace and comfort. He felt emotionally soothed by her presence. It was hard for Genaya to make such a bold decision. He knew it would affect their relationship going forward. But he also knew it was necessary. Xevo would understand. If he was to complete his transition into a fully-fledged, Ordo-worthy Paxian, he had to make sacrifices. He knew he'd have to make many more in the near future. It was just unfortunate for Genaya, that quashing a potential relationship with Xevo had to be one of them.

Chapter 34

Night was falling once again on Manoma. Grandmaster Zeffiro sat in the Ordo Chambers, alongside the rest of the Ordo. The last light of day snuck in through the chamber's windows. Behind it, the bright sparkling lights of the capital began to dazzle their way into the night. The room lay still. Grandmaster Zeffiro was seated in the Grandmaster's chair, informing the Ordo in regard to the Federation's successes on Corvaan. Yaneema, as always, was seated right beside him.

"As you may know, we have won the Battle of Corvaan," said Grandmaster Zeffiro proudly. "The plight is over. Federation forces overran the Corvaanian Government Building in Nantan quickly after storming the plaza. Some soldiers remain behind to clear out any lingering threats. From a battle standpoint, we can consider it a victory. Premier Finkel is now under arrest and being tightly monitored. Her treason will see her suffer the consequences with a long-term incarceration. However, we suffered decent losses ourselves. Our forces have been weakened, and as we have subsequently found out, there is more at risk than we thought. We must pay more due diligence to the Federation and its activities. Supposedly, we have adversaries that have infiltrated our democracy and seek to destroy it. We cannot afford to let them gain the upper hand. This war is far from won."

The room lay quiet. Vice-Master Yaneema proceeded to speak, given there were no questions. "Genaya and Heysen took on two Vondur's during the battle. One has been arrested and has been detained for questioning. He goes by the name of Vondur Jeppora. The second one escaped though, through no fault. Her name is Vondur Sombria and she's extremely dangerous. She has been identified as a former Paxian from decades ago. She fled in hatred of the Federation and Paxian alike. As for now, that is all we know," said Yaneema.

"Wait!" said Heysen eagerly. "I have one more piece of information that Genaya had discovered."

"And what might that be?" asked Vice-Master Yaneema.

"The name of the Supreme Malum," said Heysen, much to the shock of the Ordo members present.

"Who?" enquired Grandmaster Zeffiro with deep concern. Zeffiro could feel the fear entrench itself on his face like a leech. Zeffiro looked around the chamber to see if anyone interjected, but everyone fell dead silent. They were evidently intent on discovering who this man was.

"Genaya was only given one name," said Heysen with seriousness. "Veneticus!"

Grandmaster Zeffiro sunk in his seat. His eyes closed, unwilling to reopen. He placed his hand on his head and sat there in momentary silence. He could not believe it.

The entirety of the Ordo members present turned to Zeffiro with shock and confusion. Zeffiro's angst deepened. He was now the focal point of attention in the chamber.

"What's wrong, Grandmaster?" asked Xevo genuinely.

Zeffiro looked around the chamber with deep sorrow. His eyes were droopy. Emotionally, he was distraught. He turned to Yaneema who was looking at him with intent.

"I think it's best you told them, Zeffiro," said Yaneema.

Zeffiro nodded and took a deep breath, afraid of the reaction.

"Veneticus was my mentee," said Zeffiro apprehensively.

Zeffiro looked around the room to gage the reaction. Pairs of white, widened eyes stared at him unrelentingly. Mouths gawked at his statement.

"I've already partially mentioned to Heysen the situation with my former pupil," said Zeffiro gesturing in Heysen's direction. "But I feel it is important you all knew the rest of the story. It was roughly twenty years ago. Veneticus was greedy, but powerful. His desire to obtain more of it drove him away from me and the Federation. After he disappeared, I listed him as missing. Although, I knew full well of what he was. What he wanted to do. He is pure evil," said Zeffiro in a stern, worried tone.

"Grandmaster Zeffiro, you compared this man to Genaya," stated Heysen in astonishment. "Do you really believe that Genaya is pure evil?" he scoffed.

"Not quite, Heysen. Genaya may not yet have evil intent, but he is powerful. If Veneticus finds out about Genaya, he will exploit him, no matter how much Genaya improves," cautioned Zeffiro.

"Genaya showed so much temperament in the battle. His emotions no longer seem to affect his ability to perform Paxian duties. He is almost ready to be an Ordo member," pleaded Heysen.

"I will move in the coming days to grant Genaya temporary status as an Ordo member, but he is not a full one yet," stated Zeffiro defiantly.

Zeffiro could see Heysen was looking at him sceptically now, clearly puzzled by his decision.

"Genaya has fulfilled every task you've asked of him," said Heysen in a calm tone. "Despite that, you still won't acknowledge it because his demeanour is similar to that of a former Paxian, who happened to become the Supreme Malum?"

"I cannot, Heysen. I need to be reassured. If Genaya becomes emotionally unstable, he could be a nightmare for us. So long as Genaya has immaturity and fear, he is vulnerable to indoctrination. I will not lose another mentee again," said Zeffiro calmly, yet adamantly.

"You won't lose him, Grandmaster. He told me earlier today he longs to be on the Ordo. That's where his ambition lies," pleaded Xevo.

"Why do you fear him, Grandmaster?" enquired a baffled Heysen.

Zeffiro looked around the room once more. The eagerness of an answer from Heysen broke his reluctance. Zeffiro took a longer, deeper breath than before. He then opened his mouth and spoke in a calming, yet fretful tone.

"I cannot do it, Heysen, and none of you can afford to repeat this to anyone outside this chamber," said Zeffiro with utter seriousness. "I cannot bestow such risk onto Genaya because of the situation with his mother. If he ever found out how she really died, we would all be in grave danger."